D0287492

I KEPT A PIECE OF YOU

I KEPT A PIECE OF YOU

JOANNA WOLFORD

Joanna Wolford

Copyright © 2022 by Joanna Wolford

All rights reserved. No part of this book may be reproduced in any manner whatsoever without written permission except in the case of brief quotations embodied in critical articles and reviews.

First Printing, 2022

For my loves, Matt, Marcus, and James.

Part I: 1989

1
Alex

Alex peeked out from under the porch awning and watched the rain falling from pregnant gray clouds. He pulled his hood over his head when the rain touched his cheek. As he waited for his mother to walk him to the bus stop, a white car whipped around the bend in front of their house. His dad had said that people didn't realize just how sharp the curve was until they got right on it.

One more car flew past and kissed the edge of the ditch. Alex hopped down to the bottom porch step letting the rain soak his blue hoodie; he looked up when the rain stopped. His mother, Eleanor was hovering over him with an umbrella.

"Better?"

Alex peered up at her from beneath his hoodie, and grinned when he saw her. She was already in her work uniform for Marty's Diner, a light blue waitress smock with a white apron. His mom always smelled like lavender and honey.

"Much better, Momma, thank you."

They started toward the bus stop on the next street over. Eleanor stopped when a truck sped around the corner.

"Jesus, slow the hell down!" she yelled. "These people, I swear they're a bunch of goddamn idiots," She ushered Alex along until they reached the bus stop.

There were a few kids huddled together under their parents' umbrellas. Eleanor waved at them as they approached, and they waved back.

"Hi, Alex!" a girl, around the same age as Alex, squeaked. She bounced on her pink jelly shoes when she said it. Her friends giggled when he waved back.

"You have yourself quite the little fan club going," Eleanor said.

"Momma!" Alex said embarrassed.

"I'm just teasing," Eleanor mussed his dark hair before fixing it again. "Once you and your brother get home from school, we'll go to the arcade again. How's that sound?"

Alex's face lit up.

"Okay! Will Daddy come with us this time?"

Eleanor crouched down in front of him. She held out the umbrella for him to hold so she could zip up his hoodie; he took it with both hands. There was a hole near one of his pockets and she hooked her finger through it. He waited for her to answer, but she didn't.

"This jacket's seen better days. We'll have to save up and get you a brand new one."

"I like this one."

"You like it because it was your brother's, huh?"

Alex smiled with all of his teeth.

"And this shirt and these pants," he added.

"I know it. Still, you deserve your own stuff. New stuff. Not your brother's hand-me-downs. The bottoms of your jeans are shredded in the back," Eleanor kissed his cheek and wiped the lipstick smudge away with her thumb. She looked down the road when all of the kids began to line up. "Look your bus is coming," She took the umbrella back from him.

Alex buried his head against the apron of her uniform and gave her a hug. The bus came to a halt with a hiss of brakes; the door slid open and children filed in.

"Go on now. I'll see you after a while."

Eleanor greeted the bus driver as Alex made his way up the steps. Alex took the window seat on the side his mom was standing. He waved to her and she waved back blowing kisses to him as the bus began to leave. Alex couldn't wait to get home and tell his brother Eric that they were going to the arcade for the second time this week. His brother was almost five years older, but they were close. There wasn't anywhere Eric went that Alex wasn't right there with him. In fact, most of the time his big brother insisted. Sometimes, if Alex was ready to go home from a day of playing at the park, Eric would convince him it wasn't time to go home yet, and they'd stay out until it got dark or when their mom came to get them. For some reason their mom always looked so sad when she came for them; her eyes red and glossy, but she'd say she was just tired from work. Then they'd walk home together, and his daddy would be gone.

The bus ride was loud as usual. Kids screamed over each other from one end of the bus to the other. The bus driver, a heavier set woman in a white overstretched shirt and short stringy hair, looked in her rearview mirror and told the kids they'd better park it and quit their hollering, but it did little good. Alex sat by himself until more kids began to fill the seats from the other stops. He waved at his classmate, Adam who took a seat beside him. Adam greeted him with a nod. Their mothers knew each other from working at the diner though they weren't friends, in fact, they rarely spoke and when they did it was usually about homework or what they packed for lunch.

Adam sat with his *He-Man* lunchbox on his lap, and Alex spent most of his time staring out the window at the woods as they drove by, imagining there were people and creatures living there.

Sometimes he could swear they were really there, even after he blinked his eyes. Today he was almost sure there was something tall and dark walking between the trees. He jumped when he felt something brush against his shoulder.

"I'm having a party at *Peter Piper's* on Saturday."

Alex looked over to see that Adam was resting a birthday invitation on his arm. The kid watched him from behind Coke-bottle glasses waiting for him to take it. Alex took the invitation. Above an image of colorful balloons, it read: BIRTHDAY PARTY! On the back were the details. He was surprised that Adam had even thought to invite him.

"My mom told me to give one to you," Adam said it as though he were thinking the same thing.

Alex looked the details over, "Your birthday is at *Peter Piper's*? That's my favorite place! I go there all the time."

"Mine too," Adam pushed his glasses up with his stubby fingers, "but I don't go there all the time."

"My mom likes to take me and my brother there a lot. I wish my dad would go, but Mom says he needs his sleep."

"Maybe she doesn't want him to go," Adam blurted. His face flushed surely regretting he'd said anything.

"Why'd you say that?"

Adam shrugged and shifted in his seat, "I don't know. I heard my mom talking about it. Something about her leaving."

Alex put the invitation in his backpack and turned back to the window. He knew his parents were fighting, but he didn't think that she'd want to leave. Where would she go? And did that mean she would leave him behind too?

When the bus pulled in front of the school, Alex slipped by Adam and pushed past the other kids to get off the bus. His face was getting warmer and his sweater suddenly seemed too tight. He thought he might fall over until a soft breeze grazed against his cheek when his sneakers hit the wet pavement. Would his mom really leave him behind?

In class, Alex gazed out of the wall of windows from his usual seat, while his teacher wrote out math problems on the chalkboard. Her voice was background noise to the lingering thoughts of his mother. She loved them. There's no way she would leave them, so he shook the thought from his mind. Outside, dark clouds blotted out the sky, the rain was light but steady. He found himself staring past the parking lot to the woods. There was a squirrel on a tree facing the ground with its tail flicking in measured warning pulses. Alex tried to catch a glimpse of what it was looking at, but he couldn't quite make it out through the red truck blocking his view. The squirrel, apart from its tail, was frozen with its beady black eyes steady on whatever was spooking him. Alex searched through the truck's back window and the hairs on the back of his neck stiffened when he saw what had caught the squirrel's attention. At first, he only saw the figure's arm tight against its body, pale and shivering, but it was the figure's hand that drew Alex's eye. It twitched like a fish out of water, like it didn't belong there. *Not again, please not again.* His mind liked to play tricks on him. Sometimes they were too real. It didn't happen often, but it was enough to scare him. He hated that it was happening now.

"Alex."

Alex turned away from the window. He looked up to find the pale naked man looking down at him. He had mannequin parts, with dark wet hair matted to his forehead, and water dripping down his bloated face. The man's cloudy eyes bore into his. His mouth was contorted in an odd way, and his hands still twitched like he couldn't control himself, like something was retching its way out of him. And then he shrieked.

"Alex!"

Alex squeezed his eyes shut and plugged his ears, shrinking into his chair. When a heavy hand landed on his shoulder, Alex cried out, and all of the kids laughed. Alex peeled his eyes open to find his teacher standing in front of him. The man was standing beside her, frozen in time and staring at him. Alex looked around the classroom. Everyone watched from behind their desks, a safe and comfortable distance from the man. They didn't seem affected by him. They couldn't see him. A few nervous giggles lingered after the laughter had died down. It was only then that he realized his teacher, Mrs. Shelby was glaring at the kids. When she looked back down at him her eyes had softened.

"Are you okay?"

He wasn't, because the man was still here. Staring with those wide cloudy eyes, with thin brows turned upward, a string of black saliva slid from the corner of his twisted mouth.

"Yes, Mrs. Shelby," he whispered. Maybe if he said it low enough, the man wouldn't move. Maybe he wouldn't hear him. "I'm sorry, I think I fell asleep."

"If you're coming down with something you need to stay home and get rest," Mrs. Shelby looked him over and brought a hand to his forehead before crossing her arms. "I should probably send you to the nurse. You're not warm but your forehead's a little clammy."

"I'm fine. I'd like to stay please," Alex swiped at his forehead.

Mrs. Shelby looked him up and down again. "Okay. How about you answer one of the problems on the board for us?"

Alex nodded and Mrs. Shelby went back to her desk. He scooted his chair away from his desk, and the chair screeched across the floor. Alex looked up to see if the man had moved. He hadn't, but his eyes had. Alex took a deep breath, before using his feet to scoot himself back until he was pressed against the desk behind him. He turned in his seat and forced himself off of the chair. He was directly beside the man now who still had not moved but he felt his gaze on him. When Alex looked again, the man was giving him side-eye. *Please don't move.* Alex didn't want to squeeze between the man and another kid's desk, so he went one row over.

"Why are you going this way?" one of the kids snickered.

Alex ignored him. He refused to look back. He kept his feet light, as if doing so would keep the man from moving, but as he stepped, he heard the first slap of a wet foot on cold linoleum. For every hurried step Alex took, the man took one slow, uneven one. When Alex made it to the chalkboard the sounds stopped. He picked up the chalk and brought it to the board. His hand trembled ever so slightly. He wanted to look back just to see where the man was. *Just one look.* Alex turned to face the class. Mrs. Shelby's desk was off to the side of him. She was watching him. Everyone was. Including the man who stood only a few feet away from him now. Alex turned back to the board and worked out the problem. Chalk tapping and skidding across the board. He focused on those sounds when he heard the man's feet squishing and padding across the floor. Out of the corner of his eye, he saw him lurch out of the classroom. Alex exhaled and finished the problem.

At lunch the Principal, Mr. Rivera, made an announcement about early dismissal. As it turned out, the rain and warm weather had turned into what his teacher, Mrs. Shelby, had called a Nor'easter, and it was only going to get worse over the next few days. Mr. Rivera said their parents had been called and were aware. He said that if their names were called, they needed to wait in the cafeteria for their parents to come pick them up, and if their names weren't then they were to report to their bus line. Alex's name wasn't called so he grabbed his backpack from Mrs. Shelby's classroom and ran down the hall to the back of the school to wait for his bus.

His brother was already waiting on him when he got off the bus, his oversized Metallica shirt billowed against the wind, and he did his best to keep his umbrella from blowing away.

"Eric!" Alex cried when he hopped off the bus.

"Hey, Buddy," Eric held the umbrella higher to cover them both. He struggled against wind and rain to keep it steady, his mousy hair blew over his eyes.

"Guess what?!"

Before Eric could even ask, Alex blurted "Mom's taking us to the arcade again!"

Eric looked straight ahead doing his best to keep the umbrella steady. He didn't look as excited as Alex thought he'd be.

"Eric?"

Eric looked down at his brother.

"That's great, Buddy," was all he could say.

They took the shortcut home, cutting between houses and backyards. They stepped over small puddles collecting in the grass. Alex managed to step in one and his feet sloshed the entire time. He picked up a stick and ran it along fences as they passed.

"You think Daddy will come with us this time?" asked Alex, dropping the stick between tall blades of grass.

"I doubt it."

Eric stopped at the corner of their neighbor's fence which was directly behind their own backyard.

"Yeah. Adam Warner said Momma wants to leave him. You think that's true?"

"Don't listen to Adam, Alex. His mom likes to talk. Remember when she told Mom that her neighbor was cheating with the grocery boy because she saw him help put groceries in her car, and it turned out that he really *was* just the grocery boy helping put groceries in her car?"

"But I know they've been fighting, Eric. I'm young, not stupid."

Eric's eyebrows came to an arch. "You're a little stupid," he teased.

Alex raised a fist at him, and he scrunched his face at Eric. His middle knuckle started to raise, he hesitated before flipping his brother a rigid bird.

"I think I'm going to ask Daddy to come with us to the arcade this time."

It was a bold statement to make.

2
Eric

Eric peered out from under the umbrella. The skies were heavy with clouds that seemed low enough to touch. The rain was coming down harder now, and water was soaking the bottom of their jeans. Against the soft clap of distant thunder Eric could faintly hear their parents yelling. He had thought, *hoped* his mother would still be at the diner. If it wasn't storming, they could go to the park or play outside somewhere. Now he'd have to think of something else.

"Hey, let's go to Jack's house and play some video games until we go to the arcade tonight," Eric suggested. "We're not even supposed to be home yet anyway."

Alex gave Eric the stink eye.

"In the middle of a storm?"

Eric made it seem as though it wasn't an issue. "Sure, why not? We can ride our bikes there as fast as we can."

Alex shook his head.

"I just want to get out of the rain. It's in my shoes," He looked at the house. "I know what you're trying to do. I'll be okay."

Eric patted him on the shoulder and nodded.

"Okay then. When we get inside go straight upstairs and turn on the TV. You can play video games if you want."

They could hear yelling from the porch, but it stopped as soon as Eric shut the door behind them. Eleanor peered out from the kitchen just as Alex was heading upstairs. He stopped when he saw her.

"Hey, Momma. You're home early?" Alex greeted, leaning over the open banister.

"Hi my babies. Yes. Marty sent me home early."

Eleanor clung to the kitchen entryway. Her eyes were red. She forced a smile and glanced at Eric. Her eyebrows creased, pleading with him to take Alex anywhere but here.

"Storm's getting worse, Mom," Eric replied. "We're going to head upstairs and play video games."

Eleanor nodded. "Yeah, okay honey. Are you two hungry?"

The boys shook their heads.

"Okay then, I'll be up to check on you in a minute."

When Eric saw his dad appear behind his mother, he ushered Alex upstairs.

"Hey, son," said Gabe. There were heavy shadows beneath his eyes. He rubbed at the coarse scruff on his chin.

"Dad," Eric said, following Alex upstairs.

Eric dropped his backpack onto his bed. Alex plopped down in front of the TV looking through a shoebox full of game cartridges.

"What do you think they're fighting about now?" asked Alex.

His brother shrugged and sank onto his bed.

"Who knows," he said, pulling his Geometry book and a notebook from his bag.

"I wish momma would go out with her friends. Maybe they wouldn't fight so much."

"She doesn't have any. Why do you think she's always hanging out with us?"

Alex nodded, slipping a cartridge into the Atari. He reached beneath the TV stand for the game controller and stared quietly at it for a moment. Eric rested his book on his lap and looked down at Alex.

"What is it?" Eric asked.

Alex looked over his shoulder.

"Daddy doesn't really like me, does he?"

"What makes you say that Dummy?"

"Because he doesn't talk to me. He talks to you all the time."

Alex powered on the Atari, and the screen flashed once before cutting to the start screen. *Food Fight* was scrawled in bubble letters across the screen with the option to choose level difficulty and number of players below it. He started to choose Advanced but decided against it and instead went with Beginner. He looked back at his brother and waved the extra controller at him, but Eric shook his head and lifted up his book.

"I need to get this out of the way, so I don't have to worry about it later," Alex picked one player and started his game.

It was true. Their dad rarely talked to Alex. Eric wondered if it had anything to do with the way he was. Sometimes they'd find his brother staring absently at a wall or sometimes he'd be on the front lawn or the backyard. One time they found him inches from the ditch across the street and their mom had a full-on meltdown because of how fast the cars usually whipped around the corner. A few inches short of the ditch and he could've been crippled by a car, a few inches too far and he would've been headfirst into the rocks and any garbage littered there. His mom even petitioned to have the city put up a yellow sign warning oncoming traffic to slow down, but it didn't do much good. Cars still wound up in the ditch across from their house. Thankfully no one had ever been seriously hurt.

The other night, their mom said Alex was standing in the middle of their bedroom. Eric asked if his brother was sleepwalking, his mom said she didn't think so because his eyes had been wide open, and he was blinking. Alex told them that he sometimes daydreamed, and when he came back, he found himself in a different place.

"Don't think about it too much," said Eric. "That's just the way he is. He only talks to me when there's chores to do."

Eric opened his geometry book to the chapter they were currently working on at school. Alex went back to playing his video game, moving his entire body with the controller as he tried to dodge obstacles while eating all the digital ice cream cones. Eric regarded him for a moment. He had their mom's bright eyes and their dad's dark hair. He was small for his age and quiet. He wished his brother had more friends so that he could spend more time away from the house when their parents argued, which lately seemed to be an everyday occurrence. But Alex seemed content spending time with his big brother, and if Eric was being completely honest with himself, he didn't mind the company either. It helped take away from whatever was going on between their parents.

3
Eleanor

Eleanor waited for Eric and Alex to get upstairs before talking again. This time she tried to keep her voice low so her kids wouldn't have to hear. She leaned against the kitchen counter, staring blankly at the refrigerator. There was a picture Alex had drawn of apple trees along with one of Eric's outstanding report cards. She smiled thinking of her boys, but it faded when she looked at her husband, Gabriel. She watched him long enough for him to take a sip of his coffee before looking away. They had been arguing about the bills again. It was almost always about the bills. She didn't know what she expected from him, finding jobs in Landstown, Virginia was not easy, finding jobs that would be enough to support an entire family without some sort of trade was damn near impossible. Eleanor had tried to get her medical degree, she wanted to be a doctor. She started some college but couldn't finish, because how were they supposed to keep up with the mortgage and car payments? How many times did they need to refinance the house? Three? And there were liens on it now, she'd known it was only a matter of time before that would've happened, so she wasn't surprised when it finally did. They were sinking in something they weren't sure they knew how to get out of, and she had come to resent Gabriel for it.

It wasn't his fault, she knew it, but things between them had grown stagnant, and their marriage was suffocating. To make things worse, she was still working at Marty's diner where she'd been working when she first met Gabriel, and he was still working for the same construction company he'd worked at since high school. Still, it wasn't his fault, and she knew it, but she couldn't bring herself to admit it, not when they had strayed so far from the way things were between them. Now, even petty arguments were turning into screaming matches, and trivial things became consequential.

"This isn't how I pictured my life would be."

When Eleanor saw Gabriel looking at her, she realized she had said it aloud. She cleared her throat, anticipating a response for what he might say next. He said nothing. "I don't know how much longer I can keep doing this, Gabe. I'm so tired."

Gabe drew in a breath and shook his head.

"Darlin' I don't know what else I can say."

"Really? Have you even said anything? Because I haven't heard you. All these things we scream about, and I can't hear a single word you've said. Why don't you say it again? Say it a little louder so that I can really hear you."

Eleanor sank into the chair across from him with her head cocked to the side, the way she did whenever she had decided to shut him out.

Eleanor watched her husband scoot himself back from the kitchen table. He looked down at his old steel-toed boots. The rubber on the soles were damn near worn to the nub.

"I can't keep doing this with you. You're not the only one who's tired, you know it? I've loved you since the day I met you Eleanor, but if you are not where you want to be with me, then maybe we should start thinking about the alternatives."

Eleanor propped her arms on the table and covered half of her face with her hand. "You're a real piece of shit you know that?

Alternatives? You mean you were going to let me spend damn near twenty years of my life with you, then divorce me without a leg to stand on? I have no skills, Gabe! None! I have been a waitress at Marty's since my twenties. I don't even have a college degree and you're going to, what exactly? Just leave me and the kids behind so that we can be in the same boat we're in without you?"

Gabe reached out to touch her arm when she shot up from her chair, but she backed away from him.

"Eleanor," Gabe cried out. It was almost a plea and it caught Eleanor off guard that she nearly lost her balance when she moved away from him. She was waiting for him to spew venom right back at her, it was what she was used to, but he didn't.

"I've loved you for too long, Ellie, but how much longer are we going to do this?"

She took a few steps back until she was at the kitchen entryway.

"I don't know."

Eleanor headed upstairs and tapped on Eric's bedroom door before opening it. Alex set his game controller in his lap. Eric looked up from his textbook. They knew she and Gabe had been fighting, it was the silence, and the pitiful way they looked at her that gave them away. "Get your coats and shoes on. Let's go to *Peter Piper's.*"

Eleanor pulled the hood of her raincoat over her head and shut her car door. The skies were even darker now that night was approaching, and rain was coming down in sheets against the wind. She ran toward Peter Piper's. All of the lights outside were off, and the door was locked. It was absolutely closed, she knew it would be, but she pushed and pulled on the door just to be sure. She pressed her forehead against the glass door, cupping her hands around her eyes, and peered inside. All of the lights inside were off too. Eleanor looked back at her car. She had left the engine running with the headlights beaming in her direction – like a spotlight on her failure. There were no other cars in the parking lot. Her boys were staring at her through the windshield, waiting for her to get back to them. She shook her head with her hands at her sides and shrugged.

"What were you thinking, Eleanor?" she mumbled to herself, feeling insane for taking her kids out in this weather. She watched as the rain found its way to the grates while it began to flood in other parts of the parking lot.

She ran back to the car and pulled the hood off her head.

"Jesus it's pouring out there," she said catching her breath. "I'm sorry guys, it's definitely closed. Let's try again tomorrow, okay? Maybe the storm will have moved on by then. We could come here for lunch?"

Alex looked down at his shoes and his smile waned. She knew he had been looking forward to going through the giant tubes and the ball pit and watching the giant animatronic animals dance and sing. He leaned forward and looked at his brother who was sitting in the passenger seat.

Eric nodded.

"Yeah, Mom that sounds good. You're right, maybe the weather will be better tomorrow."

Eleanor smiled at him, and then looked back at Alex who gave her a half-smile and nodded too.

"I think that's a great idea, Momma," said Alex, trying his best not to sound disappointed.

Eleanor sank into her seat. She gave the steering wheel a squeeze before putting the car in drive. "Okay, then, tomorrow it is."

They didn't go home right away. They drove past some of the fast-food restaurants, a Bojangles, McDonald's, and a Wimpy's. They were all closed too. When the weather got bad in Landstown, everything shut down because the roads liked to flood. It took them nearly an hour to get to the main part of town where the restaurants were because they had to take roads that weren't buried underwater.

"Mom, it doesn't look like anything is open. Should we just go home?" Eric had suggested.

Eleanor looked at the time on the clock radio. It was close to five in the evening now. She wiped away at the condensation on the windows and turned the dials on the defogger until the windows cleared a little. She peered between the wiper blades, hoping to find anyplace with their lights on. Did she have enough money for them to stay in a motel for the night, so she didn't have to go back home? She knew she didn't. She had enough tip money to maybe get them some dinner and so they could go to the arcade tomorrow. If it was open. She drove a little further down the road, there were a few cars driving past her, just as slowly as she was in her little blue four-door Toyota. One truck swooshed past and she gripped the steering wheel tighter when turbulence tried to sway her off course.

"These trucks just do not care!" She drove a little further down, maintaining the safest speed possible which was no more than thirty miles an hour on a road where cars usually did fifty, when her eyes lit up. "Ooh look! *Burger Hop's* lights are on!"

Burger Hop was a drive-in diner which recently added their new drive-thru feature. It was taking business away from Marty's diner, but Marty refused to add a drive thru. He wanted people to sit down and enjoy their hot food, not get it home only to have it lukewarm. Eleanor felt guilty for going to Marty's competitor, but they needed to eat something. *Sorry Marty.* She pulled into the drive-through. She had thought briefly about pulling into one of their car stalls but thought better of it. Those poor employees were likely to spit in her food if she'd made them come bring it out in the rain. She pulled around to the drive-through menu and rolled her window down. Rain was getting into the car while they waited, but no one answered. She inched forward more, thinking she hadn't pulled up far enough for their sensors to go off, but still there was nothing.

"Momma, maybe they're closed, and they just left their lights on," said Alex. He was looking up at the menu.

"Maybe," Eleanor said under her breath. "Let me try one more thing."

She pulled forward to the drive-through window, as a last-ditch effort. To her surprise, there was an older gentleman standing behind the window. He was busy counting the till, and when he saw her car he jumped. He shook his head and mouthed *closed*.

Eleanor pointed at his window and he stared at her as though she had just asked him to strip naked. He put the money back in the register and swung the window open part way. He kept his hand on the lever, and investigated her car seeing that she wasn't alone. The old man was rail- thin with a crooked mustache that looked like it had been drawn on by a preschooler. Eleanor could barely see his upper lip. She rolled her window down just enough to keep some of the rain out.

"We're closed!" The man shouted against the rain. He started to shut the window again, but Eleanor pleaded with him.

"Wait! Please, don't shut that window just yet."

"There's a storm out there, Honey. Shouldn't you be at home with your kids?" The man's mustache wobbled every time he spoke.

"Yes, I know, and yes we should be," she looked at the name tag on his shirt, "Darryl, but we saw the lights were still on and we're hoping you might still be open. We've had quite a few disappointments tonight, and you might be our last chance at a decent meal in this god-awful weather."

She watched Darryl peer into her car at her kids, one of them, a tall and lanky teenager, and his younger, paler brother, who watched him with quiet unease.

"Won't have any ice cream or slushes I'm afraid. Not unless you want soap flavored. He looked back at the fryer. I can do tots, burgers, and bottled waters, but that's it."

Eleanor's eyes lit up, "Yes, that's perfect!"

"Okay three burgers, three tots and waters then," Darryl started to ring her up when he heard her soft voice call through the rain.

"I'm sorry, can you make that one burger, small tots, and one water?"

Darryl paused at the register with his finger hovered over the keys. "Okay. Four dollars and ninety-one cents."

Eleanor's face warmed when she handed him exact change, most of them in quarters and pennies. This man was probably wondering why she decided to have kids if she couldn't provide for them. Eric rested a hand on his mom's arm and smiled at her. It took everything in her power to keep from crying. She gave his hand a squeeze.

"I love you both so much, you know that? You're good boys."

Darryl got started on their order and Eleanor turned the radio to her favorite oldies station. She let Otis Redding sing softly about loving someone for too long, and after a few minutes, Darryl was handing her the paper sack that was larger than it needed to be for their order. She looked at him and he shrugged.

"It's the only bag I had. You have a good night now. Hurry on home before you get swept away in this storm."

Before Eleanor could say anything, Darryl was closing the window and walking away.

When Eleanor pulled forward, she watched the restaurant lights blink off in her rear-view mirror. Instead of going home she pulled into one of the stalls.

"Momma. There's about six burgers in here and a whole lot of tater tots too, and extra waters!" Eric beamed.

Alex threw his seatbelt off and leaned over his brother. He inhaled deeply, "That smells so good! Hand me a burger, Eric!"

Eric handed them each a burger and took one for himself. He set the bag between him and his mom so they could all share the tater tots. They talked while they ate, watching the rain fall in shimmering bursts against the parking lot lights. The boys talked about how school was going.

"There's this girl at school that I sort of like," Eric blushed. "I think she likes me too. I heard some of my friends talking about going to the skating rink. I want to ask her, but she's always around her friends."

He swept his bangs to the side.

"Maybe you could slip a note in her bag," Eleanor suggested, "Or you could start with a simple, hello," she nudged him.

"Yeah, I guess I could," Eric reached into the brown paper bag for a few more tater tots and popped them into his mouth. "How about you Mom, how's work?"

"Well," she covered her mouth and swallowed her food. "Marty cut my hours again. Business hasn't been too good for him. It's been really slow with Burger Hop and all the other restaurants going up. You can get breakfast, lunch, and dinner a lot quicker now," She looked at both of her kids and pointed at each of them. "Don't either of you say a word to Marty about coming here next time you see him. It'll break that old man's heart."

"Ooh, I'm telling!" Eric teased. Eleanor swatted at him and they all laughed.

Eleanor knew Marty didn't want to cut her hours, but he was getting worried that one day he'd have to close the diner for good. She hoped that wouldn't happen, not just because it meant she'd lose her job, but because she really liked Marty. He was a good old salt of the earth type, who genuinely cared about people. He had built the diner from the ground up at the age of twenty-three back in the fifties, and the diner had become his entire life, and most of the people working for him had been there with him since the beginning. Eleanor had been working with him for almost longer than she'd been married, and he treated her like the daughter he never had, so it must've been real hard for him to tell her he was cutting her hours.

Eleanor turned in her seat to look at Alex who had gone quiet. He was looking out the window, staring out at the glistening street.

"Everything okay, Sweetheart?"

Alex leaned against his seat, and fidgeted with his hands, "Adam said you're leaving. Is that true?"

Eleanor folded her burger back into its wrapper and set it inside the bag.

"Listen, I know your Daddy and I have been fighting a lot lately. Things, they've just been real tough, and I don't know what will happen between me and your Daddy, but I can promise this from the bottom of my heart, that I will never leave you, okay? Look at me," she grabbed at his pant leg and shook it to get his full attention, "I will always be here with you. Got it, Sugar Bear?"

Alex smiled, "Yes, ma'am."

4
Gabriel

Gabe waited until she left the kitchen and buried his face in his hands. He could've said more. He could've said that he loved her with all of his heart, and he didn't want their marriage to end. What he should've said was: *Go back to school, Eleanor, whatever it takes, we'll make it work. If I have to get a second job, then that's what I'll do.* And she'd come up with an excuse about who'd be home to take care of the kids while she was at school and he was working two jobs. To which he would reply: *We'll make it work. I want you to pursue your dreams. And don't worry about the money. Most marriages end over money, but that's not gonna be us, we have each other, and we'll get through it. No matter what. But alternatives? Maybe we should start thinking about goddamn alternatives?* Gabe shook his head, drew in a deep breath and exhaled slowly. He was too deep in his own thoughts that he must've fallen asleep at some point, and he hadn't realized Eleanor and the kids left the house until he heard the car pull out of the driveway. They fought so often now. It wasn't always like that, but the growing distance between them reminded him of how his parents used to be.

Gabe wasn't an easy man to get along with. Not because he was an unfeeling man, but because showing his emotions didn't come easy. He was very much like his stoic father. His parents didn't

24

express love, not the way he imagined other families might. It didn't help that his mom left his dad when Gabe was just a kid for some bad biker type –leather jacket and all. Gabe remembered the jacket his mom's boyfriend wore. It was jet black with worn creases at the crook of the elbows, and there was always a pack of Marlboro Reds sticking out of one of the pockets. Gabe remembered thinking his face looked like a raw potato because it was dry and lumpy. The bad biker's name was Randy. Gabe called him, Mr. Potato Head. He would come over on occasion to help with what Mom called, *issues* in the bedroom because Dad worked long hours, and these *issues* needed to be addressed.

One day when Gabe came home from school, he found Mr. Potato Head's jacket sprawled across the arm of Dad's blue recliner, Marlboro Reds hanging halfway out of the pocket. He took one out and rolled it in his fingers, it smelled good, he started to bring it to his lips but dropped it when he heard something bang against the wall upstairs, there was a wild scramble across the floor, followed by a heavy crash. That was when the front door swung open so hard it put a hole in the wall, and his dad came flying through it. The sound was enough to make Gabe jump, his dad didn't even look at him. He stormed up the stairs, and Mr. Potato Head with his jeans unzipped came crashing downstairs. Gabe's dad might have been a quiet man, but he wasn't soft, he was a damn bear, and you never poked the bear. He remembered his mom had come running down stark naked to help Mr. Potato Head off the floor. Dad came running down after her with their clothes, and he had thrown them on to the porch before throwing Mom and Mr. Potato Head out with them. Mom was crying and yelling, the bad biker hadn't said a word; he had been bleeding from his lip, and his eye started to look like a raw beef patty. Dad had slammed the front door shut and it had made the whole house shudder. That was when his dad realized that

Gabe was standing there with his backpack still over his shoulders. Dad's thick hair was a tangled mess, and his neck and face had been flushed, he'd been breathing heavy as though he had been put through the wringer. Then there was a soft knock on the door, and his mom called from the other side.

"Earl, I'm sorry, Hon. I'm so sorry, please let me back in the house."

His daddy's breathing had slowed, and Gabe saw something he never thought he would – tears in his father's eyes. He blinked them away when he saw Mr. Potato Head's jacket resting on the recliner; the chair his dad spent many nights sitting in after hours of hard work. Gabe watched his dad clench the jacket into his hands so tight that he could see the whites of his knuckles. Earl had taken it with him to the front door. There, Gabe saw his mom slumped down on the porch sobbing and naked with her baby blue dress crumpled in her lap. Mr. Potato Head had taken off on foot. His motorcycle, a cheap black and red, Harley Davidson knockoff, was tipped over in the driveway. The bumper of Earl's station wagon had pinned it to the ground. Gabe had noticed that Mrs. Turner and some of the other nosey old bitties gathered across the street watching a real-life daytime drama playing out before their very eyes. Gabe's daddy shot them a look and some of them had huddled together, but they hadn't left. It was better than any soap they had ever seen.

Earl looked down at his wife, Patty, a tired woman with wide patches of dull gray hair, bags under her eyes and matching crow's feet to boot. The afternoon sun made Gabe's mom look much older than she really was, and the deep lines on her upper lip hadn't helped. She'd pushed her wild hair back behind her shoulders and clutched the dress to her pale breasts and wept.

"Let me in the house, Earl. Please. I'm so sorry. I was so lonely. You're never around anymore."

Patty had looked behind Earl and seen her son in the doorway. Even she hadn't realized that Gabe had been home from school. She stifled a cry when she saw him.

"Baby? Oh God, Son, you go on up to your room 'kay? Don't look it Mama this way. Let me talk to your daddy a while. Go on sweetheart."

Gabe had hesitated. He hadn't wanted to leave her there. Part of him had hoped that Earl would bring her back in, but the other part of him had been angry as hell. How could she have done that to them? Gabe had seen the entire world collapse in his daddy's green eyes. Earl had nodded his head at the young boy, and he had done as he was told. He never did hear what Earl told his mom that day. All he knew was that she never set foot in the house again. The last thing Gabe remembered was watching his mom walking down the empty street in her baby blue dress, wearing Mr. Potato Head's jacket until she had disappeared from view. He never saw her after that day.

Gabe had quit school when he turned sixteen. He'd started working at R.W. Construction with his daddy to help pay the mortgage on the house and bills that were months past due. They worked long hours; they came home late. They ate TV dinners or anything from a can, and conversation was short and to the point. Every once in a while, they did laugh together, usually it was at work having conversation with the fellas, and it mostly revolved around their boss's comb over or a joke about Stan's boy being the milkman's kid. That was their usual routine, and it lasted that way for several years. That was the life that Gabriel Meier knew. That was all he knew.

He did think of his mom sometimes, and he wondered if she thought of him too, and why she never made the effort to see him. One day over supper, when Gabe was in his twenties, he had finally mustered the courage to ask Earl what happened the day his mom left. His daddy was now a very old man whose eyes had seemed a little dimmer these days and his thick hair was just a little whiter.

"I told her to make the choice. If she stepped foot inside the house again, she needed to stop what she was doing. I told her I was sorry that I hadn't been the man she needed me to be. She thought about it for a short while, she wiped her tears away, put on her dress and took that old leather jacket from me, and she said 'Goodbye, please tell Gabe I love him'," Earl had set his fork down where remnants of baked beans had been and leaned back in his chair.

"We said our vows before God in a small white chapel on Alabaster Street, you know it? Married for nearly eighteen years, but I'll tell you the truth son, she stopped loving me a long time ago. I guess I always knew it. That part didn't hurt. What hurt was that she hated me so much that she was willing to cut you out of her life, just so she didn't have to put up with me anymore."

It was the deepest conversation Gabe had ever had with his father, and it also ended up being the very last. He and five others from the construction company buried Earl on a Tuesday morning, in the spring of 1960 on an empty plot beside his own home.

Months later Gabe found an obituary in the back of the morning paper about a woman named, Patty Dickson. Next to a short post that said, **Beloved Wife and Mother** was her picture. There was no mistaking the woman in the photograph. Her hair was shorter and fully gray, the bags under her eyes and crow's feet were more pronounced. Her last name had changed, but she was still the same woman that had walked out on him and his daddy all those years ago.

Gabe had continued on working for the construction company. The house seemed quieter and bigger without Earl. He didn't realize how much comfort he'd found in his daddy's company. Now he felt very much alone. Every once in a while, the guys at work would convince him to come out and have a few drinks at the local bar, but he was usually the first one to leave. It happened to be one of those nights as he was walking home that he saw Eleanor, the only woman that he would ever love.

Gabe pushed himself away from the kitchen table. Maybe he could try to talk to Eleanor when she got home, but he always thought that was a good idea, until they were screaming at each other all over again. Gabe didn't understand why it always ended up that way. Had he been the one to start yelling? He could never remember how it started, but he always knew how it ended. They had come a long way from the husband and wife who used to cuddle up on the couch watching movies, and the happy couple who used to have sex damn near every place in the house when the kids weren't home. Eleanor used to come home before her second shift started, and Gabriel would come home too, sometimes on his way to pick up supplies for the job, and she would tear away his clothes the minute he walked through the door. He used to surprise her with flowers, but even flowers had lost their meaning. They used to enjoy the little things between them, the subtle glances across the room, and the gentle graze of their fingertips in passing. Now she couldn't stand to be near him or much less look at him. He wished they could go back to those days, somehow, he knew they never would.

5
Alex

Alex and Eric followed their mom through the front door. The light in the dining room had been left on, as well as the stove light in the kitchen. Since school was canceled for tomorrow, she told them they could stay up as late as they wanted, but they needed to make sure they brushed their teeth before it got too late. She kissed and hugged them goodnight before heading upstairs. Alex watched her go into the spare bedroom and shut the door. She liked to read in there. Sometimes Alex would find her sleeping in the Papasan chair with a book on her chest.

Alex and Eric debated on what they were going to do for the rest of the evening. Eric was up for a movie or game marathon and staying awake for as long as they could. Alex was on board but not without the snacks.

"I'll get them," Alex volunteered.

"Okay. My vote is movie marathon first, then video games."

Alex shrugged and was already headed for the kitchen, "Sure."

"Bring up the Doritos!"

"Duh," Alex called back before disappearing into the kitchen.

Alex stopped at the refrigerator when he saw his dad taking a glass down from the cupboard. He never once averted his eyes from what he was doing, even when he heard Alex come in. Alex started moving again, he padded across the tile floor as gently as he could and slid past his dad to the pantry as if to avoid a sleeping bear. He exhaled upon reaching the pantry, realizing he had been holding onto his breath ever since he saw his dad standing in the kitchen. Alex had folded his fingers around the pantry door handle when he felt the weight of his dad's eyes on him.

"Where did you all go tonight?" his dad asked.

Alex let his eyes turn in his dad's direction, he knew the rest of him wouldn't be able to.

"We tried to go to the arcade, but it was closed, so we went looking for something to eat. There's extra burgers in the bag if you want some. Eric has it upstairs. The manager gave us more than we ordered."

His dad set his glass down and cleared his throat.

"That was real nice of him. Did she know him?"

Alex opened the pantry door, reached past the cereal and saltine crackers, and took the half-open bag of Doritos by the yellow chip clip. "No. We never seen him before." He was going to get something for him and Eric to drink too, but he didn't want to be in the kitchen anymore. When his dad put his empty glass in the sink, Alex skirted past him. "Night, Dad," he called back as he high tailed it out of there.

"Can you go downstairs and get the soda?" Alex pleaded, nudging the door shut with his foot.

Eric looked up from their VCR with his eyebrows raised. "Why didn't you just do it?"

"Daddy's there," Alex set the Doritos on the floor beside Eric and the bag of burgers. He plopped down next to his brother, unfolded the crumpled fast-food bag, and pulled out the other two bottles of water. "We can just drink these, I guess."

"No, it's okay, I'll go down there later."

He pressed play on the VCR and when the warning message came up, he fast forwarded to the beginning of their movie.

"What'd you put in?"

"*Monster Squad.*"

Alex's eyes lit up, "Nice!" He reached for the bag of Doritos and tossed the chip clip aside before planting himself against the headboard. He offered some to Eric who shook his head and opted for another burger.

Alex popped a few chips in his mouth and delighted in the crunch of each one. He looked down at his brother who reached for more tater tots. "I saw the bloated man today."

Eric stopped what he was doing and turned to face his brother. "What?"

"The bloated man. I saw him in class. He was really close this time. His lips are like super purply- blue. I thought I was going to poop myself."

"I haven't heard you talk about him in a while. Mom and Dad must be getting to you. You only see him when you're really stressed out."

"Felt real this time. He didn't go away when I opened my eyes."

Alex grabbed another chip and took the tiniest nibble.

"How did you make him go away?"

"I didn't. He went away by himself. Walked out of the classroom."

Eric sat at the edge of the bed.

"You know he's not really real right? Your imagination is too strong."

Alex smiled at his brother. Eric was always good about making things seem not so scary. Even though it did almost scare the living poop out of him, the bloated man never showed up when Eric was around. Eric wasn't scared of anything and maybe that's why Alex never saw him when he was with him.

"I know, but just in case I'm going to sleep in your room for a while."

"Oh, so like what you've been doing then."

Alex threw a pillow at him and Eric swatted it away. The pillow smacked against the wall. "Ooh, check out those skills!"

They made it through *Monster Squad* and *Silver Bullet*, but Eric was struggling to make it through *The Gate*, and it wasn't long before he was curled up on the floor. Alex made it to the part in the movie when the little demon monsters made their first appearance. Flashes of light reflected on their sleeping faces and after a while the tape had reached the end and began to rewind itself, leaving Eric and Alex sleeping to the sound of TV fuzz.

When Alex opened his eyes he was teetering, barefoot on the edge of the curb in front of his home. Clouds sailed past a half moon that lit the sky in silver, and a cool breeze rustled through trees across the street. He wasn't sure how long he'd been standing there but it was long enough that a chill had crept under his pajama shirt. He glanced back at the house. All the lights were off. His parents never kept the porch light on because it attracted moths and brown beetles. The screen door tapped lightly against the frame, and the front door hung wide open like a gaping maw. He turned back to the road, watching the trees across the street as they swayed and shifted, a soft tangle of branches danced in the shadows. When something moved in the woods, he expected to see the bloated man, but it was a woman this time. Her hair was wild and knotted with leaves. When the clouds parted, moonlight revealed her eerie grin. There were parts of her missing: a hand, a few fingers, and some skin peeled away from her cheek. She stared at him. Why do they always stare? Twigs snapped beneath her feet as she limped in his direction. She stopped just shy of the ditch. Alex turned from her and started for the house, but he stopped himself.

"Alex."

Mom? He turned back and stepped down onto the main road. Grit from the asphalt dug into his bare feet as he walked towards the woman, and he stepped as lightly as he could but doing so only made his feet hurt more. Alex stopped on the other side of the ditch. She was wearing the same waitress smock his mom wore, only it was in tatters. Her eyes were cloudy, and she was looking at him but not really seeing him. Black uneven stitches held her neck together and her lips were forced into a wide grin. There were little things that reminded Alex of his mother, like the shape of her eyes and the waves of her hair. He knew this wasn't her, and yet, somehow, she was.

"Mom?"

The woman's eyes began to water like she wanted to blink but something was keeping her from doing it, and her smile was strange. Her chest heaved and he couldn't tell if she was laughing or crying. Alex took a step back when she stretched her arms toward him. He stumbled onto the middle of the street and when he turned his head, he was watching the bright lights of a truck barreling down the road towards him. He didn't have time to move out of the way. He turned to the woman whose mouth was hanging open now, and when the truck horn blared, she screamed.

Alex blinked and he was in his parents' room. The bedside lamp was on and it was a welcome change from the harsh headlights he'd seen only moments ago. His face was planted against his brother's shoulder who was patting the back of his head the way his mom sometimes did when he wasn't feeling well. Tears were leaking from his eyes onto his brother's shirt. His father was sitting in the bed wiping the sleep from his eyes. His hair was sticking up in different places, and he crossed his arms against his chest. His dad flinched when his mom stormed into the room. The door smacked against the wall and it made Alex flinch too. She ran to Eric's side.

"What happened?"

She turned Alex toward her and looked him over. When she saw that he wasn't hurt, she hugged him tight. He had stopped crying, but occasional short sobs still escaped. She cooed over him, until he was calm enough to speak.

"You're shaking, Sweetheart."

"Bad dreams, Momma," he whispered. There was a rasp in his voice now. *Was I in here the whole time?* He cleared his throat, shrinking deeper into her arms when he saw his dad staring at him from his bed. There were crazy red lines in the whites of his eyes. Alex turned his head to the wall.

"Okay, Sugar Bear, we don't have to talk about it tonight. Eric, help him get back into bed? Clean his face first. I'll go get him some warm milk."

"Sure, Mom."

Eric reached for his brother's hand and led him to the bathroom in the hall. Alex turned the light on, and Eric pushed the plastic curtain aside and reached for his brother's washcloth hanging over the faucet. He ran it under the sink water and wrung it out before scrubbing his brother's face with it. "You've got cheese dust all over your face."

Alex wasn't sure if he wanted to tell Eric about the woman in his dream. He didn't want to scare him, but he also thought maybe if he told him, he could keep her away like the bloated man.

"What?"

Alex looked at Eric in the mirror. "Nothing."

Eric tucked the covers under his brother. "You're in a cocoon!"

Alex giggled. Eric unrolled a sleeping bag next to the bed and crawled in.

"What are you two laughing about?" His mother had a mug of milk cupped in her hands and walked it over to Alex.

"I put him in a cocoon," Eric grinned.

His mother smiled at them, she offered the milk to Alex, but he shook his head.

"I'm okay for right now. Thanks, Mom."

"All right," she set it on the nightstand and sat beside Alex and kissed his forehead. "No more scary movies for a while, got it?"

"Yes ma'am."

"Now get some sleep so we can get to the arcade at a decent time tomorrow," His mom tapped Alex on the nose and leaned over to kiss Eric on his cheek before making her way to the door, "Oh and boys, please remember to lock the front door. Otherwise the wind will nudge it right open if you don't. You let all the cold air in."

"Yes, ma'am," they both called.

"Love you," She flipped the light switch off and shut the door behind her. Alex's heart thrummed in his chest. He glanced towards the window, streaks of moonlight seeped through the cracks in the blinds and turned his back to the window. He heard Eric shifting around in his sleeping bag and felt some relief just knowing he was there.

6

Alex

It was barely eight in the morning when the sound of his parents' muffled voices woke him. His brother could sleep through nearly anything, and he was still curled up in a ball on the floor at the foot of his bed when Alex snuck across the room to the stairway, the floorboards lightly creaked beneath his feet. The dining room light was on and so was the light in the kitchen. Sunlight usually poured into the living room through the sheer window curtains in the mornings, but not today. Rain pelted against the roof sounding like a million M&M's falling overhead, and a harsh gust of wind pushed against the house, forcing a high-pitched whistle through the cracks of the front door as if begging to be let inside.

Alex perched himself on the lower steps next to the open railing and pressed his head between two of the guard rails, hoping to catch a glimpse of his mom. He couldn't see her, but he could definitely hear her. She was talking about the nice man from Burger Hop, and his dad was asking about him.

"So, he just *gave* them to you out of the kindness of his heart?" he heard his dad say.

"And just why is that so hard for you to believe, Gabe? No one does anything nice for people anymore?"

"Not without getting something in return."

Alex's mom groaned and he heard something slam against the table. "That's real good, Gabe. On top of everything else we're going through, toss in an affair with the old man working at the Burger Hop while we're at it."

"Well it would make a lot of sense. All of this fighting we've been doing, it would make more sense to me if there was someone else."

"I don't believe this. You are so goddamn blind! Our marriage is falling apart, and it has nothing to do with anyone else!"

"What do you want me to do?" His dad was yelling now. "Jesus, Ellie, I'm at a loss here. I am sorry this isn't how you pictured your life would be. I'm sorry you ended up with someone like me, and I'm sorry I couldn't give you what you wanted! Is that what you want to hear?"

His mom sighed deeply, but no words followed. She was whimpering and sniffling. Alex thought about being brave and going to her, and he tried to stand, but he just couldn't muster the courage to do it. His mom cleared her throat, and Alex saw her appear in the kitchen entryway. Her back was to the dining room. She was shaking.

"It was a mistake," she said.

Gabe shuffled somewhere in the kitchen, "I'm sorry?"

"Marrying you. It was a mistake."

Alex watched his mom walk out of the kitchen to the living room in a series of movements that seemed too fast and too careless for her. In a flash she was at the coffee table fumbling for her keys and her purse, and in another she was passing the staircase and heading for the door. This was his moment to comfort her the way she always did when he was feeling sad or afraid. This was his moment to hug her tight and tell her that everything would be okay. And then she turned her head, a subtle glance in his direction, a moment suspended in time between them, and he watched the tears fall from her eyes when they met his. Alex reached his arms out to her, but she didn't stop for him. Instead she mouthed the words, *I'm sorry,* and left through the front door.

Alex heard the car door slam, followed by the start of the car engine, and his mother peeling out of the driveway. That's when it happened. He heard the screeching of wet tires and sickening crunch of metal –absurdly, he thought of Eric crushing empty soda cans against pavement with the heel of his sneakers, except so much louder. He watched his panicked father running out of the house. He heard Eric stumbling downstairs after him and the door swinging closed behind him. He sat quietly beside himself. Even the house stood still.

Alex zoned out to the sound of the clock ticking and the low hum of the refrigerator. He couldn't focus on anything else except those sounds, and they had grown so loud that he barely heard the sirens blaring down the street or saw the flashing blue and red lights through the white curtains. He wasn't sure how long he had been sitting there, but it must have been hours because it was even darker outside now, and the ambulance lights had long since gone. A burst of wind nudged at the front door; everyone left so fast, there wasn't time to make sure the door was closed. *There wasn't time to remember me.*

Alex jumped when the door hit the wall, forcing his attention outside to the glistening road, orange in the reflection of the streetlights. The rain had been temporarily reduced to a drizzle, but the winds were still heavy, and the skies still thick and gray as smoke. Alex slunk down a couple of steps until he reached the foyer and walked through the open doorway. A dirty white shoe leaned against the mailbox like someone had purposefully set it there, and shards of metal littered the street. A swirl of red foam washed into the storm drain. There was a glint in the grass that caught his eye. It was his mother's ring.

He walked down the porch steps and scooped the ring up in his little hand and he kept walking, but he couldn't feel his legs moving. It was as though he was watching himself from behind his eyes, but he wasn't in control. Alex stood in the middle of the street and stared at the wreckage. Broken pieces of glass sprayed the road. A side view mirror reflected Alex's empty gaze. He barely recognized himself. His eyes were drawn to something he could not process – clumps of brown hair and congealing blood clinging to debris. Water and blood washed over his shoes, but he hardly noticed. He didn't even notice the screech of tires of a van stopping inches behind him. An older woman jumped out from the passenger side of the car, and the driver pulled into Alex's driveway. He hopped out almost as quickly as she did.

"Alex!" she called. "God, Alex! Come on Baby, let's get you into the house!"

The woman ushered Alex away from the wreck, looking over her shoulder, eyes fixed in horror at the pooling blood. She forced herself to look away, hurrying Alex into the house, and the older gentleman followed behind them.

"Tom, can you find him a towel, and a blanket, and maybe his pajamas? Check upstairs." Tom didn't ask questions, he shuffled upstairs and after a few minutes he was back down the steps. The woman led Alex to the sofa in the living room, threw his shoes off and peeled his socks off of his wet feet.

Tom handed her the towel and rested the blanket and pajamas over the arm of the sofa. "Pretty sure these are his, Mary. Had to go through some drawers to figure out if it was Eric's or Alex's room, but these look to be about his size,"

"They're fine," She kneeled in front of Alex, "Okay, Alex. I'm going to take these wet clothes off and dry you with a towel so I can put some fresh pajamas on you okay?"

Alex gave a meek nod. She dried the boy's hair, his arms, legs, and his feet. Mary slipped on his pajamas and helped him to lie on the sofa. She draped the blanket over him and tucked him in. "Warm?"

"Yes Ma'am."

Mary jumped when the phone rang. Tom had started for the kitchen, but she motioned for him to sit, and ran for the phone, her thick white hair bobbed as she did.

Mary's voice carried in the stillness of the house, "Hi, Eric," There was a pause. "We found him outside." Another pause. "I know. He's fine now. No, Jack wanted to come, but we told him it'd be better if he stayed. Yes, we leave next week. San Bernardino. We're excited. We'll be living closer to Tara. She just had her baby last week. I'm officially a grandma. Oh, Sweetheart, no need to thank us. Really. Would you like to speak with him? I understand. We'll be here until you get home."

Mary returned to Alex whose eyes were growing heavy. He watched her lips moving and heard the words but couldn't understand them.

"That was your brother. Said he was real sorry they left you here by yourself, but that's why he asked us to come here and look after you until they get back. Why don't you get some sleep for a bit, Alex. They might be gone for a while. When you wake up, they'll be home."

Alex fixated on the popcorn ceiling, eyes closing and opening slower each time, until he drifted off to sleep.

7

Eric

It was long past midnight when Gabriel and Eric arrived home. Eric rushed into the house, before his father even had a chance to cut the engine. Mary and Tom were sitting at the dining table talking softly while Alex was sleeping on the couch. They stopped talking when they saw Eric's face. His eyes were puffy, and his nose was red, and he almost cried again when he saw his brother. Mary hugged Eric so tight, and he sobbed quietly into her shoulder. "Oh, Eric, oh baby, I'm so sorry."

Tom stood close, resting a hand on the boy's back, and once Eric was able to calm himself again, he pulled away from Mary and looked at the ground, and thanked them again for watching Alex. "If you need anything, you don't be shy to ask. We're always here for you."

Eric nodded, and he walked them out. They would've said something to Gabe, but he was still sitting in his truck right beside Mary's van, and wouldn't look up to meet their eyes.

"I'm sorry about my dad," Eric called out. Mary insisted there was no need to apologize.

"He's grieving, just like you. My heart goes out to you and your family, Eric," and with that they were gone.

When Eric walked back into the house, Alex was sitting up. Eric rounded the couch and knelt beside him. He started to hug him but stopped himself when Alex asked about their mom.

"Hi Eric, where's Momma?"

That question caused a hard lump to form in Eric's throat, he choked it back as best as he could to answer him.

"She's gone, Alex, Mom's gone," Eric's voice cracked, and then he fell back into a fit of sobs.

Alex didn't cry which Eric found strange at first. There was a vacancy in his eyes, missing any semblance of emotion. He thought maybe this was just how Alex coped, everyone grieved in their own way, but what he said next disturbed him.

"I can't wait until she comes home. She promised we'd go to the arcade today."

8
Eric

There was a warm oak smell in Sullivan's Funeral home, almost like wood burning in a fireplace at Christmas time. The vertical blinds in the parlor were closed, and dim electric lights ranged the walls in glass sconces with gold trim. There were cheap metal chairs arranged in neat rows on each side of the room parted by a thick deep brown carpet leading from the entryway to the open mahogany casket. The casket was surrounded with flower arrangements, and a wreathed photo of Eleanor was displayed on a stand. There were few visitors, one of them being Marty who owned the diner where Eleanor worked, and a few other women that worked with her. They expressed condolences to Eric's dad, and to him and Alex, seeming genuinely saddened by the tragic news that sweet Eleanor Meier had passed so suddenly.

"She was such a strong intelligent woman, Gabriel. We loved her so much. You were so lucky to have been married to a woman like her," said one woman.

"Eleanor always talked about traveling the world. I'm sad she'll never get to do it. I'm so sorry for your loss," said another.

Eric looked at Alex who stood close. He was searching the crowd of people.

Marty, a stocky solid wall of a man with short gray hair approached Gabe with his eyebrows turned down into a scowl.

"I'm sorry for your loss, Gabriel. I'm real sad about it," his voice was a smooth baritone. "At first I didn't believe what they told me. They said Eleanor had been in a car accident days after I dun cut her hours. Told my wife I felt responsible. Thought maybe I caused her stress, but you know how it is out here, work's been real hard to come by, and business hasn't been the best."

He looked down at Eric and Alex. Alex was looking around the room as though he were waiting for someone in particular.

"We can't predict how life is going to play out, Marty. No one can," said Gabe. "Believe me, this wasn't your fault."

It was yours. Eric thought.

Marty gave a slow nod and patted Eric and Alex on the shoulder with a heavy hand. "You boys ever need something to eat you come see me at the diner. I'll hook you up for free anytime."

"Thank you, sir," said Eric.

Eric watched Marty walk off, and he could feel his dad's eyes on him, he couldn't bring himself to look at him, he hadn't said a word to their dad since they arrived at the funeral parlor. Eric gritted his teeth. The thought of speaking to his dad made him seethe.

"Are you ready?" his dad asked.

Eric said nothing but waited for the last person to leave the parlor before taking Alex's hand and leading him to the casket. It was a slow walk from the parlor entrance down the thick padded carpet with black and beige diamond shapes. Eric could see the shape of his mother's face where the casket was open.

"I see her, Eric," Alex's eyes lit up as he tugged on Eric's shirt. "I see her! Momma! Momma, we're right here!" Alex slipped his hand from Eric's and ran to the casket, his feet padded along the carpet.

Eric's eyes widened, "Alex, hold on, Buddy."

"Momma! Momma it's me, wake up!"

It didn't take long for Alex to reach her. Eric looked behind him and saw Walter the funeral director, and his son, Bobby peering in from the hallway. Their mouths hung open and Walter called out with urgency, "Mr. Meier, please make sure he doesn't touch her, we had a really short time to get her ready given the nature of the situation. You can understand, I'm sure."

Their dad gave a short nod. He apologized and pulled Alex back just inches away from the casket. "Alex, we can't touch her, okay? It's very important."

Alex didn't understand. He didn't even seem to hear him. He reached out to touch her face, but Gabe moved him away. "Stop, Daddy. She needs to know we're here. I have to wake her up."

"Alex, please. We've been through this already. Momma's not alive anymore. She's not just sleeping."

Eric walked over to Alex; he was usually good at calming his brother down. He patted Alex on the shoulder, "Hey let's go outside and talk for a minute okay?" but Alex refused to listen to him this time.

"Eric, she needs to know we're here. We have to wake her up now!" Alex pulled away from him and his dad. He gripped the side of the casket trying to get a better look at her, trying to get her to wake up and see him.

"Momma, I'm here! Mom!"

Eric's dad pulled Alex away, but he had a good hold on the casket, he reached out to touch her face and smears of wet paint came off in his little hand. Eric and Gabe tried to redirect him, but Alex held on with all his might. He held on so tight that when they pulled him away from his mom, the casket tipped over and all the pieces of Eleanor spilled onto the floor. Her head rolled against Alex's feet, her shoes and her legs slid out from the lower half of the casket. Eric and Gabe began to yell.

"Oh my God!" Gabe tried to shield Alex from seeing too much, but it was too late.

Alex stood still looking down at Eleanor's face, and he began to shake uncontrollably with his hands at his side. Walter, Bobby, and his dad lifted the casket back onto the stand. They put every piece of Eleanor back into the casket and shut it. Eric rushed Alex outside to get him away from the chaos.

Even outside, Eric could hear his daddy yelling at the funeral director and his son. So, he led Alex into the woods in the back of the parlor until they could no longer hear Gabe's voice. The sun was hidden behind gray clouds, Eric felt a drizzle of rain on his cheek. He looked around at the wet golden leaves on the ground. Most of the trees were bare now. Alex stood shivering, pale, and unblinking. Eric wrapped his arms around his little brother and cried, but Alex remained quiet.

"Eric, let's go back to Momma."

"What's wrong with you?!" Eric cried. "Momma is dead, Alex! She's not hurt or sleeping. She's dead!"

"No, Eric. She's right next to you."

Eric looked beside him. Eleanor was standing there smiling down at him. Her eyes cold and ice blue, her skin was abnormally white, and her head hung off to one side exposing the bones and tendons in her neck. Eric screamed and watched his mom lean in to hug Alex, one of her legs was a bloody stump and her arm was barely hanging on by a thread. Her neck slumped over Alex's shoulder; blood soaked his blue button-up shirt.

"See, she's never going to leave me. She promised."

9
Eric

Eric woke up sobbing. He stifled his whimpers with his hands pressed against his mouth until he was able to calm himself and wiped his tears away with his shirt. He sat up from his sleeping bag and leaned over Alex who was sound asleep, snoring softly. It was still in the early hours of the morning, and a hint of blue was just beginning to creep in from the window. Eric pulled the blanket up to his brother's chin before stepping out of the room. The floorboards in the hall creaked beneath his feet and he stopped at the top of the stairs. The light was on downstairs in the dining room. His dad was either getting ready to hit the road again or he was just getting back. They barely saw his dad, even when he was home, so it was hard to know for sure. Eric started down the stairs when something creaked behind him. All of the hairs on Eric's arms prickled, but when he turned around no one was there. Eric hurried down to the dining room. His dad was sitting at the table drinking coffee from a ceramic mug with a newspaper in front of him. His work bag was on the floor next to him. He was wearing his flannel work shirt and blue jeans and his boots were still on. His dad looked up when he saw him.

Eric went past him to the kitchen and got himself a plastic cup from the cupboard and filled it with tap water and drank it until he'd had his fill before putting his cup in the dishwasher. He needed to talk to his dad. He didn't want to, the thought of talking to his dad made his chest tighten, but he was taking care of things around the house now and they needed things. Eric told himself he would start mowing lawns. When the weather got better, he planned to offer his help around the neighborhood so he wouldn't have to ask his dad for help, but for now they needed things, and he had no other choice. He met his dad back in the dining room and sat down at the other end of the table. "Are you coming or going?" He asked it in his best grown up voice even though his knees were jelly.

His dad looked up from his paper, "Just getting back."

"I'm gonna need money for groceries. We're getting low. We're already out of lunch meat and bread. Almost out of milk too. You're not around enough to know that," He hoped he was doing a good job masking the tremor in his voice.

His dad regarded him for a moment then nodded. He reached for his wallet from his back pocket and handed him a wad of twenties. Eric took them from him and folded the wad in half.

"I'll leave more on the table for you next time I go."

Eric nodded, "Thank you," he pushed himself away from the dining table and started to head back upstairs.

"Eric?"

Eric looked back at his dad with one foot planted on the first step, "sir?"

"We got all our money back from Bobby and Walter Rickman. On account of what happened last month at the memorial service. They can't fix what happened, so this is the best they could do."

"Okay."

"Money's yours. Use it to help take care of you and your brother. I'll be on the road again in a few days."

"Yes, sir," Eric waited a moment to see if there was anything else his father wanted to say. Maybe he wanted to ask how Alex had been doing since the memorial service, and maybe Eric would tell him that he hadn't been the same since. That he'd been completely off and even talking to him now was different because he hasn't been able to laugh or smile, that he's barely even cried since their mother died, and the last memory he'll ever have about her was the way her head rolled to his feet, but he didn't ask or say anything else and instead went back to reading his paper.

Eric went back upstairs. He planned on crawling back into his sleeping bag for a few more hours before making the trip to the grocery store. He stopped at his bedroom door when he heard his brother's muffled voice.

"I eat. Yes, I'm sleeping okay. No, I don't see him anymore now that you're here," Alex chuckled.

Eric rested his hand on the doorknob and turned it as gently as he could and opened the door just a smidge. His eye caught something, a pale figure, standing at the foot of the bed. Alex was sitting up looking at it too. When Eric opened the door all the way, it was gone.

Alex smiled, "Momma came back."

Part II:2004

1
Alex

Alex's head throbbed behind his eyes and his ears. He had fallen asleep on the couch again and must have stayed in the same position all night because his body had gone rigid. There was a sharp crick in his neck, and he soothed it with the tips of his fingers. Memories of the previous day clouded his mind in a thick fog. He rubbed the sleep from his eyes until they adjusted to the light streaming in through broken blinds. He saw the empty glass bottles on the floor and a deep yellow stain on his shirt. He wiped his dry mouth with the back of his hand. The air was stagnant enough to make him heave. Alex stood up and continued working the kinks from his neck before pulling off his shirt. He threw it across the room with the rest of his soiled laundry and walked to the window. Two young kids were playing downstairs in the parking lot of his apartment complex. Their parents were nowhere to be found. *Where the hell were their parents?* A pudgy blond toddler was picking up broken pieces of asphalt and throwing them at the parked cars. When she moved toward Alex's black pickup, he tapped on the glass and the little girl looked up. Her slightly older brother made her put the rocks down and she kicked his shin before moving along. Alex waited until they were out of view before turning on the TV. He had three working channels but the local news station on Channel 2 was the only one that ever came in clear enough. It was the only one he found worth watching anyway.

"Twenty-two- year- old Brenda Coswell has been missing for three days now," said the news anchor, Angela Montoya from behind her perfect desk. "Neighbors last saw Brenda on Tuesday somewhere between the hours of ten pm and two am and reported that a black SUV was parked in her driveway. This makes the second missing person report in two months. Officials have been questioned regarding the possibility of a serial killer, but they refused to confirm." They cut to a brief encounter with the chief of police, Collin Whitaker.

"At this time we have no reason to suspect there is a serial killer at large. It is a possibility that these two cases are purely coincidental. The camera cut back to Angela.

"If you have any information regarding Brenda Coswell or would like to leave an anonymous tip, we ask that you please call the crime line located at the bottom of the screen."

He shut the TV off and went into the bathroom. He took a long look at his pale face in the mirror. His face was gaunt and deep circles framed his eyes. All the alcohol from the night before had done a number on him, and his throat was bone dry. Flecks of brown stained his cheek and he scratched them off with a fingernail. Alex leaned in close to the mirror staring back at his icy blues. Class would start in an hour and he wanted to look decent for Catherine, a girl in his Sociology class. She smiled at him the other day. *What was that about?* Did she think about him the way he did about her?

Alex grabbed a brown-stained bar of soap sitting on the wide rim of the sink and worked it into a thick lather under scalding water. He scrubbed coarsely at his face ensuring he had gotten every dry fleck of red on his skin, and beneath his fingernails, and when he was done, he dried his face with a towel lying next to the shower. His gaze drifted to the plastic shower curtain and he peeled it back. Alex looked down at the tub numbly before pulling the curtain shut. He went back into his bedroom and retrieved a key from the top drawer of his dresser. He used it to secure the deadbolt he had installed on the bathroom door without the knowledge of his landlord.

He threw on a fresh pair of jeans, a black polo shirt, and his jacket. Alex closed the bedroom door behind him and put the key in his shirt pocket. He snatched his truck keys from the coffee table and slid into his sneakers before leaving his apartment. Alex secured the deadbolt and the lock on the doorknob; he jiggled the handle making sure it wouldn't turn.

"Wild night, huh?"

Alex turned to see his downstairs neighbor, Frank, already half-way up the metal steps to greet him. "Sorry?"

"You were having a lot of fun in there last night. I could hear your lady friend," Frank winked and gave him a nudge.

Alex smiled and nodded, "Sorry about that, I'll try to keep it down next time," One more jiggle on the doorknob reassured him.

"Oh hey, it's all right man. I'm a single guy. I know what that's like. There are gonna be days when you might hear me and my special lady. Especially if it's a good night, right? Anyway, I'll be out of town for the next couple of weeks, so go fucking nuts if you want to." His lips curled upward into a thin smile. Alex slipped past Frank who followed him down to his car. "I was actually coming up to thank you again for buying that gun off of me. See how it was working out for you. I really needed the money for the trip to Barbados and you're really helping me out,"

"Not a problem."

Frank was always trying to sell him something, an old stereo, some knock-off shoes, last week he even tried to sell him a timeshare in Florida. Alex wasn't even sure if he really had one or if he was just trying to scam his friendly upstairs neighbor out of a few thousand dollars a month. Alex had rejected his sales pitches so much that by the time Frank approached him about the gun, he finally gave in. Alex didn't know much about guns, but Frank had said it was a decent one. He said it was a simple .357 Magnum revolver, and he didn't have to worry about kickback. It even came with the bullets fully loaded, with an extra box in case he wanted to go practice sometime. Frank did warn him not to go brandishing it out in public because it wasn't registered, it was some off the market deal, and the serial numbers had been filed off of it.

"Do you need a lock box for it? I could sell you one if you need."

"No, I didn't want to keep it in the apartment so it's in my glovebox."

"Huh, okay well whatever works I suppose."

Frank reminded Alex of a low-budget porn star. He even sported the sleazy thin mustache and the partially unbuttoned silk shirt that showed a generous amount of chest hair. The eighties must have been the best years of his life.

"Listen, I know you just moved in a couple of months ago, but no one really cares what other people do around here. So, the *loud sex*," he emphasized with air quotes, "the parties, drugs... anything goes. You'll find that out real quick."

"That's good I guess," Alex looked past him to the little kids he had seen earlier. The little barefooted girl was now focused on throwing rocks at the windows of the first- floor apartments.

"Where are their parents?"

Frank turned around and watched the kids.

"Probably passed out drunk. Their mom works real late. The boyfriend comes and goes. I see the kids more than I ever see their mom. It's a shame really. Kids go missing all the time. I doubt they would even notice if those two were gone. Hell, they might even be happy about it. Well anyway, I gotta get ready for work, I'm sure I'll catch you around, and hey, just between us, if you ever need something that will give you a really good high, let me know. I can get my hands on anything," he said before heading back to his apartment.

Frank waved at the children's mom as she stepped out of her apartment.

"Speak of the devil," he whispered to Alex.

She looked at Frank briefly and waggled her fingers at him before crossing her arms in front of her.

"Anna Lynn! Bryson! Get your stupid little asses in this house before I knock your goddamn teeth in! I'm trying to sleep in here, and I can't with all the goddamn noise you're making!" she screamed hoarsely. She was a rail- thin woman, and her shorts barely covered her crotch, from the looks of it, Alex didn't think she was wearing any panties. Her gray tank top draped loosely over her sagging leathery breasts. Alex watched her kids run into the house. She shoved Anna Lynn and Bryson inside and slammed the door behind them.

Alex stepped into his car and threw it in reverse, careful to avoid the potholes as he made his way into the main road. Alex thought about how the two little children. What good was a mother that wasn't there?

He drove down old back roads to get to Azalea community college. It was a nice drive there. Leaves had just started to turn into a deep gold. In a few weeks they would all be dead. Eventually, the back roads opened onto the main road and after a few minutes he was turning into the main campus.

College students traveled in packs on the sidewalks and along the cross walks. Alex drove past them and turned into a parking garage. Cars lined every space of the first and second floor and he wound his way on the third level. There was one narrow space between a Jeep and the cement wall. Alex looked at the clock on his dashboard; if he didn't take it, he would be late for class. He took his time sliding into the space, but his passenger side mirror scraped along the wall. *Fuck!* He put his car in park and took the keys out of the ignition taking his books with him. The damage was done and there was no time to assess how bad it was, so he slammed the door shut.

Alex took his seat in the middle of the classroom, a few students looked up as he passed them, but they went back to what they were doing when they saw who it was. Two girls in the corner of the room looked over their shoulders and smiled at him, but Alex didn't pay attention. Catherine wasn't here yet; she was the only one he ever noticed. He opened his book and skimmed the first few lines before she finally walked in. She looked at Alex and smiled taking the seat next to him. He pretended not to notice her, but he couldn't help it; she smelled warm like she had bathed in the sun. He wanted to say something to her but didn't know how to start a conversation with a girl like her. When class started, he could feel her eyes on him. Alex focused on the Professor's dry lecture on social structure. Eventually his eyes drifted from the whiteboard to his notes, and eventually his gaze drifted toward Catherine. She looked up from her notebook and smiled at him again. Alex turned his attention back to the professor, an awkward older gentleman, with a high- pitched voice. He scribbled on the whiteboard more than he spoke and rarely made eye contact with anyone.

After class, Alex stayed behind to jot down the last bit of notes that were written on the board.

"Do you always write like that? Catherine asked. She was standing over him. He didn't know how long she had been watching him. Alex stopped writing, he couldn't find the courage to look at her and instead overanalyzed the uneven block letters on his paper.

"Yes," he replied and resumed writing.

She took the empty seat in front of him, "So what are you majoring in?"

"I haven't decided," he answered without looking up.

"Is this your first semester?" She asked pushing a few strands of loose hair behind her ear. Alex put the pen down and finally managed to look up at her. She had the brightest eyes, almost as warm and inviting as her skin. She wasn't overly perfumed – she smelled clean. There was a cool simplicity to her and to Alex she was perfect.

"Yeah, I just started," he finally replied.

"This is my last year before transferring to Altman University so I can finish out my Psych major."

Alex couldn't help but watch the way her lips moved when she talked. They were a subtle shade of pink.

"Anyway, I'm Catherine," She held out her hand and he took it into his. Her skin was as soft as he imagined it would be.

"Alex," he said before gently releasing her hand.

"Do you get out much?" Catherine sat back in her chair, "That came out wrong. I basically asked you if you had a life. What I really want to say is, would you like to grab some dinner with me some time?"

The question caught Alex off guard, and he must have kept her waiting too long because she brushed her hand over his to get his attention.

"Okay, yeah I would," Alex said finally. Catherine smiled and took his notebook from him. She wrote her number with his pen at the top of the page.

"Call me, okay?" Catherine slid the notebook back to him and started to leave but not before taking one last glance back at him. Alex watched her leave, he thought he would be excited that he had managed to catch her attention, but all he could think about were the preparations he would need to make at his apartment before he saw her again.

2
Eric

The phone rang. It seemed to go on forever, and each ring seemed a little longer than the last. Eric took the blue handset off the wall cradle. Its long curl of cord had tangled in the middle, and he did his best to straighten it out before bringing the phone to his ear. He looked on the kitchen counter where the small caller ID box sat. **Gabriel Meier** had come up at least five times today. Before that, Eric hadn't spoken to him in nearly fifteen years.

"Hey Son," Gabe said. He hadn't even said hello yet, but it was the static on the other end that gave him away.

"How'd you get my number?" Eric asked finally. He heard his dad clearing his throat.

"I looked your name up in the phone book. Not too many Eric Allen Meiers."

"Is there something I can help you with?"

"No, nothing like that Son. Just been thinking about a lot of things. Especially today. It would've been her birthday today, you know," Gabe's voice trailed off.

"Yeah, I know what today is."

Eric's voice couldn't have been sharper; there was silence on Gabe's end followed by a deep sigh. After Eric's mom died everything fell to shit, but the worst of it was how it affected his brother, and that was something he knew Gabe would never be able to undo.

"I'm really trying here," Gabe replied. "I know you blame me for that day, Eric. I blame myself,"

Eric didn't know what to say. He ran his fingers through his brown hair and stared absently at the kitchen sink. Water dripped from the spigot in slow rhythm. "It's not just that, you know that right? It's who you became after she died. We needed you, we needed our daddy. You weren't there."

There was a long pause then Gabe finally said, "Yeah, I know you're right. Listen, I'm sorry I called, but I'm really glad you picked up this time."

Eric sighed, "Daddy?"

"Yeah, Son."

"Please don't call here again," Eric returned the phone to its cradle. He pressed his thumb and forefinger against the bridge of his nose. *Why now? After all these years old man?*

Eric thought about his brother and a pang of guilt weighed heavy on his chest. He remembered the last time he saw his brother's face. Alex was fourteen then, and to Eric he still seemed so small and fragile, but it was the fight with his dad that drove him to leave. He remembered it like it was yesterday.

Leaving had been hard, but Eric didn't want to end up like most of the people in his town did, taking a job at the factory or driving trucks. He was determined to set a new path for himself, and if that meant leaving for college at seventeen, then that was what he would do. His grades in high school had been good enough for him to ride on a full scholarship. He couldn't pass that up, but that hadn't made leaving any less difficult. Eric hadn't wanted to leave Alex alone with their dad knowing he wouldn't be there for him like Eric was, especially since Dad wasn't around much anymore.

Alex had already been awake, and was sitting at the dining table tracing his fingers along the dark glossy woodgrain. Eric had gotten them each a plastic bowl of cereal. He sat one in front of his little brother.

"Here."

"Thank you." Alex swirled his spoon around the sugared O's before shoveling a heaping spoonful into his mouth. The sound of soft rain had filled the silence between them.

"You're big enough to fix your own lunches and your suppers. You have to poke the plastic film with a fork and stick it in the microwave for three minutes. Take it out. Peel off the cover..."

"I know." Alex cut in without looking up at him and continued to eat more of his cereal.

"And you need something, you ask Daddy. I know he doesn't talk much and he's never really here but you could leave him a note. Stick it on the fridge. If you run out of something, you tell him. He'll usually pick stuff up from the store, but just in case, don't be scared to ask him. You hear me?" Eric chewed at the inside of his cheeks.

"Okay." Alex pushed his bowl aside and ran upstairs to his room. Eric followed after him. His little brother was lying on his bed with his back turned to him; his shoulders bobbed up and down, and he could hear quiet sniffles. Eric plopped down next to him and Alex scooched over to give him room.

"Everything's going to be fine. I'm going to come back every chance I get." He rested a hand on his shoulder but Alex never said a word. He looked down at his plastic wrist watch. His bus would be coming in half an hour. "I have to get going, Alex, or I'm going to miss my bus."

He gave him a lingering hug and started for the door but not without looking back. "I love you, little brother," he said and he was gone.

Eric had visited as often as possible during the first year, and Alex was always happy to see him. He kept clean enough but with every visit Eric could tell he was losing weight.

"I've been leaving the TV dinners for him in the freezer like you said to. He just doesn't eat very much," his dad had said once. Eric didn't feel he should have to tell his own dad that sometimes you just have to man up and make the food for him because he's just a kid, a kid who lost his mother, and whose brother wasn't around to take care of him as if he were his own son. Did he help him with his homework? Did he stay up late to play video games on the weekend? Eric had known the answer to that.

Alex said he had done well in school. He'd shown him his report cards which were average. The teacher's comments had started off good, which was how every good intentioned piece of constructive criticism started – he's a well-mannered student and follows directions but... His teacher wanted to see him participate in class more, particularly in group activities. She wanted dad to schedule a conference so they could discuss Alex's withdrawn behavior, and possibly get him to meet with the school counselor at least once a week. Eric knew his dad never made the effort and this was confirmed by the comment in the fourth quarter with a final request for his dad to reach out to them. He wondered how many failed letters and phone calls Alex's teachers attempted, and if they ever made special visits to the house. If they did, they would have wasted a trip, Eric was certain of it.

Alex was in Eric's room playing the new video game he had brought home for him. It sure was good to see him happy at least. "Be right back, and then we can play that game together."

"Okay," Alex didn't have a chance to look up. He had been too invested in fighting some tall lanky opponent with rapid button mashing.

Downstairs, his dad fixed himself a plate of lunch before heading back to work. He remembered the smell of burnt coffee warming up in the microwave. He'd been wearing dark jeans and a checkered red and black shirt that made Eric think of a lumber jack.

"Daddy."

"Hey, Son," He didn't look up from the deli meat he was pulling from a plastic container and slapped it on some white bread.

"You got a minute?"

Gabe looked up briefly from smearing mayo on his bread. "I'm sure I can spare a minute."

Eric held up Alex's report card. "You happen to get back to the teacher about Alex?" His dad glimpsed at it.

"I had planned to, but with work and all it's just been real tough trying to schedule a conference with his teachers. Alex is fine anyhow. He doesn't need a counselor. He just gets spells sometimes. Hell, I think your great grandma Lindy was the same way."

"Daddy. This is serious. He's withdrawn, doesn't socialize. He could have anxiety or something. Could be depressed, you know, since..."

"Don't. Just don't," Gabe was shaking his head. "There's nothing wrong with that boy. He just gets spells is all."

"Maybe there's nothing wrong with him, but would it hurt for you to meet with his teachers and hear this counseling thing out? Might do him some good to talk to someone."

"No, Eric. He's not sick. He doesn't need to see anybody, and I sure as hell don't need to talk to his teachers." He threw his plate with the turkey sandwich into the sink, sending lettuce and tomato flying and a smear of mayo across the basin. He took his coffee mug out of the microwave and walked into the living room. Eric walked out behind him.

"Dad. I'm not asking for much. You know how Momma's death affected him. You owe him enough to get him some help. Please just…" Eric saw his daddy tense when he brought up his mom. A chord had been struck, he thought that it was one that would light a fire under his ass so that Alex could get the help he needed, but it wasn't.

"Goddamn it, Eric! You are not his parent. I am."

"Then act like one for a change. You could start by being here more for him. I may not be his parent, Daddy, but I am the closest thing he has to one since momma died!"

Gabe whipped around so fast, grabbed Eric by his gray t-shirt, and shoved him against the wall. His mug crashed to the ground, sending coffee splattering across the baseboard. His hand was balled into a red shaking fist at his side. Eric had been caught off guard that all words were lost to him. Through gritted teeth he managed to ask, "What are you going to do, kill me like you killed my mom? Do it then," he seethed. "I hate you, and I hate you for what you did to her."

Hot tears collected in Eric's eyes, and he looked over his dad's shoulder to find Alex trembling by the foot of the stairs, all the blood had drained from his face.

Gabe didn't kill his wife, but there was a tremendous weight in the room that ruled otherwise. He let him go, and Eric headed straight for the front door.

Eric was already halfway down the street when he heard his brother's timid voice and the sloshy patter of his bare feet on the wet pavement. He spun around and watched Alex catch up to him.

"Eric!" The rims of his eyes were red, and he shivered against the cold rain pelting against him. "Don't leave."

"I'm sorry baby brother," he shouted against the rain, "I have to," He hugged Alex tight. "You listen to me. You're gonna be okay. First chance you get, you get the hell out of here. You get yourself a job, and you put yourself through school. I am proud of you. You don't ever forget it, okay.

Eric looked down again at the caller ID. He pressed the back button until he came across a number. It didn't have a name, only a number, and the state—**Virginia.** He picked up the phone again and dialed the number on the caller ID. There was static with each ring. He hoped this time someone would answer, but it only rang.

3
Gabe

Gabe looked down at the small open box sitting in his lap. His name was written with blue sharpie in block letters in the center of the box, and it was missing a return address. It had been sitting on the second porch step when he came home from work early this morning. Gabe never received packages, he didn't have any extended family, and he knew they wouldn't be from his sons considering their history. The thick white box was worn and slightly dented in two corners, it wasn't the type of shipping box you could buy from a Wal-Mart or the UPS. It looked like something re-used that Gabe had only ever seen used for small hardware items like nuts or bolts. The box had been wrapped securely with brown packing tape around all edges and once across its length. It had been taped so well that Gabe needed a box cutter to tear away at it.

He examined the letters in his name again. There was something familiar about the shape of the **M** in Meier, and the way the letter was segmented as though two vertical lines had been drawn followed by a **v** in the center to create the point of the **M**. Gabe wasn't the type to pay special attention to those types of things, but this stood out to him, it was the way the package had been waiting for him beneath a dim porchlight, casting its own small shadow on the wooden steps, and because the penmanship resembled his own. Stranger still was what had been inside the box. There was a singlet of fine honey-colored hair bound together by a black ribbon, a fabric pressed neatly into a square in a clear zip lock bag, a square card that simply said Happy Birthday, and a newspaper clipping of his wife's obituary. Gabe held the obituary gently between his fingers as though he was holding onto something sacred, as though mishandling it would somehow be disrespecting her. There was nothing unusual about the obituary, at least not a first glance. The only thing missing from it was Eleanor's picture. When he looked more closely, he noticed a single pen mark before the start of the sentence, 'We'll meet again,' followed by another pen mark at the end of it.

There was a hint of lavender in the cloth and hard little fragments inside that felt like rough plastic, and when Gabe unfolded it whole fingernails dropped into the box. He jumped flinging the box onto his living room floor pushing himself against the couch. Some of the fingernails fell beneath the couch. He leaned over the edge looking at the brittle pieces that now inhabited his carpet. They were short, dainty, and gray crescent moon shaped nails. At first, he thought they might've been the plastic kinds he'd seen advertised on TV, but these weren't plastic; there were flakes of dead skin still attached to some. He used the cloth to pull the fingernails from the carpet ensuring he had collected every single one and dropped them into the box. He set it beside Eleanor's framed picture on the end table next to the sofa. Who could send a package like that? Who else could've known today was her birthday? He knew the answer to that. Gabe looked at Eleanor's picture. Her eyes were bright and alive, and her smile was sweet yet artificial. A smile to hide the pain, he thought.

4
Alex

Alex sat in his car at the corner of Newbern Street and Dalliance in downtown Bridgford where all the shops and restaurants were. It was a big college town, but there were also a lot of retired folks that liked to do their holiday shopping here too, and being so close to Christmas, these streets were full of people. It was eight o' clock at night and especially busy for a Friday, but he didn't mind. He liked watching people and how they went about their lives. A mother and father walked with their toddler into a toy store. He imagined being part of their lives somehow. He could be the older brother and they would have dinners together every night just like his mom used to make, only they would talk to one another like families are supposed to do. An older couple walked hand in hand down the street to a restaurant. He wanted to be their grandson; he could ask them to be his new grandparents, but that's not what he wanted. He was looking for something more meaningful with someone he could connect with. He continued watching people; many of them enjoying their weekend; some of them walked alone. Those were the ones he watched the most. There were so many beautiful women, and most of them didn't know it, but he wanted them to know how beautiful they were, and he was going to show them. Alex pulled a silver flip phone from his pocket when he felt it buzzing. **Mom** flashed on the small outer screen and he watched it ring until it went to voicemail. After a minute, the phone vibrated twice. **1 Missed Call** and **Voicemail** appeared. He slid the phone back into his pocket and went back to what he was doing.

After an hour of watching he finally saw the one he would give his love to. He liked brunettes with small frames and a warm smile. This woman was perfect. She greeted her friends outside of The Dandy Lion, a local pub most college students spent their weekends; she seemed friendly and outgoing. He enjoyed the way her scarf draped around her neck and subtly touched the top of her breasts, and she had a smile that could probably brighten anyone's day. Alex watched them go inside the pub. He waited a few more minutes before going in too.

It was a busy night. Music blared from a vintage juke box across the room and people chattered endlessly about random things. Alex sat at the bar watching the woman standing at the other end waiting to get the bartender's attention. She caught Alex's eye briefly and smiled, he smiled back at her and turned his attention to the bartender who had just finished closing out the tab of an older gentleman next to him.

"What can I get for you?" the bartender asked.

"One of your draft beers. Doesn't matter which," the bartender nodded. He took a glass from behind the counter and put it under one of the nozzles and pulled back on one of the levers. Cool amber spilled out from the spout. He filled the glass to the brim before placing it in front of Alex. "Three fifty," he said. Alex slipped a crisp five from his wallet and handed it to the guy. Alex recognized him; they passed each other on campus every once in a while. He was the typical frat guy, sociable with all the charm. Alex doubted he even knew who he was. He thanked him and told him to keep the change.

"Thanks, Man."

Alex looked over at the woman again. She was looking at him again. That was all he needed to know that he could win her over, and he didn't acknowledge her again. Instead, he found a cozy table to sit at in the far corner of the bar and occasionally checked his phone as though he were waiting for someone.

"Hey!" a sweet voice called. Alex looked up expecting it to be the woman, but to his surprise, it was Catherine.

"Hi," Alex adjusted himself in his chair. It was a wonder he could say anything at all. Seeing her there was enough to throw him off kilter.

"I didn't know that you come to this bar," she said taking a seat beside him.

Alex was having a difficult time looking into her bright eyes, "It's my first time here," he replied.

She smiled at him, "I'm glad you're here. Were you expecting someone?"

Alex shook his head, "No, I actually just got off work, and needed some place to unwind,"

"Nice, where do you work?"

"I work at, Dusty's," Alex replied. Dusty's was the local hardware store at the end of the street. The old man who owned it took him in when he first came to the small Virginia town in Bridgford County. He said he reminded him of his own son, back when he was still in his twenties.

"I love Dusty, he's such a nice guy! I never knew that you worked there," Catherine beamed, "I was so sad when I saw him on the news talking about his granddaughter,"

"Yeah."

Her phone went off and she retrieved it from her purse. She checked to see who it was and dismissed the call.

"Sorry about that," she looked up at him. She carried a warmth that he wouldn't mind being around all the time. "Why haven't you called me?" she asked curiously.

Alex was taken back. She genuinely seemed interested in him. He shook his head. "Between work and school there's not much time for anything else. I would have called you tonight, but I wasn't planning on staying here long."

"Well now that you're here, you can hang out with me and my friends."

Alex had his reservations, and he discreetly looked past Catherine to the woman who had been standing at the bar. She wasn't standing there anymore, she and her friends had moved to a table close to his and had engaged in light conversation about movies they've seen.

"Okay, sure," he said.

Catherine smiled, "Come on," she took his hand into hers and led him toward the back of the bar. He watched her walking seamlessly past the crowd of people. She looked back at him every once a while and smiled. He liked the way she looked at him. He even liked how much thought she put into her clothes. She was wearing a nice floral top with a brown leather jacket and jeans that hugged her small frame. She took care of herself.

They walked past the girl he had been watching. She looked up at him briefly but didn't smile when she noticed Catherine holding his hand. They walked through a door in the back where the pool tables were. The smell of cigarettes wafted through the air; it was almost too thick to breathe. Catherine's friends were busy playing a game when she greeted them, "Hey guys," she called to a man and a woman in their mid-twenties.

"It's about time!" the woman took the cue stick from a stocky man with thick burly hair that sat perfectly still atop his masculine head.

"Sorry," Catherine laughed. "I want you guys to meet my friend, Alex. He's in my Sociology class."

"Hi, Alex," the woman held out her hand to shake his. "I'm Cara. This is my husband Aidan."

Aidan stood next to her and Alex shook his hand.

"Hey, how's it going?"

"It's good," Alex felt out of place standing with Catherine's friends, but she smiled at him, and it was the only thing that kept him from leaving.

"How about a game?" She turned to Alex. Why was it impossible to say no to her?

"Yeah, okay sure."

"Good, you're on my team."

She took a pool stick from the rack along the far wall. There weren't many to choose from. Most of them were warped or the tips were worn down to the point of being useless. Catherine had picked the best one she could find and handed it to Alex.

"I should warn you, I'm not very good."

"They're not either," she joked.

Cara shot her a look and they all laughed. The game went well. Alex managed to sink most of his shots but scratched on the eight ball, and Catherine teased him for costing them the game. Occasionally, she subtly leaned against him. Alex didn't know if it was intentional, but he didn't mind. The warmth that he felt when she was near him was a welcome change. He enjoyed listening to her telling stories about when she and Cara were younger.

"Cara slept over and we had this big plan to watch our first real horror movie after my parents went to bed. So, when they fell asleep, we snuck downstairs and flipped it to channel 32. They always had the late- night horror movie presentations, do you guys remember that? The host was a guy who wore a lab coat and black rubber gloves, what was his name? Dr. Mad Blood!"

Cara and Aidan nodded. She looked over at Alex and he shook his head, he could feel his face begin to warm, but Catherine just gave him a smile and a quick wink.

"So anyway, the movie was C.H.U.D, a creepy and typical cheesy movie about these weird creatures that came from the sewer. We were joking it until one of those stupid things came from out of nowhere. This dork grabs my arm and we screamed so loud that my dad came flying out of his room and slid halfway down the stairs only to find us watching TV. He grounded me for a week."

They all burst out into a fit of laughter. Aidan made some crack at Cara still being a big wuss when it came to scary movies.

The night went on that way, one light-hearted conversation after another, and though Alex said very little, Catherine managed to include him in every single one. After a few more games, Aidan was ready to call it a night. He explained that they had been up earlier than normal because of work. Catherine didn't want the night to end yet and pouted her lip when Cara checked her phone to see what time it was.

"You know we have to," said Cara.

Catherine shook her head, "I understand, but let's do this again soon, okay?"

They closed out their tabs and walked out together. The temperature had dropped much more than when Alex first went into the bar, but there were still so many people walking around downtown Bridgford. Cara clung to Aidan's arm.

"It's so damn cold! Let's get out of here," she hugged Catherine tightly and looked over at Alex who had been staring back at the silhouettes of people through the frosted window of the bar, "Take care of her, okay?"

"Of course."

"Bye guys!" Catherine watched them walk to their car. Aidan opened the passenger door for Cara before making his way to the driver side. Catherine and Alex watched her friends drive off.

"They seem nice," said Alex. He followed her down an alley lit with white Edison lights that crisscrossed over their heads; they followed it behind The Dandy Lion to a small parking lot. Wet gravel glistened beneath their feet as they walked. There were a few people smoking outside in Dandy Lion's beer garden.

"Oh, they are really good people, I've known Cara since I was a little girl. She and Aidan are high school sweethearts. They're still so much in love. It's refreshing you know?"

Alex nodded. He walked with Catherine to her car.

"So, what should we do now?"

Alex looked into her kind eyes, catching himself smiling.

"Actually, I should be getting home myself."

"Really?" You don't want to stay out just a little longer?"

Part of him wanted to stay. "Believe me, I do, but there are some things I need to take care of early in the morning."

"Tomorrow night, then. You could come over; we'll order a pizza. Rent some movies."

Alex studied her face. A sweep of dark hair fell over her eyes and she pushed it aside. She was different than the others, so what was it about her that drew him to her? "I'd like that, but I have some things to take care of. Rain check?"

"Okay. You have my number. Send me a text so I can program yours into my phone."

"I actually lost my phone, but I'm going to be getting a new one soon. When I do, I promise I'll text you with my number."

"Okay, you better or I'll hunt you down," she pointed a sharp finger at him with a pout and a scowl.

He couldn't remember the last time someone made him smile the way she did.

Catherine slipped a pen from a pocket on the side of her designer purse and reached for his hand. She turned it over and leaned in close to him, cradling his hand in hers and wrote her address in his palm. Alex winced when she had to press down a little harder at the creases to get the ink going again.

"Here, write your address on my hand now."

Alex took her hand into his, gently unfolding her delicate fingers so he could write on her palm. He looked at her briefly before scrawling his address down.

"There."

"Now I know where you live. You can't get away from me," Catherine said, seeming reluctant to take her hand back from his. She wrapped her arms around him. When was the last time anyone had ever held him like this? Alex wrapped his arms around her waist.

"Bye," she smiled.

Alex waited for her to get into her car. She waved as she drove past, and he watched her until she was out of view before he headed for his car.

"She's not like the others," his mother's voice whispered behind him, and hearing her was enough to stop Alex in his tracks.

"No," He swallowed hard.

"You gave her your real address?"

"Yes," He felt her icy breath on his shoulder and the hairs on his neck prickled. "I really like her."

"But you're forgetting me."

Now he felt his mother's hand on his shoulder. It weighed him down like cinderblocks, and he could feel himself sinking into the gravel. Her grip was so cold, he could feel it through his jacket.

"No, Mom, I could never."

"What will you do when I'm gone?" Her voice seemed to echo though it was no louder than a whisper.

Alex swallowed hard, "Please don't say that. You promised you'd never leave me, remember? All I've done is honor you. They were my perfect girls and I've given them to you." Her eyes were filmy and unblinking, staring directly at him. He turned and nodded at a few people as they walked by. They smiled and hurried into the Dandy Lion through the beer garden. When Alex turned back, she was gone.

He headed back for his car when he noticed the woman he had spotted earlier walking out with her friends. She looked over at Alex briefly before walking off. Alex sat in his car for a moment watching the woman say goodbye to her friends. He saw her long honey-colored waves bounce as she hugged them. His window had fogged over, and he wiped it away with the back of his jacket sleeve. He couldn't help noticing she was by herself now and he wondered if she lived alone. Alex knew he should be driving home, but the last thing he would want was for this woman to be lonely.

The headlights to her Corolla flooded his car as she pulled away from the curb and on to the main road. Alex did the same, but instead of going in the opposite direction, he made a U-turn and followed her behind at a comfortable distance. Headlights glared in his rearview mirror, and he flipped it upward so that he could focus on what was in front of him. The woman took a few turns down the side streets until approaching an older neighborhood; she didn't live far from the city. When she turned into the neighborhood, Alex slowed down. When she turned a corner, he followed the corner ten seconds later. After a few minutes she turned onto her street and pulled into her driveway. Alex stopped in front of the curb of a vacant home with a "For Sale" sign just two blocks from hers. He cut his lights off and watched the woman get out of her car. She fumbled with her keys until finding the right one, and he watched her pull the flimsy screen door back to get into her house. Alex drifted past her home so slowly that he could hear the friction of his tires against loose asphalt. *She left the porch lights on just for me.* His eyes moved along the fancy black numbers on the porch post, *Eight-Nine-One.* 891 on Camila Street. He committed it to memory.

Alex drove home taking the usual back roads. It was a quiet ride, but his mind stayed busy. His thoughts kept drifting to Catherine. She really seemed to take an interest in him, why was it so hard for his mother to see that?

When he got home, he walked straight into the bathroom and opened the cabinets beneath the sink. He crouched down and reached toward the back until he could feel the edge of a canvas bag with the tip of his fingers. He pulled it out and sat down on the linoleum floor. Alex carefully unzipped the bag and took a peek inside. There was a box of latex gloves, a small bone saw, a painter's mask, and a box of black trash bags.

He shimmied himself close to the bathtub and drew back the shower curtain. Inside were pieces of his old love, Brenda – packaged neatly and buried in ice. The ice hadn't thawed yet, it was too soon, he knew. He had his procedure down: drain, cut, wrap, ice. The organs were trickier, sloppier, so he always took care of that first. He would put them in a trash bag and take them out to the dumpster on trash day. The rest of her was preserved in plastic wrap, which he found to be more reliable than grocery store bags he used the first time.

Alex sighed. Saying goodbye was hard, but he hoped that she would understand. Alex opened up a trash bag and carefully placed the wrapped pieces of her inside. He tied the bag off before taking it into the bedroom. Then he reached beneath his bed for a large gym bag and put her inside. Even though she was a petite woman, it was still a tight fit, and for a second he worried that he would need to make two trips, but he pushed down on the bag and forced the zipper across the tracks leaving only a small gap. He secured it further by clasping the Velcro handles together. Alex changed from his regular clothes into a pair of workout shorts and a black shirt and threw on his brand-new gym shoes, and he was sure to take his cell phone with him, slipping it into one of the pockets on his shorts before heading out with gym bag in hand.

As he made his way to his truck, he heard tiny feet approaching. He looked down to see the pudgy little toddler, Anna Lynn, behind him.

"Hi," she said.

"Hello," Alex replied, sliding the bag into the passenger seat of his truck. "Where's your brother?"

He clicked the key fob and it beeped twice. Anna Lynn looked up at him and shook her head.

"Bryson got a 'owie. He won't wake up."

"Where's your mom?" Alex pulled on the handle to ensure that it was truly locked.

"Mama lef wif Tim affer Bryson gotted hurt. He beated him bad 'cause Bryson didn't wunihm to hut me. Mama wus scream'un real loud. She wus mad at Bryson un me."

Alex looked past her toward her apartment. The door was wide open like it usually was, but it was pitch black inside. He looked back at his car. *She* wouldn't be angry at him if he had to call the police. *She* would be proud, and no one would bother her because there was no need to. *She* would wait. Alex followed the little girl to her apartment. He entered cautiously before flipping on the kitchen light switch. After a few clicks and a hum, the fluorescent bulbs in the ceiling cut on, and Alex could get a clearer picture of Anna Lynn's living situation. A draft crept in through the open door. In the kitchen, the lights cast a bluish hue on the cheap folding table, piled with half-eaten chicken fingers on broken plates. A plastic cup of orange juice had spilled across the table and it pooled into a puddle on the floor. Week old dishes lay in a sink of standing water, and the dingy linoleum flooring was beginning to curl upward at the edges where the living room separated the kitchen. It was quiet, apart from the low hum of the fluorescent lights above them.

"Where's Bryson?" Alex looked down at Anna Lynn and she pointed toward the open living room. Alex walked toward the back of the apartment, flipped a light switch he thought might be for the living room, but nothing happened. Alex didn't see Bryson, at least not right away. The living room was dim, partially lit from the light in the kitchen. Toys were strewn across the floor. There was a brown couch against one wall and beside it a pile of laundry. He looked down at the dark Berber. It must have been the original carpet from when the complex was built in the seventies. There was a strange pungent odor emanating from it. A small TV sat on the floor on the other side of the room, and the walls were bare which somehow made the room seem colder. Alex's gaze swept across the room again. He looked on the couch and around it, and to the small pile of laundry on the floor. Beside the clothes were small shoes. Only then did he realize that attached to those shoes were legs, and the pile of laundry wasn't laundry at all. Alex walked over to the boy and crouched down. The little girl followed close behind him. The boy wasn't moving. His eyes were partially open, but they were dim. His face was purple and stretched tight from the swelling, and his arms had been contorted into a sickening position behind his back. Alex was almost sure that Bryson was dead until he heard a whistling coming from his throat. He was hanging on within an inch of his life. Alex looked down at Anna Lynn who was now huddled close, not once taking her eyes off her brother. He glanced back at the open front door letting the draft in and the soft orange glow from the streetlights. "Where's your telephone?" Anna Lynn pointed over his shoulder at the white phone sitting on the end table. He picked up the receiver and dialed for help. It rang once before dispatch picked up.

"Nine-One-One what's your emergency?" asked the dispatcher. She said it as though he was calling to order pizza.

"Yes, I'm at 101 Azalea Cove. I'm with a little girl who says her mom's boyfriend hurt her brother. He's not looking so good."

"Are you with him now?"

"Yes, I think he's alive but he's not moving. He's going to need serious help as soon as possible. The mom and boyfriend aren't here," Alex looked back at the little girl who had mimicked the way Alex was crouching beside Bryson.

"I have dispatched emergency services and nearby officers to that location. They should be there shortly." Alex stayed on the line with the dispatcher answering questions. The little girl sat quietly beside her brother. It was a long ten minutes before they heard the sirens outside. The officers announced themselves from the doorway before entering.

"They're here now," he waved them over, "We're right here," he called out to them.

"Okay Mr. Meier, I will be ending the call now."

"Thank you," Alex returned the phone to the receiver.

Two officers and an older man in a dark gray suit walked in and the paramedics weren't far behind with a stretcher in tow. Anna Lynn shied behind Alex. One of the officers searched the other rooms and the other went to the little girl. The older gentleman, who introduced himself as Detective Howard Tamblin, took Alex aside for questioning and Anna Lynn stayed by her brother.

Alex watched the officer and two paramedics tending to them.

"What's your name, Sweetheart?" the officer asked. She was shorter and rounder than the man who was standing with him. Anna Lynn didn't answer, she scooted closer to her brother and touched his shoulder.

"It's okay we won't hurt you. You can tell me," she said. The little girl fidgeted with her stained My Little Pony shirt and looked down at her brother.

"Anna Lynn Baker," she squeaked, but it sounded more like, Anuh len baykoh.

"Anna Lynn, that's a beautiful name. I'm officer Cadence," she looked down at the young boy, "Is this your brother?"

Anna Lynn nodded.

"What's his name?"

"Bryson."

Officer Cadence looked the boy over. She kept her eyes and her voice steady, but all color emptied from her face. She waved the paramedics over.

"Anna Lynn, they're going to check for Bryson's pulse, okay? We need to see how strong it is. Is that all right?" The little girl nodded shyly, and she sat as close to her brother as possible. Officer Cadence moved aside to let an EMT move in. The woman crouched down beside Anna Lynn and she waited for a good long minute. "The pulse is weak but it's still there," she put her fingers close to his nose. "Breath is shallow but also present," she motioned for her partner to bring the stretcher to her. "He's in pretty bad shape but he's still with us. Let's get him on the stretcher," Officer Cadence looked at the little girl, "They're going to take good care of him okay?"

Anna Lynn didn't say anything.

The paramedics slid the couch away from the wall and put the stretcher as close to Bryson as possible. They lowered it down to his level. As carefully as they could they hoisted him onto it and lifted the guard rails to secure him. They had to reposition his arm because it was horribly twisted behind his back, and the poor kid whimpered.

"Let's get him out of here and get the IV started," said an EMT.

Alex watched as they wheeled him out.

Officer Cadence looked at the detective, "I'll go ahead and call CPS. Shouldn't take them long to get here."

She looked back at the little girl; she was trying to go with her brother, but Officer Cadence told her she would need to stay.

"We're going to help your brother get better. As soon as he is, you'll be able to see him okay?"

Anna Lynn stared at her with big glossy eyes. She didn't believe her. Alex wasn't entirely sure if Officer Cadence believed what she was telling Anna Lynn either. She patted Anna Lynn on the shoulder and urged her to sit down on the sofa, she promised she wouldn't be gone long. The little girl sat quietly, looking toward the door every once in a while. Alex wondered who she hoped it might be. Who could she turn to, now that Bryson was gone?

"What's going to happen to her," Alex asked.

Detective Tamblin shook his head.

"CPS will try to contact next of kin. If they can't get a hold of anyone or if there isn't one, she'll go to foster care until this whole thing gets straightened out. As of now we'll be on the lookout for her mom and step- dad."

After a few minutes, Officer Cadence returned. Tamblin nodded to her and he walked out with Alex. Anna Lynn tried to wiggle herself off the couch to follow Alex, but Officer Cadence convinced her to stay.

"Do you know them well?" Detective Tamblin asked.

Alex shook his head.

"No, I just moved here a couple of months ago. They're always outside by themselves. Do you think their mom will come back?"

"No, I don't. You saw the condition the kid was in. They left in a hurry. Left the girl to fend for herself. Left her brother to die. Little man's brave though, sticking up for his sister like that."

"Yeah. I hope he makes it."

Tamblin followed Alex to his truck. A flood of red and blue lights flashed along the walls of the apartment buildings. A crowd of people was now forming in the middle of the street trying to make sense of what was happening. When Officer Cadence stepped out with Anna Lynn, Alex heard a few gasps among them.

"Oh my God."

"Where's her brother?"

Alex looked across the parking lot. The ambulance had just started to pull away from the neighborhood. He felt sorry for him. How could his mother go with a man who hurt her child that way? How could she abandon them?

Alex watched Anna Lynn and the officer approach a white government vehicle that had just pulled into the parking lot as they were walking outside. A lanky woman wearing a serious gray suit with a neatly pressed collared shirt stepped out and shook firm hands with Officer Cadence. She looked down at Anna Lynn who was hiding behind the officer. Alex could tell that Officer Cadence was explaining the situation to her from the way the woman was shaking her head. At one point she held out her hand to Anna Lynn, but the little girl clutched on to Officer Cadence's pant leg.

"I want my bruder! Where's my bruder?!"

Alex heard her yell, and she began to cry. She swatted at the woman's hand and screamed when she reached out to her. Alex watched her kneel down in front of the little girl. She didn't smile; she didn't even wag a finger at her. Instead, she said something to Anna Lynn that managed to calm her down. He wondered if she promised to take her to Bryson. Officer Cadence helped her into the back seat and buckled her in. After a few minutes she shut the door and the woman drove away.

"Detective! Can you tell us what happened here?"

It was a local news reporter from Channel 2 waving a microphone in his face. Tamblin shook his head.

"I'll give you a statement in just a few minutes, David," Tamblin said without looking over as he followed Alex to his truck.

It didn't take long for the reporter to head toward the crowd of people.

"Thanks for staying with those kids. You did a good thing. So many people these days would have looked the other way," Tamblin said.

Alex unlocked the door to his truck with one push on the key fob. "It was no problem. I'm happy I could help."

He lifted the door handle and sank down into his seat before starting the ignition. Detective Tamblin started to shut the door for him but hesitated when he caught a glimpse of the gym bag. Alex followed his gaze.

"Headed to the gym this late?"

"Yeah. I like to go to the gym when it's not crowded"

"I didn't realize there were twenty-four- hour gyms around here. I've been looking for one. Where do you go?"

Tamblin kept a hand on the edge of the door leaving an uncomfortably short distance between them.

"It's not a gym. My buddy has equipment in his garage," Alex rested a hand on the steering wheel.

"Oh, I could have sworn you said you like to go to the gym when it's not crowded."

A cool sweat started to collect on Alex's forehead, but he wiped it away, hoping Tamblin didn't notice.

"No, I'm sorry, I should've explained myself better, I like to go to my buddy's gym because it's not crowded. We just call it the gym. It's set up exactly like one except it's in his garage," Alex swallowed hard. "I should probably get going though. He was expecting me an hour ago."

"Of course. Well listen, we may need to come by to ask you some follow-up questions in the next day or two. Which apartment is yours?"

"Yes, sir. It's 214, right up there," He pointed to his apartment, the one with blinds bent unevenly toward the bottom of the window. "I keep meaning to fix those blinds," He wished he had done it right after *She* broke them. Tamblin looked up.

"Oh, they don't look so bad," but something had caught Tamblin's eye. "Sorry, I won't keep you. You have a good night now. We'll talk real soon."

Alex nodded, and he reached for the door handle. Tamblin released it from his grip and the door shut with a thud.

He caught the officer's eyes flicker toward his apartment one last time before walking off. The young man pulled out of the parking lot. He looked in his rear- view mirror. Tamblin was watching him.

5
Alex

Alex wound his way down the old back roads as if he were heading back toward the college. His headlights guided his way on the dark streets. Cars rarely took those roads at night: there were too many twists and turns and there had been too many accidents. Few wanted to risk it. Elbow roads people called them because the curves were as sharp as the crook of an arm. Alex had become good friends with that road and particularly with the woods that had surrounded it where he had found, and there was a special place for his girls – a safe place from the rest of the world. It was down a small path off the beaten track just big enough to accommodate his truck, and dark enough to hide what he was doing. Tonight was perfect. There was just enough moonlight to help him find his way to his special place, but it was still dark enough to hide. No one would find them there.

Alex slowed down when he saw the small wooden stake planted firmly in front of a decaying maple. He almost missed it because it had been partially obscured by soggy leaves. He cut his headlights off and turned onto the old dirt road just before his marker. Thick trees surrounded him, and he drove forward at two miles an hour until the front of his car met resistance from trees that refused to let him go any further. He put the car in park and cut the engine off with two clicks before shoving the keys in his back pocket. Alex hoped she would be happy here just like the other one. He took the gym bag and scooted out of the truck, and he shut the door as softly as possible before heading to his special place. It was a long walk to get there, and it had rained so much over the last few days that mud and debris sloshed beneath his feet. He sank a few inches with each step. The conditions weren't ideal, but *She* couldn't stay with him anymore and Alex knew it.

He continued walking for nearly half an hour with only a sliver of moonlight casting down between crooked branches to help guide him. His feet grew heavy with mud collecting in the crevices of his sneakers, but he trudged on until he came to a small clearing beside a pond. Alex looked next to him and he set his bag down next to a tree that had a shovel propped against it. The bluish hue from the light above made the ground look as black as tar and just as thick. Beyond the trees he saw his mother's eyes glinting in the moonlight. She limped out from the shroud of darkness and waited by the pond.

Alex reached for the shovel, carefully guiding his hand along the tree's coarse bark until his fingers tipped it. He took the shovel and hoisted the gym bag onto his shoulder with some strain from the weight of her. He tried to find the perfect spot for her, a place close to the other one. He thought *She* might like to be near the pond. He remembered most of the pictures in her living room had been of her fishing with her family. His favorite picture was of her sitting on a dock with her legs hanging over the edge in jean shorts and a white tank top. Her hair was pulled back in a messy bun, and she was smiling. Yes, *She* would be happy next to the pond, he thought and began to dig a hole beside it.

An hour had passed before Alex was finally satisfied with the job he had done. He had dug a perfect grave, even on all sides, and deep enough to keep her safe from the elements. It had taken him longer than he had hoped, the ground was too soft and mud from the sides kept sinking into the middle. Alex looked down at his work and smiled, "You're going to be happy here."

Sweat beaded on his forehead, and he carefully slid the gym bag to him and cradled it close. "Does this make you happy Mom?

His mother stood over him; her head was bent at an angle. The black wire stitches were taut against her rotting flesh. Her lips were pressed into a thin smile and occasionally, her entire body twitched. Alex set the gym bag in the grave and began shoveling earth into it until it was level with the ground. He packed the soil down tight hammering it with the flat side of his shovel but dropped it when his ear caught something rustling in the leaves. He watched his mother lurch into the opposite direction past the pond. It could have been the wind or some animal, but they sounded like footsteps. Alex didn't wait to find out. He sprinted for his truck, fighting his way through the mud and trying not to run into the trees that crowded in around him. He looked back, but he shouldn't have. That carelessness caused him to run straight into the front end of his truck. Alex fell hard but he picked himself up and crawled his way to the driver side door. His hands were wet and gritty, and he slid his hand along the door until he felt the handle and pulled the door open. Alex hoisted himself into the truck, trying to catch his breath. His hands shook, but he kept them steady enough to put his key into the ignition, and once he felt the engine fire up, he peeled back onto the main road. He wiped the sweat from his brow which just seemed to smear mud across his face, his eyes shifted to his mirrors trying to see if anyone was following him.

By the time Alex made it back to his neighborhood, the ambulance, the police, the reporters, and the crowds were all gone. A small circle of orange light hung over the otherwise dim parking lot. He walked upstairs, his shoes clanging heavily against each metal step, and fell through his front door, locking it behind him. He felt for the light switch and a soft light filled the room. He dropped his keys on the ground and sank into his couch with a groan. Alex wasn't even sure what time it was. He reached into his pocket for the phone, but his pocket was empty. He felt in between the couch cushions. Nothing. Alex ran back downstairs to his truck. He searched beneath the car seats and between them. He checked the dashboard, and the floorboards, he checked the back seat and even in the bed of the truck. It wasn't there. Alex went back to his apartment and collapsed on the couch. A slow panic took root inside him. He knew exactly where it was.

6
Detective Tamblin

Tamblin pulled into his driveway. The porchlight was on, but none of the lights in the house were. He figured his wife Lorraine went to bed early, but when he looked at the clock, he realized it was damn past midnight.

"Late again, Old Timer," he said to himself. That's what Lorraine would've said had she been waiting up for him.

Harold Tamblin lived in a quiet suburban neighborhood of about twenty evenly spaced houses, with grass always trimmed to a regulatory two inches, landscapes perfectly pruned, and sidewalks devoid of cracks or thistle weed. His wife, a retired naval officer, was a gardener at heart, and so the front porch had its fill of large potted plants and she even had her square patch of garden in front with what she called perennials and butterfly bushes. It always tickled him to see the Monarchs coming to pay Lorraine a visit every spring; she'd be sure to take pictures to keep in her scrap book. He smiled at the thought of his wife and couldn't wait to snuggle up beside her.

He walked into the house and was welcomed by the smell of apple cinnamon potpourri and the wagging nub tail of his English bulldog, Buddy. He knelt down to scratch the old boy behind his white ears, and when Buddy was satisfied, the dog hobbled over to his bed in the corner of the living room. He was a hefty little thing, with foggy eyes, and brown patches in the folds of his white fur; and he was one hell of a guard dog, the kind that would lay in the middle of the floor for belly rubs if he saw an intruder.

Tamblin disarmed and rearmed their house alarm after securing the door. Down the corridor he could see the kitchen light was on which meant Lorraine had left him some dinner in the oven. That was the first time he thought about food since breakfast. His wife would've given him a piece of her mind if she knew he was skipping meals again and he hoped not to stir that nest. The problem was that the case had taken over and he wouldn't be able to think of much else until it was solved. He honestly didn't know how Lorraine had managed to put up with him for the last twenty-six years on the force where late nights and early mornings were the norm. It took a special kind of woman, and Lorraine was certainly more under-standing than most, what with her having served in the military.

The faint aroma of something savory lingered in the kitchen. There was a note on the microwave that read, "I hid the salt so don't even think about it. Love you."

Tamblin shook his head and smiled; she knew him too well. In the microwave was a plate of rotisserie chicken, mashed potatoes with a pool of gravy on top, and a side of peppered green beans covered with plastic wrap. Tamblin removed the plastic wrap, pressed the number three on the microwave, and let it do its thing.

He took a seat at the island in the center of his open kitchen and mindlessly thumbed through his phone while he waited for his food. He wasn't sure what he was looking for, nothing in his phone would give him a break in the Delaney/Coswell cases. He would be making a visit to Brenda Coswell's family later in the week, and tomorrow a visit with the Delaney's. It would be his third visit with the Delaney's, but it was necessary to go back. Sometimes you end up finding things that weren't there before, important things that friends or family forgot to mention. Eventually there had to be new leads, he just hoped they wouldn't lead him cold.

"Were you going to let that beep all night, Baby?"

Tamblin looked up, his wife, Lorraine was standing in the doorway, his food was ready, and the microwave had started beeping to remind him something was still in there. He was so far deep in his own thoughts that he didn't even realize his food was done. Tamblin started to get up but Lorraine was already walking past him to the microwave, patting his shoulder on the way there.

"Sit," she told him.

She came back with the plate of food, and a fork and knife wrapped in a cloth napkin and sat it in front of him, but before she would join her husband, Lorraine poured him a glass of milk with a splash of dark cola.

"Thank you, Dear Heart," he said when she set the glass beside him.

"I don't understand why you like it, but if it makes you happy then who am I to judge?"

"You don't know what you're missing. Nice little fizz, coupled with the smoothness of the milk. It's almost like a root beer float, except it's milk instead of ice cream and cola instead of root beer. Give it another chance."

He waved the glass playfully in front of her.

Lorraine shook her head with her nose scrunched up like a rabbit.

"I'm not missing a thing. You can go ahead and keep that to yourself, Baby."

Tamblin laughed, "Okay, okay, Lord knows I'd never be able to change your mind."

They talked while he ate, mostly about plans to visit their daughter, Tina in the fall, and about vacations they intended to take. Lorraine suggested Hawaii as she had always heard about the Aloha spirit and she wanted to experience it for herself.

"We just need to go somewhere sunny and absolutely breathtaking," she said, "and warm," Lorraine said she had a friend who went to Hawaii for a vacation and she just decided she wasn't going to come back. "Maybe we could do the same thing and get away from it all. What do you say?"

"That would be mighty fine."

Tamblin pushed at the mash potatoes with his fork and gave it a good dip in what remained of the brown gravy pool before shoveling it into his mouth.

Leaving Bridgford, Virginia would be a mighty fine idea, but Howard Tamblin was never the type of man to just leave everything behind, especially with these cases that had him coming home so late at night. He set his fork down and took a sip of his drink. Even though he was sitting right here next to his wife, he was miles away. Every time he blinked, he found himself walking through the possible scenarios, revisiting crime scenes, rewinding the footage in his mind while searching for the missing pieces of a broken puzzle. He was good at what he did, solving nearly twenty missing case files over the course of his career, a small feat for anyone who knows how many cases go unsolved, but to the twenty families whom he had brought closure to, those small feats had meant the world.

Howard Tamblin had a late start in his career. Long before law enforcement, he was a sous chef in some cushy five-star restaurant, and it was a good job, but it wasn't the job that he was meant to do. So, at the age of thirty-eight, during what may have seemed like a midlife crisis, he applied to the Baltimore police department. He passed all his preliminary tests, the psych evals, the physical exams, maybe better than some of the young bloods. He went on to graduate at the top of his class at the academy, and the first time his feet hit the pavement in full uniform, he knew he'd found his place in the world. No, it wasn't the easiest job, but it fulfilled him in a way no other job would be able to. For once in his life he had a true purpose.

"Must be a really tough gig, Old Timer. I don't think you've come home this late since we were back in Baltimore, and that was what, nearly twenty years ago?"

Tamblin couldn't believe it had been that long, but she was right, here in Bridgford the biggest offences usually involved domestic disputes, traffic violations or the occasional theft. Bridgford wasn't a rural town, and it wasn't the big city. It was stuck somewhere in the middle. Now, here he was with three big cases. Trouble always seemed to find him, and it always came in threes.

"You're right about that. Tonight especially." He told her what he could, avoiding things he knew he couldn't, and she never asked for more than he was able to tell.

"That poor kid and his little sister. Lorraine, I've never seen anything like that in my entire career, and I've seen some pretty terrible things."

"Well good on that young man for calling it in when he did," Lorraine had commended, but Howard kept quiet as he stared off into his glass.

If Alex hadn't been there to help, that little boy wouldn't have made it. He saved his life whether he wanted to be involved or not, and yet despite the act of heroism something didn't sit well with Tamblin. It wasn't just the obvious either. He knew Alex was lying about the gym; he remembered exactly what he had said the first time. It was his placid demeanor, there was no trace of genuine concern. But what really stood out to Tamblin was the deadbolt on his apartment door, hard to notice at first because it was placed unconventionally near the bottom left corner and painted green to match the color of the door. He didn't pick up on it right away. The only reason it stood out to him in the first place was because of the red and blue flashes coming from a police vehicle's light bar as it drove by. The lights had struck the deadbolt just so, and it had caught Tamblin's eye. Maybe there was something more to this Alex kid than he led on.

"Something wrong, Sweetheart?" Lorraine asked, pulling Tamblin from his thoughts.

Howard came back to her, taking his eyes off the glass; he smiled softly at Lorraine and shook his head, "Not too sure yet, Love. There's something off about him. I haven't quite figured it out. Might be nothing."

Six a.m. snuck up on Detective Howard Tamblin who sat behind a metal desk looking over complex reports of the two women that had gone missing within the last month. There wasn't a doubt in his mind that both cases were related, but there wasn't enough evidence to make the connection, not yet anyway. What he did know was that Brenda Coswell went missing just one month after Jessica Delaney. Both women lived alone in a rural neighborhood. Neither one had many friends, but they did have a solid relationship with their families. Brenda Coswell's dad said they went fishing every Saturday morning at the Portman Docks. It had been a tradition of theirs since she was seven years old. He had told Tamblin that she rarely missed a Saturday, and if she did, she would call. When she didn't meet them, he knew something was wrong. It was a similar story for Jessica. They had regular Sunday dinners in her parents' home. Her mom had mentioned that the last time she spoke with Jessica, she was supposed to pick up some crescent rolls on the way to her house, but she never made it to dinner. The problem with both cases was that there was little evidence to provide any strong leads. There were no signs of a struggle, or a break in, and no reason to believe they might have been followed. Two witnesses did report seeing a black SUV at the Coswell residence the night she went missing, but another witness stated that it had been a black pickup truck.

Tamblin leaned back in his chair. He looked up at brown water stains on the ceiling tiles in the far corner of the room. It was a small precinct, one where the city budget didn't include fixing leaks in government buildings and calls about missing women just didn't happen. He looked over the reports again and for some reason his mind drifted to thoughts about the call that had come in the other night from Alex Meier. He'd run the plates on the young man's truck that he had committed to memory as he was driving away; he was as Tamblin predicted, squeaky clean. Still, that feeling was hard to avoid. It added to the strange happenings in Bridgford County. First, two girls go missing within weeks of each other, and now a boy was in critical condition because of a violent stepdad with a long criminal history.

Law officials from other counties were now on the lookout for a brown 1976 Buick with expired Virginia Tags. The car belonged to Timothy Beaumont, a violent sex offender who had recently been under investigation for the suspicion of sex trafficking. To make things even more interesting, Timothy had been working in the deli department at the same Quick Save that Jessica Delaney went to the day she disappeared. The only reason Tamblin's department knew this was because they had run the database for a list of new parolees and sex offenders in the area. If Tamblin was a betting man, he would've put all his money on Timothy, but the damn fool had an alibi. During the time Jessica allegedly went missing he was being held at the county jail for assaulting a prostitute, and with that in Timothy's back pocket there was nothing else connecting him to Jessica.

Missing cases were the hardest ones for Tamblin to accept. He found the idea of someone disappearing from their everyday lives without a trace unsettling. He still hoped someone would come forward. Tamblin knew there was always a witness, even if they don't comprehend exactly what it is they're witnessing. He just needed one person who had been at the Quick Save the same day that Jessica had been, or near Brenda Coswell's home when someone abducted her from it. He needed one person who would remember an unusual detail, something that stuck in their mind from that day. If he could find that, then all the pieces just might fall into place.

7
Alex

Alex had an obsession with things. More accurately, he had an obsession with *their* things. Hairclips, bracelets, toothbrushes, watches, or cell phones – whatever they used the most, he wanted it. For Brenda Coswell, it had been a bracelet from her mom that she wore all the time. Inscribed on a silver heart charm were the words, *I believe in you,* and on another identical heart charm, *love mom.* He kept that in a tin watch box in the nightstand next to his bed. He liked to tell himself that Mom let him have it so that she'd always be with him. For Jessica Delaney it had been her cell phone. She had been talking on it the day she was walking into the Quick Save, and she had tried to use it when he met her for the first time.

Alex had bought a brand- new charger for Jessica's LG flip phone, a cheap one from the corner gas station beside his neighborhood. He took it everywhere. Everyday there would be a new call from her mom, wondering where she was. Sometimes he could hear her crying, sometimes she begged her to come home. There were a few calls from her sister, her dad, and her grandpa. He liked to listen to them. Sometimes he would replay the messages and pretend her mom was talking to him. Eventually, Jessica's mailbox was full, so they stopped leaving messages, but that didn't stop her mom from calling at the same time every day. He was surprised that her phone service hadn't been disconnected yet, but he figured her parents were still paying for it. Maybe they figured as long as the phone kept ringing there was a chance she'd still pick up. Now that the phone was missing in the woods near where she was buried, he would need to go back there and retrace every step to find it. He couldn't go back last night. There's no way he would be able to find something so small in the dark. That phone was dear to him, it was a small piece of Jessica that he needed back. Without it he felt alone, even with his mother around. Alex planned to go back to take a long walk through the woods early this morning to look for it.

He sat up in his couch and rubbed the sleep from his eyes. He didn't remember falling asleep in the living room, but he was still wearing the same clothes from yesterday. There was mud on the back of his gym shorts and white shirt from when he fell in the woods. There were mud and leaves on the couch now too. Alex headed to his room to change but froze when he noticed a shadow moving across his living room blinds, very shortly came three solid knocks on his door. He looked through the peep hole; it was the Detective from the other night. Alex backed away from the door and made his way to the bedroom. He threw on a fresh pair of gym shorts and a new white shirt, scrubbed his face in the bathroom, flung a sheet on the couch to hide the dirt, and headed back to the front door with his keys in his hand. He heard two more knocks at the door.

"Open the door sweetheart, it's rude to keep people waiting," his mother whispered in Alex's ear.

"Sorry, Momma."

His mother stood over his shoulder wearing her stained green dress, her gray skin was peeled away from bone, the gap in her neck caused her head to rest on his shoulder. Parts of her arms were broken showing splintered bone and black congealing blood, and though her mouth was wired shut her teeth were exposed through a large gap in her rotting flesh. Her milky blue eyes bulged from their sockets.

"That's my good boy. Good, good boy," said his mother though he never saw her lips move.

8
Detective Tamblin

At seven, Tamblin took a drive to Alex's apartment with the intention of asking him follow up questions regarding the kids, and maybe to get a little more on Timothy Beaumont, and if he was being completely honest, to get to know Alex, and see if there was anything more to the nagging feeling in the back of his head. The smell of dew and wet leaves wafted across the chilly air. He thought it best to catch him early before the young man started his day, and it was a pit stop before visiting Jessica Delaney's mom. It would be a quick visit, he decided, just to get to know him a little better. He needed to know if there was something to that uneasy feeling in his gut, the feeling that sat just below the bony protrusion where his ribs met the sternum. He knew his job, and he knew people, and what seasoned officers always tell you is more times than not you stick with your gut. Years of walking the beat when he was just a rookie cop living in Maryland had taught him well. He walked up the concrete steps supported by shoddy metal framework. His black Oxfords landed with soft clacks as he ascended the steps until he reached the door. He looked down at the painted deadbolt. It wasn't painted over by mistake; it was there with a purpose, and it had been used recently. There was a distinguishable slit in the center of the lock where the key split the paint apart. Tamblin glanced at the window; three of the lower blinds were bent away from the window. There were uneven creases in the white aluminum Venetians. *A struggle? Maybe.* He couldn't be sure, but that feeling was there, and it wrenched at his insides like his intestines had been caught in a vise. Tamblin gave three good solid knocks on the door with a heavy fist and listened. With the exception of some distant cars driving on the main roads, he heard nothing, at least not right away. Tamblin knocked again, this time much louder. Not long after, there was the sound of a door shutting and the shuffle of feet across a carpeted floor. He heard the slight jingle of keys and a series of clicks and turns from the top of the door toward that bottom unconventional lock, and the door handle turned. Alex had opened it just enough for Tamblin to see part of his face. The young man only seemed half awake, peering at the detective from the narrow opening.

"Morning, Alex, did I catch you too early?" Tamblin looked down at his wristwatch, pretending not to realize just how early it was.

Alex rubbed the sleep from his eyes and blinked a few times; he squinted against the sun until he could focus on Tamblin. "Detective? I wasn't expecting you."

"I know, I'm sorry to show up unannounced but I was in the neighborhood following up with some of your neighbors, I thought you might like an update on this case and I also wanted to ask you a few questions. Do you mind if I come in for a bit? Promise I won't take too much of your time."

Alex was awake now. Tamblin wondered what excuse he would give.

"Detective, I'm sorry, this isn't the best time. I have a lot to do today."

There it was. Tamblin gave half a smile, "Okay, another time then," He tried to catch a glimpse inside the apartment, but it was difficult to see anything past Alex. "Hey, would you mind if I use your bathroom real quick? I've got quite a few stops to make today and it would really save me some time. This old man's bladder isn't as strong as it used to be."

How could Alex refuse an old man the bathroom? Alex stared at him blankly now. There were no excuses to make without making him seem suspicious. He opened the door for the detective.

"Sure, of course."

Tamblin's smile grew. "I appreciate it very much," Alex let him by, and Tamblin caught him stealing a glance at the 9-millimeter, nestled safely in his shoulder holster, beneath the front panel of his unbuttoned suit jacket. Alex shut the door behind him.

Even with the thin stream of morning light coming in through the blinds, the living room was still dim. There was an uncomfortable chill in the room that penetrated straight through Tamblin's gray suit, and a there was a faint smell – something rotten hiding behind the smell of cleaning products. He looked around. There was an old floral sofa with a wooden coffee table in front of it, and a silver Magnavox, the one with horizontal, Tic Tac shaped buttons on the upper right side. Directly in front of him was a small kitchen with a narrow bar counter, and to the left of it was a door with more locks.

"The only bathroom I have is in my bedroom," Alex said. "The landlord had these apartments split off so he could sell more of them. It's right through there."

He pointed to the door with deadbolt locks. Tamblin noticed that the young man stayed close to the front door.

"Safety an issue for you, Son?" He pointed to the deadbolts on his bedroom door.

"Yeah. Whoever lived here before me must've needed them."

"I bet," Tamblin said to himself. He made his way past the coffee table and into the bedroom.

"You know they say that little boy's going to be just fine, thanks to you. Yes, sir, little Bryson is going to be okay. Still can't find his mom or stepdad though. Damn shame."

He looked back at Alex who hadn't moved from the front door. In the dimness, Alex looked like a stone-faced statue.

Detective Tamblin looked around at the second-rate furniture in Alex's bedroom. There was a recessed bookcase with a few of Alex's college books in the far corner of the room, a tall dresser, a bed with a wooden headboard and a blue floral comforter, another door with extra locks to the right, and that smell, stronger in the bedroom than anywhere else in the house.

"Door on the right is the bathroom?"

"Yes," Alex's voice had carried from somewhere else in the apartment now. Tamblin glanced back toward the living room. He was no longer near the front door.

"Okay," the detective turned the knob and felt along the wall for the light switch. A rectangular wall lamp above the mirror flicked on with a low hum followed by soft light. The smell was strongest here. It was the unmistakable smell of decay that Tamblin was no stranger to. There were baby blue towels covered in dirt on the floor. A bar of brown-stained soap and washcloth lay on the rim of the sink. He locked the door behind him and lifted the toilet seat. A dark ring lined the inside of the bowl. He didn't really need to use it. It was all for show. Tamblin put the seat back down and flushed. His eyes moved toward the translucent shower curtain that was drawn closed and carefully peeled it back. Nothing. Nothing, except a few strands of long brown hair that had collected together in the drain. He ripped a small piece of toilet paper from the roll and swept up the strands, before sliding them into his pants pocket. He pulled the curtain closed, ran the sink water for a few seconds, and shut it off again. Tamblin unlocked the door slowly and peered into the bedroom before stepping out. No sign of Alex. He called out from the bedroom.

"Feels like an icebox in here. Your heater broken?"

No answer. He stepped out of Alex's room and shut the door behind him. His fingers brushed against his gun, an involuntary response to the sudden absence of his host. Tamblin advanced further from the bedroom door and looked at the deadbolt on the bottom of the front door. It was a double-sided lock. He rounded the bar counter and into the narrow kitchen. Alex wasn't there. He had half expected a sink full of dirty dishes from the way the bathroom looked, but it was empty. The detective skimmed the rest of the kitchen. There wasn't really much else to see apart from a beige refrigerator and a spotless electric stove, but what he did eventually notice toward the darker end of the small kitchen was another door. It was partially open. He leaned in to listen. Was that the sound of his own breathing or someone else's? He reached for the handle but pulled away when he heard a knock at the front door. Tamblin ignored it. He waited for something, a shift in the door, a slow creak on the cheap laminate, but there was nothing. He started for the handle again. Something in his gut told him to open it, but the knock at the door came again, this time with fierce determination.

"Alex, I know you're home! I can see your truck," a woman called.

Tamblin didn't budge, he pulled the door open. It was just the laundry room with a double stack washer-dryer. Alex wasn't in there. He went to the front door in long strides across the living room, half expecting it to be locked. Outside there was a young woman hugging her denim jacket tightly against her. Her brown hair fell over her eyes in soft waves and she swept it to the side. She looked at the numbers on the door frame.

"Oh, I'm so sorry, I must have the wrong apartment," the young woman took to the first few steps.

"I don't live here, ma'am. I was just following up with someone. Who was it you're looking for? Maybe I can be of some help."

"I was looking for Alex Meier," She took notice of the badge clipped to his belt.

"You've got the right place."

"He said he lost his phone so I can't call him. I was going to see if he wanted to grab breakfast before my class starts. Is he okay?"

"Seemed fine, but..." he let out a small laugh and shrugged. The whole thing seemed odd to him, "he was here just a few minutes ago, I'm not entirely sure where he's run off to."

"Okay, well if you see him, would you let him know I stopped by? My name is Catherine."

"I'll be sure to."

Tamblin watched her drive away in a newer Chevy Malibu that was parked across from Alex's truck that had mud caked into the tire tread and more smeared across the lower half of the bumper and a scratch on one of the side-view mirrors. He couldn't recall if he had noticed that yesterday evening and decided to take a closer look. Tamblin looked behind him contemplating about knocking on the door but decided against it. He had what he needed from there. Questions would come later.

Some of the mud in the deeper crevices of the tread was still wet and the stain along the bumper had been a hand- print. Just then, Tamblin heard the door shut from Alex's apartment and he looked back to see the young man walking downstairs to meet him. He was wearing a fresh pair of jeans and a blue polo. His dark hair had been brushed back perfectly to one side. He smiled at Tamblin. There had been a drastic shift in the way he carried himself. He walked with his shoulders square and a vigor in his stride as he hurried down the stairs to greet him.

"I was wondering where you had gone, Detective," he said casually.

"Alex, I didn't see you in the apartment. I thought you might've left, but I come down here to find your truck still parked."

The detective looked down at the bumper again. Alex followed his eyes and crouched down beside the front end of his truck.

"Yeah, sorry about that. I was in the closet getting dressed for work."

"Where do you work?"

"At Dusty's Hardware Store," said Alex.

Tamblin watched as Alex rubbed some of the dried mud off of his bumper with the side of his closed hand.

Tamblin was all ears now. "You work for Dusty?"

"Yes, sir. I've been there for a little over a month now."

"Well that's good to know," *That was really good to know.* "He helped me put my deck together. Dusty's real good people, and so is his family. Did you ever get to meet his granddaughter? Jessica Delaney? She'd be about your age."

Alex froze for half a heartbeat but continued wiping away at his bumper.

"No. I never got the chance. It's real sad though, Dusty told me she disappeared before I started working there. Some of the other people I work with think she might've run away. Are you the one working that case, Detective?" He looked up at him, squinting his eyes against the sun.

"I am, and you're right, it is truly sad. Dusty loved Jessica as though she were his own daughter."

"I hope you find her," Alex said, once again working hard to get the mud off of the bumper, "I've got to get my truck washed sometime this week. It gets so muddy so fast. Especially going down those back roads on my way to school."

It's true this fall hadn't been the driest, and many of the cars in the parking lot had mud on their tires too, but it didn't explain the handprint smeared across the bumper.

"Looks like someone's handprint don't it?"

"It is. My handprint actually. I was running real late to school yesterday, thought I'd cut through a trail in the woods, but it was a mistake. Truck got stuck in some mud. Spent an hour trying to get it out and going again."

"That right? Hey, before it slips my mind, a young woman stopped by to see you. Said her name was Catherine? She was banging on your door pretty hard. I'm surprised you didn't hear it."

Tamblin watched Alex brush away what he could off of the bumper until the smeared handprint was reduced to nothing more than a few specks of dirt.

"She did?"

Tamblin nodded, "Said she doesn't have your number because you lost your cell phone. No landline?"

There was a subtle flicker in Alex Meier's eyes when he mentioned the cell phone. If Tamblin blinked, he would have missed it. Alex stopped messing with the bumper and turned to him.

"Yeah, I misplaced the damn thing somewhere. I've been looking everywhere for it. I'm gonna have to get a new one after work tonight, and no I don't have a landline. I can't afford to have both right now. I figured one of those Pay As You Go phones would be smarter."

"I see. Well, you might look into those woods you tried to cut through yesterday. If I could put money on it, I'd say that was the likely place," *More than likely.*

Alex gave a nod, "Good idea."

"Well, I'll let you be on your way. You let me know if you want to go visit little Bryson. I'm sure he'd appreciate it. Could even ride together if you want to."

Tamblin stepped aside so he could let Alex get to the driver's side.

"Yeah, okay I will."

"Hey, since you're working for Dusty, do you think you could help me with a ceiling fan? I know he's got a lot on his mind. It's just sitting in a box. My wife's been on me about putting them up, but I'm going to be honest with you, I don't know the first thing about hooking up ceiling fans," None of that was true. If she ever wanted anything done bad enough, she would've done it herself or gotten someone who could. "If you help me do that, I will guarantee you a steak dinner and a cold beer. I wish I could say I was the grill master but in the Tamblin household, it's my wife. She makes some of the meanest steaks you will ever eat. They're so mean they bite back. I'll never admit that to her."

Alex smiled at him, "Okay."

"Great. What time do you get out of work today?" Tamblin followed Alex to the side of his truck. There was a smudge of moisture on the door handle when Alex moved his hand from it.

"About two," Alex had one foot in the truck now.

"Okay then, how about I pick you up at three p.m. Give you some time to get home and changed. It'll be a late lunch, early dinner situation."

"That works."

Tamblin reached his hand out to Alex. He seemed to hesitate and wiped his hand on his jeans before shaking Tamblin's hand. Alex was getting into his car, but the detective stopped him. "One more thing before I forget. It would help me out greatly if you could come by the station over the next couple of days so we could ask you a few questions."

"To be honest, Detective, I've told you all I know about those kids. Frank, he lives below me, he knows."

"Oh, it's not about Anna Lynn or Bryson. It's about Jessica Delaney. You see we questioned all of Dusty's employees, but since you came after Jessica Delaney went missing, it would really help if you could give us some insight on some of his employees. There's one in particular that we've been keeping an eye on," That wasn't entirely true. "Also, we'll need to ask you some standard questions. Strictly protocol."

Tamblin watched Alex's jaw muscles tense and then relax, "Sure."

"Great. Try not to worry too much, like I said, this is just protocol. We have to cover all our bases."

The detective waved at Alex as he watched him drive away, over uneven asphalt in the square lot. The young man was becoming a much more interesting person than Tamblin had anticipated.

9
Alex

Alex took the streets in the opposite direction of Elbow Roads. He wasn't sure if Tamblin would be following him, so he was careful not to go back to the woods right away. Alex drove back through town which comprised of boutiques, cafes and restaurants with outdoor seating, clothing stores, and of course Dusty's Hardware Store. Dusty's wouldn't be open for another hour and he was certain he could be back before his shift started. He thought about sitting somewhere for coffee at least until he was sure that Tamblin wasn't following him, but his mother was getting restless. She watched him in the rearview mirror. The glint in her eyes pleaded with urgency. *Find the phone, or he'll find our secret place.*

And so he took the long way back to the woods winding his way back onto Elbow Roads, passing the only convenience store nestled there. He had to slow down as he neared his marker. There was a cop car parked in the dirt beside it, and the entire road had been blocked off by a barricade. Blood drained from his face; his whole body went numb. There was an ambulance on the other side of the street. Their flashings lights reflected off of his car. He tried to see around the cop car but couldn't. An officer rounded the barricade and met Alex. Their eyes met, and the officer kept his eyes steady on him.

The officer tapped on his window, and Alex lowered it just enough to hear him.

"Everything okay, officer?"

"Bad accident. You're going to have to turn around," was all the officer would disclose.

Alex nodded. "Yes, Sir."

He swallowed hard and looked behind him to make sure there were no cars before throwing the truck into reverse and making a U-turn. The officer watched him the entire time. Alex looked in his review mirror but could only see his Mother's face. Black sludge trickled between her teeth and bubbled in the corners of her mouth. She wouldn't be happy, but he'd have to come back another time. His mother glared at him, but he flipped his mirror up so he couldn't see her and focused on the road ahead.

10
Detective Tamblin

Detective Tamblin stood outside of the Delaney residence. It was a cookie cutter ranch style home, a picturesque scene with skies as blue as an ocean, and a few scattered fluffy white clouds. Jessica Delaney's mom peered out from one of the windows. Tamblin gave a wave. A few moments later she met him at the front door.

"Good afternoon, Mrs. Delaney," Tamblin greeted.

"Mr. Tamblin. Come in, and please call me Audrey," Mrs. Delaney always spoke as though she had just run a marathon.

Tamblin obliged and followed her into the living room where she directed him toward the sofas. Mrs. Delaney made her way to the wet bar and pulled a crystal glass from one of the shelves.

"Can I offer you something to drink? Water, juice, something stronger?"

"No, but thank you, Mrs. Delaney, and thank you for seeing me on a Saturday morning."

Mrs. Delaney poured herself a short glass of an old reliable, Tennessee whiskey before joining him. "Of course."

Tamblin looked around the living room while Mrs. Delaney swallowed her first drink of the morning, before pouring herself another. A double skylight in the vaulted ceiling let a refreshing amount of daylight in. There was a picture of her family on the mantle of her fireplace: Mrs. Delaney, her husband, and their two daughters. It must've been an older portrait because Jessica's face looked much younger than the woman's in the newspaper sprawled across the glass coffee table in front of him. The headline read: **Missing: The Search for Brenda Coswell and Jessica Delaney Continues** in bold letters, with their pictures side by side, and **Read More on pg.14** in smaller print right below it. Their hopeful eyes and smiling faces watching Tamblin in black and white print pleaded for him to find them.

"I know it's more than a coincidence that my daughter and Brenda Coswell look so much alike, Mr. Tamblin. It doesn't take an educated woman to figure that one out," she said as she joined him in the living room. She planted her glass on the coffee table and sat herself in the other couch. Though Tamblin wouldn't outright admit it to her, Mrs. Delaney was right.

"I'm not fooling myself into believing this will end happily. She's been gone over two months now. I've watched enough of them shows to know what the odds are."

She took a slow drink from her glass, swiping a tear that had managed to escape from the outer corner of her eye.

Right again, Tamblin thought.

"I know we've gone through this before, but can you recall anything else that might've stood out to you? Even the slightest sounds in the background when you last spoke to her. Maybe something in the tone of her voice? Did it sound like she could've been in any kind of distress?"

Mrs. Delaney set her glass down on the table and sank back in her chair. She pulled her robe tight against her thick cotton nightgown and settled her arms across her chest.

"The only thing I remember about that day was that she was in a hurry. I could hear the wind blowing against the phone. She was just supposed to meet us for dinner. I told her not to rush, but she didn't like being late for anything. She said, 'Mom, I'm just going to run into the store real quick and grab these crescent rolls.' Then she told me she loved me, and she'd see us soon," Mrs. Delaney cleared her throat and with a sigh she said, "I don't know of any other place she would've stopped between our house and the Quick Save parking lot where they found her car."

When officers had arrived at Jessica Delaney's silver Mazda, the driver side window had been rolled down about two inches. The car itself was about two feet out of the stall. From the way the tires and the steering wheel were slightly turned, Forensics could tell she had been getting ready to leave. The problem was that she was parked just outside of *Quick Save's* surveillance camera range in the lot closest to the woods. She probably parked there because it was closest to the exit and she was in a big hurry. It could've been because everyone did their shopping at the Quick Save and parking was always a nightmare to get into. No one would ever know except for Jessica.

Tamblin and his team had combed through those woods and the parking lot, but there was no evidence that someone had been with her or been waiting for her which wasn't surprising. It rained a lot and wildlife was always trekking through the woods. The crescent rolls Jessica bought were still in a plastic grocery bag on the floor of the passenger side. Beside the grocery bag was her brown leather purse with everything still in it, and the keys were missing from the ignition. They found them later near the interstate heading East on I-64. They followed the trail, stopped at every gas station, every rest stop, and the woods in between. They searched in the opposite direction and did the same, they even searched beneath the overpasses. Nothing. The keys could've been a red herring, another thing to throw them off the scent, just like every tip that came in and led them cold.

"Mrs. Delaney, does the name Timothy Beaumont ring a bell to you?" asked Tamblin.

"Sounds familiar," Mrs. Delaney shook her head. "Where have I heard that name before?"

"Timothy Beaumont had worked at the same Quick Save your daughter was last seen. He has a damn good alibi, but I'm curious to know if Jessica has ever mentioned him to you. Or was there ever a situation with any of the Quick Save employees that didn't sit well?

Mrs. Delaney ran her hand against the arm of her sofa, trying hard to put a face with the name, then she looked at Tamblin. "Did this man happen to work in the deli department?"

Tamblin nodded, "Yes, he did."

"The name on his tag was Timbeau. I suppose that makes sense, could've been a nickname for Timothy Beaumont."

"That's right."

"Jessica and I had stopped at the store for sliced turkey nearly a year ago. It had only been a few days after Thanksgiving, and I made a joke that the Quick Save deli turkey could've saved Thanksgiving dinner. She swatted at me for that because it had been her year to roast the bird," Mrs. Delaney laughed at the memory. "Jessie's never been much of a cook. That girl could burn water, but she will deny that up until the day she dies."

Mrs. Delaney went quiet when she realized what she had said. Tamblin watched the pain grow behind her eyes as her smile faded. He reached out and rested a reassuring hand on her arm.

"What happened next, Mrs. Delaney?"

"So, this man behind the deli counter took our order, but he just kept smiling at Jessie. It wasn't a friendly smile, Detective. He was leering at her. I get the willies thinking about it. He had the brownest teeth I'd ever seen. It was enough to make you lose your appetite. To make things even more uncomfortable, while he was putting the turkey through the meat slicer, he kept winking and licking his lips at Jessie. Gave us the creeps. I'm not sure what type of drugs he was on, but I'm certain he was on them."

"Did he say anything to either of you?"

"I didn't want Jessie anywhere near that man, so I paid for the turkey, and I told her to wait for me outside. Well, he leaned in real close and he says to me with breath fouler than a steaming porter john on a summer day, 'You'll never have to pay for turkey again if you let me and my friends have some fun with your daughter.' Well, I told him as calmly as I could that that was just not going to happen. Then I also told him to fuck off. You can't give scum like that the satisfaction of watching you squirm. That's how they get off, Detective. I've worked at enough bars in my college years to know diseases like him."

"What happened after that?"

"He laughed and called after me as loud as he could. I'm pretty sure he called me a few misogynistic names. *Cunt,* I think was one of them. You better believe I let his supervisor know it too. Never did see him working behind the deli after that day, and we never had another issue at the Quick Save since. I didn't think about him after that day. He wasn't worth remembering." Mrs. Delaney finished her drink. Her eyebrows creased with worry now, and she let her eyes fall to her lap. "Does he have something to do with my daughter?" Mrs. Delaney adjusted herself in her seat.

"If I'm being completely honest here, no I don't think so, but we haven't ruled him out just yet. He had been locked away in a county jail for several months. Probably not too long after your run-in with him, but we're really interested in his connections and if they could've been at the Quick Save the day Jessica had been."

"I'm sorry, Detective, I'm trying to understand. What would his connections have to do with Jessie?"

Tamblin leaned forward, "I can't say much about it, Mrs. Delaney, but he's trouble."

"Understood," Mrs. Delaney set her hands into her lap. "Truth be told, I don't know what would be worse, finding out that my daughter is dead, or finding out that she'd been abducted to be passed around from one disgusting human being to another. You know part of me is still hoping that she ran away to start a new life, and that maybe she was secretly unhappy and needed to get away, but the realist in me is strong enough to know better."

Detective Tamblin gave a solemn nod, "At this point until we get more to go on, all we can do is hope for the best possible outcome."

He picked himself off the couch and Mrs. Delaney walked him to the door.

"I won't stop looking for her. Not until she's found," said Tamblin

Audrey Delaney gave a sad smile. "I know you won't Detective. It's how you'll find her when you finally do that scares the ever-living shit out of me."

Tamblin had barely made it out the front door when Mrs. Delaney called after him. "Detective Tamblin?"

"Yes, ma'am," Tamblin turned around.

"Did you ever find her cell phone?"

"No, we didn't. Why do you ask?"

"Jessica's a real smart girl. I just figured if she was in trouble, she might've put something on her phone. It's a silver flip phone. Motorola or Samsung or other. I can't remember. All the kids have them these days, you know."

"That's good to know, Mrs. Delaney, thank you."

"I call it every day hoping she'll pick up, then I'll hear her voice, and for a split second my heart is alive. When I realize it's only her voicemail, I die all over again. I think I'm losing hope, Detective," she said softly. "Her grandfather has taken it harder than the rest of us. He raised her, you know. Especially when Jessie's father and I were off the wagon."

"Listen, don't ever give up hope, you hold onto it like a candle in the dark, and don't you ever let that light go out. Even if that's all you'll ever have to hold onto."

She waved at him from one of the windows when he got back into his car before disappearing behind doily-patterned curtains. Tamblin looked at the case files lying beside him in the passenger seat and opened Jessica Delaney's folder. He flipped it to the back where all the pictures Forensics took of the car were. Tamblin took out the shots of the car interior, then briefly to the pictures of the surrounding area. *Where did you go, Jessica?*

11
Jessica Delaney
<u>2 Months Earlier</u>

"Jessie Bean?" A stranger asked her as she was getting ready to drive out of the parking space. He was peering at her through her partially open window. Jessica's foot went down hard on the break when she saw him. Her grandfather was the only one who called her that, hearing it from someone else's mouth made her cringe. Jessica stared at him through the crack in the window. He wasn't a difficult man to look at, with his dark hair, jeans, and a simple black t-shirt that outlined the muscles in his chest, *like a Guess Jeans poster child*, Jessica thought.

"That's not my real name," she said.

"Jessica Delaney, I'm sorry. I know your grandpa," he said. "He calls you Jessie Bean, right? Look, I don't want to scare you, but he's been in a horrible accident."

Jessica Delaney began to worry now, because she had just tried to call him a few minutes before Alex appeared at her driver side window, and he didn't answer. She didn't stop to question how he knew her grandpa because all she could think of was that he's somewhere hurt and that's what really mattered. She jumped out of the car and followed him into the woods, unsure why she had taken her keys with her and left everything else behind. She wasn't even paying attention to where they were going. She could still see the Quick Save behind her and cars whizzing by on the interstate, and it wasn't until they're both out of view that she started to get nervous.

"What's your name?" she asked him.

"Alex," he looked back with a smile that showed his dimples.

She asked him how much further they had to go, and he told her they were getting close. She pulled her phone from the back pocket of her jeans, lucky to have charged it before she left the house. Full bars but no signal. She wondered if Alex knew that. Ahead of them was a black truck parked with the engine running in the middle of the woods, but there was no sign of her grandpa. She knew in her gut that something was amiss, but the gnawing feeling that something could've happened to her grandpa outweighed any rational logic. Jessica followed him to the truck, and he opened the door for her. She looked behind her. She had a small window of opportunity to run, but she didn't take it. Alex moved behind her and now she was trapped between the truck and this stranger. She stayed calm but inside she was screaming at herself for not thinking things through. This man had caused her to abandon her inhibitions, and all because he called her by the name only her grandpa used, and because this man had approached her with such urgency. *Something happened to Grandpa,* and that was all she could process. The very grandpa she adored more than anything in the world, the person who remembered her birthday when her parents didn't, and who would make sure she was up and ready for school when they were too drunk to remember.

Alex drove them down a back road through the woods, some place she'd never been. He smiled at her. Where had she seen him before? She couldn't quite place it, and even though he seemed kind enough, she knew something wasn't right. She pretended to make a call even though there was no service, and instead she punched in the numbers that would leave a small but significant clue behind: 626-347-2539. She knew it was inconspicuous enough that if things went south, he wouldn't think twice about the number in her phone.

Alex was watching her now, so she called the number and just as she had expected it would, the call failed, but at least the number was in her phone. He leaned back to catch a glimpse at what she was doing. Jessica put the phone down at her side and stared out of the window seeing nothing but trees around them. They weren't going very fast; she could jump and make a run for it.

Alex was focused on driving again. It wasn't a back-road people usually took, he was forcing his own way through the woods, the truck bounced over the rough terrain. Jessica felt along the side of the door without taking her eyes off of him. She pulled on the handle, but it was locked, she felt around the handle for the lock and popped it open. He looked over when the passenger side door swung open. He grabbed onto Jessica's arm, but she slipped away jumping from the moving truck. She landed on her knees, picked herself up, and ran. All she wanted was to get back to the Quick Save, or even the interstate, but in her panic, she couldn't remember which way she came from now that they were so deep into the woods, and she had been too worried about grandpa to pay attention. She should've paid attention. Now the late September sun was setting in the distance, and Jessica was a stranger to the woods. Alex trailed behind her, she could hear the crushing of twigs and leaves beneath their feet even through the sound of her own heartbeat screamed in her ears. The adrenaline surging through her body threw her into a panic. Yet as frantic as she was, everything played out in slow motion. Jessica looked back just once, a mistake that cost her because though her eyes locked on Alex, she failed to see the tree root jutting from the ground like a broken arm. The last thing Jessica remembered before everything went dark was falling and seeing his face.

12
Jessica Delaney

Jessica had been out for a long time. When she finally woke up, she found her arms and legs bound together with duct tape. She was in someone's living room wearing someone else's clothes, a stained green dress that looked like something from the sixties. Her usually wild hair had been tamed into soft waves. There was a sharp pain in her head and left leg. She winced, noticing her leg wound had been dressed in a gauze bandage and white tape. She looked around the living room, the light above her seeming brighter than it probably was. She didn't see Alex at first, but he was watching her in the dark from his narrow kitchen. Jessica screamed louder than she ever thought she could, until a violent pain in her throat made her gag. She hoped someone would hear her but after a few minutes she realized that no one was coming. Jessica looked around once more; she hopped off of the couch and winced as she hobbled her way to the window. She flipped the latch and tried to lift the window, but when it wouldn't budge, she felt along the edges to find that the windowpane had been nailed shut. She went to the door, quickly realized that it had a double-lock, one you needed a key from both sides to get in and out of. Jessica's heart drummed in her chest, but she tried not to let the fear take over. *If you let it take over, you're dead Jessie,* she said to herself.

"Can I get you something to drink?" she heard Alex call from behind her.

It made Jessica want to jump out of her skin. God, she wanted to cry, she wanted to scream, and claw his eyes out, but she did her best to stay calm. So, she returned to the sofa, never once taking her eyes off of him. He seemed different somehow – scarier. She nodded slowly.

"Yes, please."

"Water or beer?"

"Water."

"Ice?"

Jessica nodded again. Alex walked into the open kitchen which divided the living room by a narrow bar counter. He took a glass from the cupboard above him and set it down. He looked in the freezer for ice but turned to Jessica with his lips turned down almost in a pout.

"Sorry, out of ice, Momma."

Jessica wondered if he really called her Momma or if she'd misheard him. Alex filled her glass with water from the faucet. His hands were doing something else too, but she couldn't see past the counter. She tried to peer over it from the couch, but he was already on his way back.

"One water just for you," he wedged the glass between her bound hands and threw himself right next to her, lifting his legs onto the sofa.

"Thank you," Jessica looked at her water. There was a slight cloudiness to the glass. "Where's my grandpa?"

Alex watched the way her lips moved as she talked. He seemed to be studying every inch of her face. A small strip of hair fell over her eyes and he swept it gently behind her ear.

"Hmm? Oh, Grandpa's fine. Probably at your mom's house eating dinner now."

"Can I go home?"

"I just want to spend a little time with you. Is that okay?"

"Okay."

Alex grinned from ear to ear. He leaned in close resting his head against her chest but pulled back instantly.

"You're shaking. Here let me help you drink some water."

He tipped the glass to her lips causing water to trickle down her chin. There was a saltiness to it.

"Silly girl, you're spilling it all over the place."

He set the glass down on the carpet and wiped her chin with his thumb.

"There. All better."

He leaned against the couch with his elbow propped on the back of it and he let his cheek rest against his fist.

"Why did you take me, Alex? Do you really know my grandpa? Have you been watching us?" Jessica couldn't look at him. Her chin quivered as she spoke and she took short gasps of air trying to catch her breath, trying not to let him see her cry.

Alex didn't seem to hear her. "I'm really glad you're here. You can't leave me again, okay?"

"Again? What do you mean by that?" Jessica wasn't certain, but her eyes started to feel a little heavier, and her words a little sluggish. She tried to sit up in his sofa, but her legs felt ten times heavier. She tried to swing at him, but her arms dropped like dead weight. Jessica tried to scream but all she could do was whimper.

Alex pulled her in close to him, rocking her gently.

"It's okay, you're okay, just breathe," he lulled. "Don't ever leave me."

13
Alex

Alex watched as she slipped into the darkness, he carried her into his room and laid her on the bed. He took his time unzipping the dress from her body and set it out beside her. She was a perfect sleeping angel with her eyes in a slight flutter, her soft pink lips relaxed and open slightly, and her arms resting comfortably over her naval. He carried her into the bathroom and lowered her into the tub, a careful descent so that he could avoid injuring her. Alex ran a fresh washcloth under the bathroom sink and worked a bar of soap into a good lather before returning to Jessica. He sat on the rim of the tub and ran the cloth over Jessica's bare body. He gently scrubbed her arms, worked his way to her hands, and between her fingers. He ran the washcloth over her thighs and behind her knees, between her toes, and the bottom of her feet. He paid special attention to her smooth flat stomach, gliding the soapy washcloth around her naval, then leaned back to admire her frame.

Her chest rose and fell in slow even intervals. Alex wanted to touch her, and his hand hovered over her breasts with a slight tremor in his hand, but touching them would ruin her, and he wanted to preserve her. He ran the washcloth over her rounded shoulders and her neck. Alex wrung out the washcloth under the sink and ran it over her body one last time with clean water before drying her off with a freshly laundered towel that had been lying at the back of the toilet. He leaned over from the rim of the bathtub and reached under the sink for a thin bottle of lotion that smelled of lavender, pushed on the lid until it snapped open, and squeezed a generous amount into his hand. He worked it into her skin in light circular motions until he was satisfied with his work. Alex reached down beside his feet not once taking his eyes off of her. He felt along the dingy linoleum floor until his fingers brushed against a black canvas bag and reached his fingers inside until he felt the wooden handle of a small bone saw. Alex teetered back and forth, staring at Jessica with an emptiness in his eyes. He leaned in close to her face, pushing strands of her soft hair away from her cheek and let his fingers trail down to a prominent muscle in her neck. Alex tilted her chin up with his fingertips, while holding the saw in the other. He brought it down against her neck and raked it against her skin. Her skin tore apart in fibrous pieces, when he struck an artery, blood sprayed over the bath tiles and across his face, but he didn't stop drudging the teeth of the saw across her skin until he was hitting bone, and even then, he didn't stop.

Jessica's eyes began to flicker, but Alex didn't take notice. He stared mindlessly as though he wasn't in his own body. Jessica screamed when she saw what he was doing to her, screamed until her sounds were drowned out by the gurgling in her throat, the horrific sound of blood and air forcing through her windpipe. Jessica flailed wildly, fighting against him until the lights in her eyes went out.

Alex blinked and looked down at her, and he let the bone saw fall into the tub beside Jessica. He didn't know how long he'd been there with her, but she was in pieces. He slid down onto the linoleum floor wiping moisture, blood, and sweat from his forehead with a trembling hand. "I did something very bad. You're not going to be happy with me."

"She's beautiful, Alex. Did you do this for me?"

Alex looked up to see his mother looming over the bathtub, eyes wide, blue lips pressed in a smile that never moved even as she spoke. "I didn't mean to."

His lips quivered and he rocked himself back and forth with his arms crossed tightly against his chest. His fingers shook as he tried to wipe the sweat from his brow.

"Oh, sweet baby boy, I love what you've done. Now she's just like me. In some ways she is me, isn't she?" She moved in his direction casting a shadow over him. Alex could see thick black wires in her neck. "You can't leave her here; you know that don't you? You have to find her a special place, somewhere she'll be happy."

"Okay, Momma."

14
Gabe
<u>Present Day</u>

Gabe rang Eric's doorbell, looking around the front yard while he waited for someone to answer. Thankfully he was in the phone book, so he wasn't hard to find. He was shocked to learn that Eric had been living in the next town over not far from his own home. They hadn't seen each other in fifteen years and Eric was only twenty minutes away.

There was a white Ford Focus in the driveway, and though the lawn was brown now it had been well-kept even with the fast-approaching winter. His house was in a newer subdivision not far from his own home. It was so new that you could still smell the freshly paved asphalt. There were smooth flat stones in a plant bed on the porch with three short bushes spaced neatly in a row identical to the houses across the street. Gabe could tell that the vinyl siding had been power-washed regularly. HOA, he figured.

This time Gabe tried knocking on the door. If Eric didn't answer this time, he promised himself he would leave. He could vaguely hear children's music and talking inside the house, possibly a TV commercial, so he knew someone was home, and he started questioning whether or not he had the right house. After a few more minutes no one had come to the door, so Gabe made the short trek back to his truck parked beside a gray mailbox with a red flag. He was already opening the driver side door when he heard a woman call out to him.

"Hello?" she said. The woman was in green and white flannel pajama pants, fuzzy house shoes, and a white t-shirt. She was holding the screen door open with one hand and trying to keep an overweight Golden Retriever in the house with her leg, while balancing a dark-haired toddler on her hip with her other hand. Her blond hair was pulled back into a messy bun.

"I'm sorry, I came to the wrong house," said Gabe.

"Are you looking for my husband, Eric?"

"Yes ma'am."

The woman shook her head, "Please don't call me that," she laughed, "He's at work today, but what's your name? I can tell him you stopped by."

Gabe looked at the cute baby in a long-sleeved onesie, who was chewing on the sleeve of his momma's t-shirt. He giggled gumming a part of her sleeve pinched between his stubby little fingers. Gabe wanted to kick himself for coming to Eric's house and was beginning to wonder what had possessed him to try in the first place. The woman squeezed out of the door pushing her dog back with her foot before shutting him inside. She stood on her porch bracing the little boy against the cold waiting for an answer. Gabe was one foot in the truck now; he just wanted to drive away.

"I'm sorry for bothering you."

"Can I ask you something before you go?" the young woman was walking across the dry grass in her fuzzy bear shoes toward him. Gabe watched her over the cab of his truck keeping himself in a comfortable space between the door and his driver seat.

"I really should get," he said.

"Are you my father-in-law?" the woman cut in.

Gabe stared for a moment, lost for words despite how easy it was to answer. Yes, he was her father-in-law, but how could he explain why he was never around? Gabe was sure Eric would've told her what a terrible parent he'd been. She probably saw him as a piece of shit the way he knew his sons did.

The baby grunted and jerked his hands away from the woman's sleeve. He had grown tired of playing with her shirt, and his cheeks had turned pink from the cold. The woman bounced him up and down and shifted him to her other hip, but the baby was having none of it. His frustration had turned into a meltdown and he wailed at the top of his little lungs.

"Listen, I'm pretty sure I already know the answer to the question I just asked you 'cause you are a spitting image of my husband, apart from your dark hair, but I have to get this grumpy little man back inside before we freeze to death. Why don't you come in for a bit and get out of the cold too? I'll put us on a fresh pot of coffee. I have so many questions."

She walked back inside her house leaving the door open. Gabe looked around, he thought coming to see Eric would be awkward enough, he didn't anticipate he'd be spending the morning with a daughter-in-law and grandson he was meeting for the first time.

Gabe walked into the house, and he immediately felt the warmth from their central heater. Even the house had a new smell to it, like fresh paint and newly installed carpet. There were pictures of the little baby with two little girls hanging on the walls in the carpeted hallway, and there were oversized blocks everywhere. He walked down the hall which opened to a large living room with vaulted ceilings, bright bay windows, and French doors which led to the backyard. The baby was lying on a blanket on the floor gnawing on plastic keys while he lifted and dropped his legs just for the fun of it. The Golden Retriever rounded the corner and jumped up to greet

Gabe. He scratched him behind the ears and tilted his head up to avoid getting slobbered.

"Buster, get down," Eric's wife called from the open kitchen. Buster eventually did as he was told and ambled past the couch to lie beside the little baby. "Have a seat at the kitchen table. Coffee won't take long. Are you hungry? I could whip up some breakfast."

Gabe took a seat next to the highchair at her round kitchen table in a breakfast nook, "No thank you. Coffee's fine."

He watched her take two mugs from a hanging cup holder just below the cabinet. She poured it three-quarters of the way and stopped.

"Do you want cream and sugar in yours?"

"Black. Please."

"Just like Eric," she said. "I need sugar and creamer in my coffee otherwise it tastes like coffee flavored cardboard to me."

She poured a little extra coffee in his mug and poured an excessive amount of dairy creamer and sugar in hers, stirred it with a spoon she took from the drawer beneath the coffeemaker, and met him at the table.

"Here you go."

"Thank you," Gabe said taking the mug with both hands. He took a short sip of it and set it down on the plastic placemat.

"Not a problem," Eric's wife set her mug down too, and took a seat next to him studying Gabe, probably trying to find all the similarities between him and Eric.

"You have a lovely home, ma'," he began.

"Carol," she interjected. She looked over her shoulder into the living room at the baby who had now rolled onto his stomach and had discovered Buster's ear. "And that little booger is your grandson, Peter. Elsie and Samantha are at school right now," Carol smiled at Gabe. "Wow. So you're really Eric's daddy," she said with her hands folded around her mug, looking him over as though she wasn't sure if he was really siting there with her. "Gabriel, right?"

Gabe nodded. "To tell you the truth, I'm surprised he talked about me at all."

"Oh, he did," she took a sip from her mug and wiped her lips with the back of her hand.

Gabe looked down at the placemat. There was a picture of apples in the lower right- hand corner and remnants of orange crayon scribbled around it. "And you still let me into your home?"

Carol smiled, "Yeah well, I figured since you've been trying real hard to get in touch with Eric lately, I might try to help you out a little. Eric's a stubborn man, Gabriel, I have a feeling you already know that, but he has a good heart, and I know deep down he wants things to be right between you. His mind has been somewhere else these days," she hovered over her half-empty mug. "So, what do you do for a living?"

"I'm the maintenance man at the Alan Tool and Die. Used to work in construction a long time ago but got laid off a few years back. I drove trucks for a little while, but I was always on the road, and I guess I was getting tired of it. When you get familiar with all the truck stops, and the truck stops get familiar with you, it's time to move on. This job I got now is pretty good. It doesn't pay much, and the hours are long, but it's reliable. What about you?"

"I'm a physician's assistant. Been working part time these days so I can spend more time with the little guy."

Carol pointed her thumb behind her at the chubby little thing scooting his way around the blanket. Buster had decided he'd had enough of Peter moving around and went into another room. Carol pulled her hair band from her messy bun and pulled her hair back tight into a high ponytail.

"Can I ask you another question, Gabriel?" she said matting down pieces of hair that refused to stay put.

"I suppose so," He scratched at the gray scruff on his chin and braced himself for whatever question she was getting ready to throw at him.

"Eric's been having these nightmares lately about his mom's funeral. He said something happened that day, something pretty traumatic. The kind of thing you'd expect to see in a horror movie."

Carol looked behind her. Her son was still content, he had rolled onto his back again and was now playing with his feet.

"You want to know if it happened the way he said it did?"

Carol nodded.

"Things can seem so much worse when you're young."

Gabe took a good long sip of his Columbian Roast coffee. "I'm afraid it did and probably exactly the same way Eric said it did. My youngest..." he started to say.

"Alex?"

"That's right. His momma was his entire world and he never could accept that she was really gone. That casket tipped over and Eleanor did too, except she didn't just slide out of the coffin, she came out in pieces. It was as horrible and traumatic as you could imagine."

Gabe looked down and tapped absently at the handle of his mug.

"That must've really affected Alex."

"That sure is a nice way to put it," he said sparing her the details of Alex's strange behavior. "He took off a few years after Eric left for college. Haven't heard from him since."

Carol jumped up when Peter began wailing, his little cheeks turning redder and redder by the second. He'd had enough of exploring the toys on his baby blanket and decided he was ready to be picked up.

"Gabriel you just sit back and enjoy your coffee. Feel free to pour yourself another cup if you want. I'm going to feed him real quick, and put him down for a nap," she said without looking at him over her shrieking baby.

"I should probably get going," he said picking his mug off of the table.

"Won't be but a minute," she said, and she was already putting Peter to her breast with a blanket over herself for privacy.

Gabe looked out the window. Even though all he could see was the back of her head while she sat on the couch, he didn't want to seem like a dirty old man staring in her direction. He looked through the white framed windows in the kitchen. Even their backyard was nice, there was an open deck with patio furniture and a stone fire pit in the center, a white fence squared off the large yard, and a small frozen pond bordered with large decorative rocks sat at the far end. It was strange being in Eric's home, having a conversation with his wife, and meeting a grandson he never knew he had. To have Carol welcome him into their home as though he had always been a part of their lives was a kindness he never expected to receive. He wasn't sure if it would last, but he was thankful to have it while it did. In a lot of ways Carol reminded Gabe of Eleanor who could bring out the best in anyone, even someone like him.

15
Eric

Eric noticed the white truck parked on the street right in front of his house when he pulled into the driveway beside Carol's car. It was an older Tacoma rusted on some parts of the bumper, Virginia license plate, and a toolbox in the bed. He wondered if the heater was broken, and if Carol called the HVAC repairman for it. That was possible but unlikely, it was a brand-new unit.

He walked into his warm house and kicked off his shoes at the door. He could hear Carol's and a man's voice coming from the kitchen. They weren't talking in formalities the way his wife did when she was talking to a coworker or even a salesman, it sounded more like she was talking to a very close friend or a family member.

"Hey honey, we're in here," Carol had heard him come in.

Had he forgotten they were supposed to have company for lunch? He didn't remember his wife mentioning anything about it. Eric went past the living room. Peter was asleep on the floor with his arms up at his sides in loose fists and his mouth open partly. The baby smiled in his sleep showcasing his gums, and it made Eric smile too. Carol and whoever was with her stopped talking. Eric could feel their eyes on him, and he got the feeling that he wasn't ready to see who was with her. Somehow, he already knew, and he'd known it from the minute he saw the old truck parked on the street.

Carol greeted him in the living room, kissed him on his cheek, and Eric gave her a gentle squeeze around her waist.

"What's he doing here?" he whispered.

"We can talk about it later," she whispered back, "Come on," Carol hooked her hand around the crook of his elbow and led him into the kitchen.

His dad was already standing, probably just as unsure how their meeting was going to go. Eric's chest felt tight, but not with anger, at least not the kind of anger that he felt for his dad back then. That feeling had died down a long time ago, only hurt remained in its place now.

"So, your father stopped by this morning, Eric. He was hoping to speak to you," Carol was speaking to them in a steady voice as though she were talking someone through defusing a bomb.

"Hi, Son," said Gabe.

"Dad," Eric replied. He thought it sounded harsh, and it probably was. He wanted to leave the house, more than that he wanted his dad to leave the house. He wanted a drink, a shot full of something that would knock him on his ass until the next morning. Carol squeezed his arm, a private message that read somewhere between say something else and get your shit together.

"I know you two haven't eaten yet, why don't you go out and get some lunch," Carol said. "I'll stay with the baby. It'll give you two a chance to talk, really talk," she elaborated. Eric could've elbowed her for suggesting it.

His aversion to the idea must've transcended onto his face because Gabe smiled at Carol's effort, and he took his coat from the back of his chair. "Carol, thank you for inviting me into your home, but this was probably a bad idea," Gabe reached out to shake her hand, and Carol cupped it into hers. "You've got a beautiful family, Eric. You've done real good for yourself. Your momma, she would've been proud."

He saw himself to the front door.

Eric looked down at Carol who gave him a half smile and a head tilt toward the door, Carol's gentle way of nudging him. "Dad?" his voice carried down the hall. The door was already open letting a gracious amount of light and cold air into the hall, and it made Gabe look like a towering shadow. "Would you like to grab lunch at Marty's?"

Eric couldn't read his dad's face from where he was standing, but after a moment he finally answered, "Sure."

16
Gabe

They went to Marty's Diner. Gabe sat across from Eric who was gazing out of the window constantly as if he were waiting for someone. Neither of them quite knew what to say or how to begin. Gabe stared down at his empty coffee mug. A brown ring had dried at the bottom. He looked back at Sally, the old bat who was chatting up one of the other regulars at the counter. She looked up at him and nodded when she saw him.

Gabe's eyes fell back onto the plastic menu and cleared his throat.

"I know this won't change a thing, but I am sorry I wasn't who you and your brother needed me to be after your mom died."

He soothed out the aches in his tired hands. His shoulders dropped and he took a deep breath in. He kept looking past him at the door. Two more people walked in, a young woman in a red overcoat and her husband wearing a nice tailored suit. They looked inside the diner briefly but decided it wasn't the place they wanted to eat and walked back out.

"You know, for the longest time I hated you for what happened to Mom, and I hated you even more after you told me my brother ran away. I couldn't find him. I didn't even know where to begin to look. Landstown PD classified him as your typical teenage runaway and they said teenage runaways usually ended up homeless. Every chance I got, I looked for him. I looked in the alleys and under the overpasses. I searched the woods. I used to check the local paper so damn much for a John Doe, it had become an obsession. I couldn't find him, and I felt so damn guilty for leaving him behind. He had no one, not even his own father, and I cried damn near every day of my young adult life for losing him and Mom. So, I hope you understand how hard it was to see you in my kitchen today. Your showing up after all this time; it's hard to take in, and I guess I really just need to know why."

Gabe's gaze shifted from Eric to the mini jukebox sitting on the table against the window. It didn't work, it was mainly there for show. The real juke box sat on the opposite end of the diner and it played all golden oldies all the time.

"I don't know if your mom ever told you, but we met here. Well, she cornered me here," he gave a soft chuckle. "I was sitting right over there," Gabe pointed at a middle seat at the counter.

Eric followed his gaze. The seat was empty, but there were dirty dishes and a half empty glass where someone had been.

He had seen her through the window of Apple's Ice Cream Parlor sitting across from another woman in a mustard yellow dress sporting a bouffant hairdo. When Eleanor smiled, she smiled with her bright eyes, and it lit up her entire face. Her hair fell over her shoulders in soft honey brown waves, she was so beautiful it was almost painful to look at her. His face warmed when she caught him looking at her as he walked by, and he averted his eyes as he hurried past the window. Gabe didn't think he would ever see her again after that night, but he did several months later at Marty's diner. He was sitting at the counter sipping coffee and waiting on the big egg breakfast special when he saw her. This time she was the one watching him from afar. When he caught her eyes she smiled. At first, he thought she might have been looking at someone else and he looked over his shoulders, but no one else caught her gaze. Just him. She was sitting near the end of the counter dressed in Marty's waitress uniform, a light blue dress and a white apron that she was tying around her waist. It somehow reminded him of what nurses wore. Even her white shoes completed her nurse look.

Eleanor walked over with a cup of coffee in her hand and she took the stool beside him. "I've seen you somewhere before, haven't I?" She set the cup of coffee in front of him.

Gabe mussed his hair back with a hand and straightened his brown work jacket.

"You probably have. I come in here almost every Sunday for breakfast."

He cleared his throat. That wasn't what she was referring to of course. She remembered him staring at her from the window of Apple's.

She shook her head teasingly.

"Nuh-uh," God, there was that beautiful smile of hers again. "I just started working here last weekend. Go on, try again."

By this time Marty was peering out from behind the metal pick-up window that divided the kitchen from the wait station. He threw the plate down on the counter.

"Elle, I got an order up darlin'."

"Be right there, Boss," Eleanor never took her eyes off Gabe. Marty shook his head and walked away. "Go on."

Gabe cleared his throat. He had never felt so uncomfortable in all his life, and here was this petite young thing, with a quick wit, and a disarming smile challenging him. She knew exactly what she was doing.

"Apple's Ice Cream Parlor."

"Now, was that so hard?" she winked at him. Marty was getting ready to put the next plate of breakfast down on the steel counter when he saw the other one still there.

"Elle! Give that man this food here, 'stead of talkin' his ear off. I've got more orders comin'. The church crowd's gonna be here soon too."

"I'm coming, Boss."

Eleanor slid off of the stool and walked behind the counter to hand Gabe his plate. Marty handed her the other breakfast special and she took it to another man sitting two seats down from him, and she went right back to him and leaned on the counter.

Gabe wiped away at the crumbs of toast that had collected in his beard with a napkin and crumpled it beside his plate. She watched him as though she were waiting for him to start the conversation.

"Your name's Elle?"

"Eleanor is my real name, everyone around here calls me, Elle."

"You like working here?"

Eleanor shrugged, "It's okay, I suppose. I was hoping to get an office job. Went to the interview and everything but didn't get it. Guess I didn't have enough experience for them. That's okay though, I have a plan. I'm gonna work here while I go to school."

She looked past him. A large group of people were coming through the door in their Sunday bests.

"What are you planning to go to school for?"

"Med school, hopefully."

Gabe sopped the last bit of toast in his over easy eggs and shoveled it into his mouth. Eleanor reached for a full pot of coffee from behind her and filled his cup to the brim. She took his empty plate and put it in the wash bin behind the counter. "Well, I better get back to it. The church crowd's finally coming in," she set his check down and started to walk away but stopped, "Hey, what's your name?"

"Gabriel, Gabe for short."

He had just brought the coffee cup to his lips and nearly burned himself from what she said next.

"Well Gabriel, are you gonna ask me out or what?"

Gabe set the coffee cup down and wiped his lips with a napkin, "Would you like to..."

"Tonight at five. Apple's."

He wouldn't have missed it for the world.

Gabe smiled at the memory, but it quickly dissolved.

"Your mom, she was a strong woman, so much so, that I missed the signs. Every fight we had, and I couldn't see what she really needed. She was the brightest light in this tired man's life, and I let it burn out," Gabe was gazing out of the window now, eyes staring into some faraway place. "Son, I'm getting old now. I don't want to reach the end of the line without at least trying to make things right with you and your brother, and if I can do that then maybe in some way, I'd be making things right with Eleanor too."

He fidgeted with the buttons on the mini juke box and re-arranged the salt and pepper shakers. Gabe had just begun to open his mouth when Sally came to the table.

"Ya'll ready to order?" Sally had a hand on one hip, and she looked them both over with a face that read, *hurry up you're wasting my time.* Her wiry gray hair was pulled into a high ponytail that swung back and forth as she spoke to them.

"I'll just have the soup of the day, Sally," Gabe replied.

"All right, one bowl of broccoli cheddar soup for Gabriel, and what about you hun?"

"BLT on wheat and fries for me," Eric responded, "Pickle chips on the side, please."

"Anything else?" Gabe and Eric shook their heads. "I'll get that right in for you boys," and she made her way behind the counter.

The diner had been remodeled many times since its opening in the late fifties. The newest version was made to look like its original model. The new owner even recreated the red vinyl booths, matching bar stools with the chrome bases, as well as the checkered black and white floors. Gabe watched her go back to the wait station.

"Sally's been working here since before your mom ever did. After Marty died, I'm sure most of us thought the diner would close for good, but it didn't. I overheard her talking to one of the other customers one day. She said she bought it, but it had been more than she wanted to put up with, so she sold it and asked the new owners to put her back on the waitstaff," Gabe rambled.

Even though he had reached out to his son to make amends, he didn't know how to tell him that there might be something wrong with his brother.

"Were you about to say something before Sally came and took our order?"

Gabe leaned back against the booth and shook his head, "Yes, there was but I can't remember what it was now," his eyes shifted to the window when he said it. "If it was important, I'm sure I would've remembered."

Eric gave a nod and poked at his empty glass. Sally swooped in with a pitcher of water in one hand and a pot of coffee in the other and refilled their drinks. Before they could even thank her, she was headed to a table at the front of the diner.

"So what are you doing these days, Dad?" Sally came by and set their food down along with extra napkins and walked off.

"I've been working at a tool and die company. Maintenance," Gabe sank his spoon into his bowl of soup and let it sit there. "What about you?"

"I teach Philosophy at Altman University. I have two classes before lunch and then two more in the evening."

Eric squeezed a good amount of ketchup on the side of his plate and dipped his fries into it before shoveling them into his mouth.

"You know, I said this earlier, but you really have got a beautiful family, and your wife, she's got a good heart."

"Yes, she does, but don't let her fool you, she'll spit fire if she needs to," Eric laughed. He took a good bite of his sandwich and wiped the crumbs away with a napkin. "And Peter, he's a handsome little guy. He looks like your brother."

"After Mom died, I would bring Alex here. We'd ride our bikes even though it took us more than thirty minutes. Marty would make us supper just like he'd said he would, and we'd stay until we were ready to go home. Sometimes we'd do our homework at the counter. Marty would tell us stories about how feisty Momma could be and we'd laugh our little tails off, and then Alex would ask him where she was, but he didn't have the heart to remind him that she was gone. I used to be so mad at him when he started in with that kind of talk, and when I could finally get him home and back down to reality, he'd cry until he cried himself to sleep. I was so angry at you for a very long time. I didn't understand how someone we needed was never around. As I got older, I realized that in your own way you were just like Alex. You were struggling to cope too, but there's a part of me that will always resent you for never being around. You forced me to grow up before I was ready, and I didn't know how to be the parent that Alex needed,"

"I know, Eric I'm..." Gabe cut in.

Eric didn't give him the chance to finish, "But more than being angry at you, I was angry at myself for leaving him behind. I was all he had after mom died, and I just left him. I always think about him. Do you know how heavy that weight is? I wonder if he's still out there somewhere cold or hungry. Is he homeless? Is he dead?" Eric took a drink of water. He wished it was something stronger. The glass slammed down on the table.

"I don't think he's dead."

"Why do you say that?"

Gabe pushed his bowl of broccoli cheddar soup aside. It had too much salt and had the consistency of pudding like it had been sitting for a long time or someone had put too much flour. The old man looked down at his watch, "My shift's starting in an hour so

I'll have to leave soon, but that's actually the other reason I've been wanting to talk to you. There was a package sitting on my porch step the other day. It had a clipping of your mom's obituary," he looked around before continuing and lowered his voice, "and a lock of hair and fingernails."

"Hair? And fingernails, like clippings?" Eric was all ears now.

"Whole fingernails."

"That's damn near creepy, Daddy."

"This has your brother written all over it, right? I can't think of anyone else it could be," he looked at his watch again and flagged Sally down for their check. "You know how much he loved her."

Eric nodded, "So what did you do with the package?"

"I turned it into the police. They said they'll hold onto it, but they don't think it's anything to worry about. Said it was probably some kids playing pranks. I don't believe that. This was too personal."

Sally was back a few moments later. Gabe handed her cash and told her to keep it. She patted him on the shoulder and walked off.

"I've gotta' head out or I'm going to be late for my shift. I want to say something before I leave, Eric. I know no amount of apologizing will ever be enough. I know that, but I am truly sorry for never being around after your momma died. You shouldn't have been the one to hold it together for Alex. It wasn't fair. And you were right, he needed help, and I didn't want to see it." Gabe slid out of the booth. "Thank you for the company. It was real good to see you again," and with that he was gone.

17
Gabe

The next morning, Gabe stood on his sidewalk looking at a small package on his porch. The sun was barely starting to peak through light gray clouds. It was a damn cold morning, the air had slapped him in the face as soon as he stepped out of his truck, and now it was creeping its way through his insulated jacket and thermal undershirt. He balled his gloved hands into fists, a poor attempt at keeping his hands warm. Some distance away he could hear the garbage truck making its rounds in the neighborhood. Gabe pulled his wool cap tight over his ears. The package was drawing his gaze; it was on the same step the last one had been. It looked to be the same size and in the same type of box the last one had been too, and the porch light put it on display just as before. This time there was an envelope attached to the top of it. Gabe looked around to see if someone was waiting in the street or peering at him from the side of the house. He wondered if someone knew he would be pulling an overnight shift at the factory.

He picked up the box and gave it a shake, something light shifted inside as he did. Gabe let himself into the house, hearing the screen door shut from the other side of the main door as he turned the lights on in the foyer. He walked past the stairs and directly into the dining room and set the package down on the table, slipped off his gloves and jacket, and laid them on the table too. Only his name was written on the envelope that was fixed to the package by brown packing tape. It was the same writing – all capital letters scribbled in blue permanent marker.

He lifted the envelope away from the package taking some of the brown packing tape with it. He peeled the envelope apart and took out a square piece of printer paper with the words **HAPPY ANNIVERSARY** only it wasn't their wedding anniversary. That had been back in June. Today marked the anniversary of Eleanor's death. With one of his short nails, he scratched away at a strip of tape then pulled it back so he could pry the box flaps open. The same lavender scent drifted from a rolled satin cloth. It was tied at the center with a pastel purple ribbon. There were two things that Eleanor loved, the smell of lavender, and pastel purple. There was what looked like an oil stain on one end of it. Under the cloth was a picture of Gabe in his dark gray suit, and Eleanor in her wedding dress that came down to her knees. Gabe's arms were wrapped tight around Eleanor; they were standing beneath a sycamore whose leaves were still lush and green. It made him think of their first date at Apples; she seemed so happy then.

At Apple's Ice Cream Parlor, Gabe and Eleanor sat across from each other at the same table in the storefront window where Gabe had first seen her. Eleanor's legs were crossed in a perfect, graceful sort of way, with her foot gently nestled against his slacks. Gabe didn't quite know how to dress on a date, so he came in the only suit he had ever owned, dark gray dress pants and matching jacket, with a white button up shirt and a crisp collar, and black Florsheim Imperials polished to perfection.

Eleanor sat back in her seat and smiled. "You look nice."

She did too. Her long waves had been tamed back into a high bun, and her bangs were swept to one side. She was wearing a white dress with various floral patterns and a high neckline. Eleanor looked like she could be on the cover of one of those *Vogue* magazines that Gabe had seen on occasion in the waiting room of a doctor's office.

"Beautiful," was all he managed to say.

They didn't order any ice cream; instead they asked for coffee and talked about work mostly. Eleanor did most of the talking. She could carry a conversation with the dullest man and still never run out of things to say. Eleanor was good at getting people to open up about themselves in a way that never felt forced. She asked him open ended questions and talked about her favorite books and movies, most of them he had never heard of before. She talked about medical school and starting college in the fall at Landstown Community College for her general studies. Gabe said little about himself. He enjoyed listening to her talk, and Eleanor didn't mind. She talked about her childhood. It was a good one, she grew up in Georgia, daughter to the late John Witty, a welder, and Marlene Witty, a schoolteacher. They moved to Albright, West Virginia when she was eight, and eventually moved to Landstown, Virginia. She said she was the only child and a handful at that. She laughed at the memory of her mom having to chase her down the road when it was time to come home for supper. It took nearly thirty minutes to catch her and the only reason she finally did was because her mom threatened to sell their brown lab, Oggie to a made-up man in Chackbay, Louisiana.

"I just wanted to be outside, you know? All the time. I was such a tomboy, always out with my friends, playing in the mud, jumping in the pond. I just wanted to be free."

That part of her never changed. Not even after they were married. Part of her would always be that little girl on the inside wanting to be free. Eleanor took a sip of her coffee and fidgeted with the cup handle.

"You sure you just want coffee? No ice cream?" Gabe gestured to the menu wedged between the napkin holder and the sugar caddy. Eleanor shook her head.

"No, I usually come here for the coffee."

"Hell, we could've gotten that from Marty's," he chuckled.

"That coffee is shit and you know it," Eleanor rested a hand on his. "Besides, it's nice here. Doesn't smell like cooking grease, and the company's nice. And it's got meaning now, you know?" She gave his hand a gentle squeeze. "So, tell me more about you. I want to know everything about Gabriel Meier."

There wasn't much to tell her, at least Gabe didn't think there was. He could sum up his life in about five minutes and that included all pauses in between, but he knew Eleanor wouldn't mind how long his life story was, she was just interested in what he had to say.

"Before the cows come home, Gabe."

"All right, here goes, but I am warning you now, there's not much to tell so don't you go expecting some grand spectacle," Gabe raised his hands in the air and shook them as though he were praising the Holy Ghost and it damn near made Eleanor spit out her coffee.

"I won't, I promise."

"Well, where to start? I was born and raised right here in Landstown to Earl and Patty Meier. I was a good kid, didn't give anybody any problems. Kept to myself most of the time, had maybe about one or two good friends in the neighborhood. We used to go out and ride our bikes everywhere, usually to the pond by the school. I used to love catching tadpoles; you ever do that?" Eleanor nodded. "We used to catch 'em in mason jars. They were big sons of bitches too. Makes me miss being a kid, you know? But you blink and you're sixteen working twelve- hour shifts at a construction site, blink again and you're nearly thirty years old still working hard at the same place. My daddy was a hard-working man, I reckon that's where I got it from. He worked at that same construction site for nearly forty years, up until the day he died."

"You were working that much at sixteen? What about school?"

"I didn't finish school. I couldn't, not after Momma left. Earl needed all the help he could get."

He almost regretted bringing up his mom as soon as those words had left his lips, and he didn't need to look at Eleanor to know that she would require some sort of explanation, he could feel her eyes bearing down on him, a gentle gaze filled with pity and concern.

Gabe told her everything that happened, Randy the bad biker potato head, the countless afternoons when he came over to help his mom with issues, the day Earl caught her cheating, and the day Patty Meier decided she was never going to come back home.

"She remarried. I found her picture in the obituary of the Sunday paper. She looked happy. I guess she never really loved us. Daddy figured she hated him so much that she was willing to cut me out of her life too."

Eleanor shook her head, "I don't believe that. I don't think that's the reason she cut you out of her life. Granted, I never knew the woman so I'm just shooting from the hip here, but what if she was too ashamed to come back for you? Maybe she really did want to come home, but she just didn't know how. Could you imagine hurting the people you're supposed to love, and then having to see their faces every day? Like daily reminders of the pain she caused. The guilt she must've felt. I don't think I could live with myself."

Gabe scratched at his short beard and leaned back in his chair. He never thought about the other possibilities for his mom not coming home. He supposed there was never a reason to see it any other way, but Eleanor grasped at ideas that were deeper than he ever cared to go, and she opened wounds he thought had long since healed. It made him uncomfortable, not in a bad way but in a way he needed. Eleanor watched him, waiting to get his thoughts.

"That is a possibility, but all those years and not even a single letter? Hell, I was just a kid when she left. My dad could've been the biggest asshole to her, and I wouldn't have known it back then, but it just would've been nice to know if she ever thought of me. If she was sorry. If she even missed me at all. You'd think she owed me at least that much."

Eleanor shook her head and smiled. "Well I can't argue with that."

She looked at the clock on the back wall, behind the register counter. It was nearly seven o'clock. Apple's would be open for another ten minutes.

"Will you walk me home, Gabe?"

They walked out of Apple's. Eleanor had wrapped her arm around his and headed down the street. It was a quiet night out in town. There were few shops here and there, a furniture shop, a bakery, the barber, and the corner market. Marty's was across the street with a *Closed: We will reopen at 6:00AM* sign in the window. He was usually open late, but never on a Sunday. The last few people who had finished their dinners late were walking out of the door. They waved at Eleanor before heading to their cars.

"That's Margie, Arnie, Louis, and Doris. Sweet older crowd. They come in for early bird but stay until Marty kicks them out. They have the entire restaurant laughing with some of the stories they tell. They may be old, but they still got that spunk."

"That's a good way to be. I'm twenty-nine but I tell you these days I feel about sixty-two."

"Heavens, you're an old man."

It took all of five minutes to get to Eleanor's house. They stopped briefly to admire the view of the sun setting beyond acres of farmland. Sometimes they talked, sometimes they were silent, but they were content either way. Gabe enjoyed listening to her talk about her plans. It made him feel as though there was something more to life than the way he was living.

Eleanor turned off the main road into a neighborhood of about four houses spaced out over large lots. Her house had belonged to her parents; after their passing they had left everything to her. It was a small cottage with a yard and a narrow driveway leading to a garage port where an Oldsmobile was parked. There were azaleas planted in the walkway leading to her front porch, and there were blue flowers, he didn't know the names of, spilling over in hanging baskets.

Eleanor stepped onto the first porch step and turned around, so she was at his eye level and she leaned in close enough to feel his breath on her cheek.

"I'd like to see you again, Gabe. I really like you. Would you like that?"

"Very much."

She wrapped her arms around him and gently pressed her lips against his. He could still feel her lips on his even after it was long over. To think of it now made his heart ache.

They married the following summer, a small outdoor wedding in front of twenty people that consisted mainly of their coworkers. Marty had been the one to give Eleanor away. Gabe wore the same suit he had worn on their first date, and Eleanor wore a simple white dress that came to her knees. Their honeymoon was an evening picnic on a blanket beneath the stars in the middle of a twenty- acre field, and they made love there for the first time. Gabe would later remember the sweet smell of her skin and the way her body felt against his, how she tightened her grip around his shoulders when she let him inside her. He would still remember what it felt like to be loved by the woman of his dreams, and the emptiness he felt when it died.

They sold their parents' houses and used what money was left as a down payment to buy their own. It was an older three- bedroom home with a decent kitchen and a huge backyard. The only thing that concerned them was that it sat on the corner of a main road, but it was the best they could afford, and for the amount of house they were getting it was almost a steal.

In the fall Eleanor enrolled herself in college like she set out to do and she made some of the best grades in her class, even better than some of the girls just fresh out of high school. Then eight and a half months later they welcomed, little Eric Allen Meier, and four years after, Alexander Robert Meier followed. Eleanor had made the conscious decision to withdraw from college so that she could enjoy being with her new little loves, and she promised herself she would go back once they were older. She took the night shift at Marty's so she could wait for Gabe to get home to take care of their kids and eventually quit when Gabe's job called for longer hours and the occasional travel.

It went on like that for years, Gabe remembered, and over those years the sad familiar story of a troubled housewife and a distant husband had begun to surface. Mortgage was always late and hospital bills from her deliveries were overdue, what little savings they had were now gone. Every time Eleanor thought about going back to school, she decided against it because that was one more payment they would have to make, and Gabe made barely enough for them to get by as it was. When the Oldsmobile finally quit, they needed a reliable car, and that was one more payment they didn't need.

Gabe could see the change, the slow decline in his once happy marriage. Eleanor's bright light was dying, and he didn't know how to fix it, so he watched her drift away until she was too far gone, until she didn't love him anymore. Gabe pulled himself from the memory of her and looked down at the picture.

It had been well-preserved with no apparent sign of wear, no warping at the edges, no tears. Gabe turned it over, expecting something to be written on it, but there wasn't. He felt around the inside the box to see if there was anything else hiding inside and didn't see anything. Gabe picked up the cloth as careful as one might do with a bomb. Whatever was wrapped inside was slightly longer than a crayon and thicker. He wasn't sure he was ready to know what was wrapped inside, especially if it was anything like the last package he'd received. Gabe was getting ready to sit at the table when he heard the screen door open. This was immediately followed by a series of tapping on the main door. It was only six-thirty on a Saturday morning; who could possibly be visiting him this early?

Gabe opened the door part-way, letting momentum take it the rest of the way when he saw who was standing on his porch.

"Hey, Dad," said Eric. His hands were stuffed in his jacket pockets, and he gritted his teeth against the biting cold.

"Eric? Damn, Son, you're the last person I would've expected to see at my door. Come on in."

His son followed him into the dining room. Gabe took a seat at the table and set the box beside his chair. Eric looked around the room which hadn't changed from when he and his brother were little. "You want to sit down?"

Eric looked at the pictures of him and Alex as kids hanging on the walls. There was a picture of a four- year- old Eric sitting on the couch holding his newborn baby brother, and a framed portrait of a smiling two- year- old Alex sitting on a white carpet. He moved from those to a collection of pictures in another frame. One of them was of his mom sporting short shorts, a midriff shirt, and big hair teased at the bangs, another of Alex and Eric playing with the hose, and one of his dad reading a paper on the sofa. Eric's attention shifted to a photo of a ten- year- old Alex pinched between the outer glass and a corner of the frame. He wasn't smiling, his hair had been combed perfectly to one side. There was a faraway gloss in his eyes. He was wearing a striped button-up shirt, and dark blue shorts.

"I took this picture shortly after," Eric started to say.

"Yeah. Found the camera on your bookshelf. There were only three pictures on the roll, that one and two that were out of focus."

Eric took the picture from the frame and made his way to the dining table. He took the seat on the opposite end. A comfortable distance from a man he no longer knew, Gabe thought. "What brings you by?"

"I was at the Food Lion picking stuff up for breakfast. It's rare for me to sleep in past six a.m. and Carol has asked me to invite you over for supper tonight so you can meet the rest of the Meier clan. The girls were all too happy to discover that there was a grandpa they hadn't met yet, and all I've been hearing is how excited they were to meet him," Eric folded his arms on the table.

Gabe let out of soft chuckle. "I'd really like that."

Eric gave a half smile.

"If you want, I can just say I'm working tonight."

His son shook his head. "No, please, I'd never hear the end of it from Carol if you didn't show up tonight. I'd like you to meet Elsie and Samantha too."

"Okay. I'll be there."

Eric was looking down at the picture of Alex laying in front of him. He seemed miles away and now that Gabe had a chance to really look at his son's face, he could see dark circles beneath his eyes.

"Something on your mind, Son?"

Eric looked up at him and shook his head.

"I've been having these nightmares lately about Alex. Carol said she told you about it, but what I didn't tell her was that there is more to that dream, and it's really been keeping me awake at night."

"What is it?"

"I see Momma and she's alive but not the way you would think. She doesn't look like the sweet woman you married, not the way I remember her when she was still alive. It's her corpse stitched together in the places she'd come apart at, and she's always walking around with Alex. She has this grin plastered across her face that I cannot get out of my head. Then this morning about three, I get a call from a number I've seen once before, comes up as a Virginia area code on the caller ID. I could hear someone crying on the other end. I was sure it was Alex. I even called out his name, but whoever it was hung up shortly after. It only ever rings when I try to call the number back."

The nightmares Eric had been having got Gabe to thinking about the night Alex wandered into his room. It was the static from Eric's TV that hurled him out of sleep. Even though the room had been dark, he could tell the door was open because he felt a draft coming through it. He thought Eleanor might've finally decided to sleep in their bed again. She had been sleeping in the guest room for a while. He looked over and swiped his hand along her side of the bed, but it was just as cold an empty as it usually was. He stopped moving when the floorboards creaked in the middle of the room. When his eyes adjusted to the dark, he caught glimpse of a shadow in the corner. Gabe was a stoic man, but damn it if the idea of some-thing or someone watching him sleep didn't give him the willies. He flipped the switch on his bedside lamp and jumped when he saw Alex standing beside him. His dark brown hair was tousled wildly to the side, cheese dust crusted in one corner of his drooping mouth, and his eyes were open slightly. A low growl was coming from the back of his throat.

He screamed for Eric. Gabe wasn't sure why his first instinct was to call his oldest, but that's what he did, and Alex's eyes sprung open, and he shrieked like the devil bit him. Gabe shook him and hollered for his eldest son again.

He heard something thwack against the floor in the next room, then there was a scramble across the wood floor, and he collapsed into Gabe's bedroom. His eyes darted across the room, delirious from being slapped out of sleep and saw his brother, he tripped over his own feet to get to Alex, and wrapped his arms around him. He pressed his little brother's face against his chest and patted his head the way their mom sometimes did. Alex wailed into Eric's shirt. Eleanor flew into the room moments later.

She crouched beside her kids, and turned Alex toward her and looked him over. When she saw that he wasn't hurt, she hugged him tight. He had stopped crying but occasional short sobs escaped. She cooed over him, until he was calm enough to speak and asked if he was okay.

There was a rasp in his voice now from all the screaming and he'd told her it had been a bad dream, shrinking deeper into her arms when he saw his dad staring at him.

Eleanor had asked Eric to help Alex back to bed. Eric, not Gabe. Never Gabe because he wasn't around enough to be involved. It was the same reason he called for Eric instead of trying to calm Alex himself. She watched Eric take Alex by the hand and followed behind them, but not before apologizing to Gabe. Why did she feel the need to apologize? *I'm sorry you had to wake up like that* she said to Gabe who had one leg tangled in the covers.

I didn't help the situation any. He scared me good. I overreacted. He thought she might say something else, but she gave a single nod and shut the door behind her.

"You think it was him calling you?"

"I think he might be in some sort of trouble."

Gabe's foot hit the side of the box when he shifted in his seat. He looked down at it and Eric followed his gaze.

"I guess while we're talking about Alex, I should show you this," he picked up the box and set it on the table. "I got another one this morning."

Eric looked at the box sitting in front of Gabe, "So what's in it?"

Gabe peeled the flaps back and reached inside.

"A picture of me and your momma and something wrapped in a cloth. I was just getting ready to unwrap it when you come to the door."

Eric scooted into the seat beside him and watched Gabe pull on the ribbon and let it fall into the box. He laid the cloth down onto the table, and they both looked at it, neither one prepared for what would be inside. Gabe unfolded the cloth just enough to see and jumped out of his seat. He cupped his hands over his mouth.

"What? What is it?" Eric shouted louder than he probably meant to.

"It's a finger, Eric. It's a goddamn finger, and I think that's your mom's wedding ring."

Eric leaned over the table and peeled the cloth open. Sure enough, there was a finger inside, missing the nail, with a wedding ring, Eleanor's ring.

"Oh my God."

The finger was bluish purple, and the smell, like that of a rotting tooth was enough to make them heave. The ring, a quarter karat diamond set into a white gold band shined as though it had been well-cared for. Had Alex done this? If so, what type of message was he trying to send? And whose finger was it? "We need to turn this into the police," Eric folded the cloth back over the finger and laid it in the box and watched his dad who was inching his way back to the table.

"Dad. Do you think it was Alex?"

"To tell you the truth, I don't know who else it would be," Gabe took the box from the table. "Go on home to your family. I'll turn this in to the station."

They walked out together.

"Let me know what they say," Eric buried his face in the top half of his coat and hopped into his car parked behind Gabe's.

"You think I should tell them about Alex?"

Eric started the engine on his car and cranked the heat up as high as it would go.

"No. It's not fair to pin something like this on him when we don't even know if he's capable of doing it."

Gabe watched Eric drive away before hopping into his truck. He drove in the opposite direction toward the precinct. What exactly was Alex capable of?

18

Brenda Coswell
<u>A Few Days Earlier</u>

Brenda was making sure she had everything for the fishing trip in the morning. Her dad had rented a charter for the entire day so they would need to leave right at five in the morning. It would be a much-needed break from everything going on in her life. She jumped when her phone rang. Who would be calling so close to midnight? She ran downstairs to the living room, fumbling for her phone that was on the couch.

"Hello? Hi Stacy!" She hadn't heard from her old college friend since they graduated nearly two years ago. "How have you been?" The call cut in and out from time to time making it difficult to fully hear what her friend was saying. She looked at the bars on her phone watching it switch between one bar and zero.

"I've been good... calling so late, but... had the... AA you went to... I've been going through...and."

"You're breaking up, my cell service is shit," she looked at the blinking power bar. "And the fucking thing is dying. I think I know what you're asking. Give me one sec, and I'll text you the info."

They hung up and Brenda thumbed through her phone but stopped when she heard someone pulling into her driveway. She made her way to her living room window, noticing a black truck sitting out front with the engine off. She could make out the silhouette of someone sitting in the driver seat. She convinced herself that someone was probably lost and went back to searching through her phone. Once she found the number, she texted it to Stacy with a short message that said she hoped that it would help her, but the text was undeliverable. *Piece of shit phone,* she thought.

Brenda double checked the front and back doors were locked before turning out the lights. She returned to the window one last time, just to reassure herself that her gut was wrong about the person in her driveway. When she peeked between the blinds again, she couldn't see the person in the truck anymore. Brenda backed away from the window, and before she could reach the steps there came a knock at the door. Her phone beeped and she looked down at it, the battery died.

"Can I help you?" she asked from the other side of the closed door. Brenda flipped the porchlight on, but for some reason they didn't come on. She hated that there was no peephole on the door.

"I'm sorry to bother you so late, but I'm lost," the man's voice was muffled as he spoke from the other side of the door. "I was hoping I could use your phone. It's kind of an emergency."

"No, I'm sorry. I don't have any service," *Stupid*, she thought, *why did I just tell him that?* Brenda recoiled, "There's a twenty-four- hour convenience store down the road. They'll be able to help you."

She waited for a response only she didn't get one. She listened for the sound of a truck engine revving up again, but it didn't. Brenda spun around with her back pressed against the door when she thought she heard something at the other end of the house. She flipped the hallway switch on, but nothing was there. She wondered if the strange man was trying to get in through the back door. She decided she wouldn't wait around to find out. So instead she pulled the door open just enough to see through it. When she was satisfied that no one was there, she bolted. She didn't anticipate that he would be hiding out of view on the side of the door, or that when she tried to scream his hand would already be over her mouth with a cloth laced in chloroform. Her eyes grew heavy, and the last thing she would remember was the black truck sitting in her driveway.

When she woke up, she found herself in a dark room lying on plastic with her hands and legs bound together by duct tape. There was something in her mouth that tasted like cotton which might have been a handkerchief or sock held in place by more duct tape. She brought her bound hands to her face and with her fingertips she struggled to find the tape seam so that she could ungag herself. She traced her fingers along the tape, scraping it with her nails forward and backwards until she found it. She scraped at it until a piece of tape came lose and pulled until it unraveled, careful once she got to the tape that was sticking to her hair. With one good yank, the tape came loose taking some of her hair with it. She yelped but she couldn't think about the pain now. She used her teeth to peel the tape around her wrists off and felt around the small room. The walls were lined with something soft and cratered and it reminded her of the egg crate mattress topper she had on her bed. She would've given anything to be in her bed right now. She padded her fingers across the floor which rustled every time she moved. *Am I sitting on plastic?*

With a deep breath Brenda sat up and scooted herself against the wall, she pulled her legs in close and worked the tape off of her ankles. She felt around the room, pressing against the egg crate foam trying to find a doorknob or a light switch. She felt along each side as thoroughly as she could and as quickly as she could, and when she spun around to try another side of the wall something grazed her cheek. Brenda shrieked, blood pulsating in her ears, she threw herself against the wall, flinging her arms wildly until whatever it was found the back of her hand. It took a minute to calm herself before she realized that it had been a pull chain that caused her to jump out of her skin. Brenda pulled it and a dull light emanated from a single bulb in the ceiling; she blinked a few times until her eyes adjusted to the light. Brenda squeezed her eyes shut and shook her head. She allowed herself to cry and she hugged her arms to her chest. She looked down at her feet. She wasn't wearing her clothes anymore; her pink pajama pants and matching shirt had been replaced by a green dress stained with God only knew what. She ran her hands over the black egg crate foam until she reached the edge and ripped a piece of it away from the wooden board it was glued to. She knocked against the boards, listening for something hollow and when she didn't hear anything, she pulled away at more pieces of foam exposing even more wooden boards. Brenda beat her fists against the wood, her entire body trembled, and she did everything she could to calm her breathing. She screamed until her voice went hoarse and kicked at the boards with her heel until she couldn't do it anymore.

Brenda jumped when she heard music vibrating against the walls, and she slinked back when a door in front of her sprang open. Brenda didn't think twice. She pushed the man out of her way, knocking him over. She sprinted from a bedroom and through an open door leading into a living room. Some punk rock song blared from a radio on a kitchen bar counter. In a frantic blur, Brenda rushed for the front door.

She twisted at the door handle, but it refused to turn; Brenda panicked when she realized it needed a key. She had staggered to the window bending some of the blinds back when she tried to regain her balance. She pounded her fists against the glass, and she screamed against the punk band, but it was too loud and too fast. The strange man was behind her now. She lunged at him and kicked him where she knew he'd feel it, but it didn't seem to bother him. She fought against him, but the man wasn't fighting back. He spun her around, pinning her arms to her body when he wrapped his arms tight around her. Brenda tried to bite him. Her legs flailed wildly. Was he singing to her? She swore she could hear something against the blaring music, a familiar lullaby. She was exhausted now, but she refused to give up.

"Fuck you, asshole! Let me go!" she cried. The strange man pulled her in tight and pressed his face against her hair. He closed his eyes as he breathed her in as though he had just taken a hit of something. He dragged her across the living room cranking the music up louder as they passed the kitchen bar counter. He pulled her into the bedroom, slamming the door shut while Brenda's screams were drowned out by the music.

19
Alex

Alex sat on the bottom steps of his apartment and waited for Detective Tamblin. His mother stood beside him and looked down on him. Her hand was clamped around his shoulder. He zipped his jacket up to his chin and stuffed his hands in his pockets. It was difficult to look at her sometimes. Especially when she was standing beside him in her tattered waitress smock. He could see every wire fiber taut against her neck, rotting flesh peeled away from bone in some places, and her eyes bulged like skinless grapes. She didn't look the way he remembered her when she used to tuck him in at night, or the way she used to call him Sugar Bear with all the warmth and glow of the sun, and her hair wasn't the tender ripples that smelled as clean as a spring rain, but this was his mother, and he would rather have her with him like this than not at all, and his *gifts* kept her close.

"Are you coming with me?" He kept his gaze steady on the trees in his neighborhood. There were few leaves clinging to branches otherwise they were bare.

"Of course," she whispered.

Tamblin arrived only a few minutes after he said he would and greeted him with the kind of smile that he was sure made people want to smile too. He was an older man, slow moving, but carried a quiet confidence like he kept all the answers to life's secrets locked away in his chest. He kept his dark eyes steady on the road, taking care and precision with every turn through the back roads and the main ones. Tamblin turned the radio on and tapped one of the preset buttons. It was the oldies station his mom loved.

"I'm old Alex, so's my taste in music," he chuckled. "Hope you don't mind."

Alex shook his head.

"No, Sir. Not at all. This is actually my mom's favorite station. I like it too,"

Tamblin's eyes lit up and he glanced in Alex's direction.

"Is that right? Who are some of her favorites?"

Alex looked in the passenger side mirror. His mother sat behind him, her eyes boring into the back of his seat. Alex shuddered in his jacket. The car was plenty warm, but he couldn't get warm enough. Tamblin must've felt the chill too because he cranked the heat up.

"She has so many, but she loves Otis Redding and Sam Cook the most."

"Well, all right."

Alex smiled but it dissolved when he felt his mother's cold breath on his neck.

A few minutes later, they pulled into Tamblin's driveway. Alex had never been in a neighborhood quite like this one. All of the houses looked the same as did the mailboxes. The asphalt on the road was smooth and smelled like it had been recently paved. The front of Tamblin's house had a full garden of flowers of all colors and shapes and bordered by flagstone.

"My wife has a bit of a green thumb. I don't know how she does it. I couldn't keep a cactus alive if I tried, but she has a talent for it. She says it's all in the soil, but I think she could grow orchids in snow if she wanted to."

Wafts of gray smoke carried upward in the back yard and for a moment the air smelled like Christmas.

"She's got the grill going."

"The flowers are beautiful. I don't think I've ever seen most of these," Alex admired them as he followed Tamblin into the house. A blanket of warmth welcomed him the minute he walked through the door. Tamblin took Alex's jacket from him and hung it on the coat rack by the door, and a pudgy bulldog came a bounding to Detective Tamblin for scratches then waddled to Alex and planted himself on his feet. He looked up at him with foggy eyes, mouth hanging open, and floppy ears resting comfortably on his head.

Tamblin watched his dog take to Alex.

"Well, look at that, Buddy likes you."

"Hi, Buddy," Alex crouched down to pet him and the dog buried his snout into his palm for more scratches. Alex had to shuffle his feet out from under Buddy's butt so he could follow Tamblin to the backyard. They stopped when Buddy woofed and snorted at the door. His mother was standing as still as stone in the foyer looking down at the hefty dog. *Sorry, Mom.*

"Buddy? Get away from that door, old boy. There's nothing there."

Tamblin clapped his hands to get the dog's attention but he kept on in short bursts of *boof, boof, boofs,* refusing to listen. Tamblin swatted at the air.

"Ol' Senile, is what he is. That's what I'm going to call him from now on. Come on Alex, let me introduce you to Ms. Lorraine."

Tamblin patted Alex on the shoulder and they stepped onto the wooded patio. In the middle of the patio was wicker furniture and there was a special place for the grill off to the side. The backyard was surrounded by a wood privacy fence, but from where he was on the patio, he could see into the neighbors' back yards. Tamblin's wife was steady at the grill with a plate of steaks in one hand and long metal tongs in the other. She put them on one at a time and they hissed and crackled, and that savory aroma wafted into the air.

"Smelling good, Dear Heart."

Lorraine set the tongs and plate aside and turned to Tamblin.

"Hey, Old Timer," Lorraine planted a kiss on his cheek and Tamblin stepped aside to introduce her to Alex.

"Alex, this is my lovely wife, Lorraine," Alex reached his hand out to her and she gave it a firm shake, never once taking her eyes off of him.

"Hello, Ma'am."

"It's very nice to meet you, Alex. Howard tells me you're the young man who'll be putting in our ceiling fans," Lorraine pierced the steaks and flipped them over.

"Yes, Ma'am. Should I get started on that now?" Alex gestured back toward the house.

"How long do you think it would take, Honey?" Lorraine said it as though he was one of her own grandkids.

"As long as it's replacing a ceiling light, it should only take about an hour," Alex could hear Buddy's muffled barks inside the house. Lorraine turned toward the sound.

"Is that Buddy?"

"That would be, Buddy," Tamblin took a seat on a wooden bench that lined the edges of the porch.

"Old boy of yours is getting senile, Howard," Lorraine shook her head and smiled. She rested her hand on Alex's shoulder, "I tell you what Alex, if it's going to be an hour or so to get that fan hooked up, why don't we just enjoy ourselves with dinner tonight and we can worry about it another time. How's that sound?"

Alex looked over at the detective, waiting for some sort of cue, but Tamblin only shrugged, "Your call, Kiddo."

"Sure, that sounds good."

Lorraine patted his shoulder, "Good choice."

Alex helped set the dinner table the way he used to do for his mom. Tamblin brought out glasses filled with ice and set them beside each plate and followed it with two pitchers, one with lemonade and another with sweet tea. Alex liked their home. They had older dark cherry wood furniture and a china cabinet propped against one wall with plates and glass figurines. The tablecloth was a simple white cloth with a plastic cover. Lorraine and the detective sat beside each other, and Alex sat on the other side. Buddy had eventually moved away from the foyer when Tamblin set his dinner down. Alex's mom was gone by then. Lorraine had served them corn and baked potatoes to go with their ribeyes. Alex cut small precise pieces off of his steak, careful not to touch the meat with the corn and the potato, wondering when his mother would come back.

"Where are you from, Baby?" Lorraine was buttering her roll and moved the salt away from Tamblin as he reached for it with all the ease and grace of a swan. Tamblin snickered and went back to his meal.

"From Landstown, Virginia, originally. Moved here after high school."

"Did you move here with your family?"

"Just my mom," Alex set his knife and fork down on the rim of his plate, and rubbed his arms when a chill crept in. His mother was sitting beside him staring straight ahead at Tamblin and Lorraine. Buddy moved from Tamblin's side and sat behind Alex's mom. This time he didn't bark or snarl, he just watched her. Tamblin looked over at him and shook his head. Alex picked his knife and fork up again and began cutting away the pieces of meat until all that remained were perfectly shaped cubes.

"But she died, so it's just me now."

"I am very sorry to hear it, Baby. That never gets easy."

Lorraine nudged her husband, "Did I leave the back door open? I feel a draft," Lorraine twisted around to see and shook her head, "No, it's closed," she buttoned her cardigan.

Alex smiled, "It's okay. She's not really gone. She's always with me."

Tamblin stopped chewing for a moment and looked at Alex, "Now, that's a good way to think about it. So, what brought you both to Bridgford of all places."

"I don't know, it has its charms, and it was the first place I was able to get a decent job. I've been all over Virginia looking for a place to settle."

"I can understand that," Tamblin chimed in, "we used to live in Baltimore, but Lorraine's family is from here, so this is where we ultimately wound up. Town's not too slow for us and it's not too fast either. It fit just right. So Dusty took you in, huh?"

"Yes, Sir. He even pushed me to go to school. I haven't decided on my major though,"

"Well, you can figure it out later. Important thing is you started. Some people don't even get that chance."

After dinner they sat in the living room with coffee and some leftover cherry crumb cake that Lorraine kept in the fridge. Lorraine retired to her bedroom for the evening to call her sister for their routine chat. Alex's mom stayed at the dinner table watching Alex enjoying his dessert next to Tamblin. Buddy didn't dare move from her side. The detective took a sip of his coffee and set it down on the glass table.

"Have you ever met Timothy Beaumont?"

Alex choked back the small piece of cake stuck in his throat and shook his head, "Not personally, no. I think I've seen him come and go a couple of times," *Timothy watched me carry Brenda Coswell upstairs to my apartment.* Alex knew this because as he ascended, he caught the spark of Timothy's lighter and the slow crackle when he took the first hit off his cigarette. The orange glow of it briefly illuminated his face as he did. He was standing in the dark leaning against the apartment building watching Alex until he reached his apartment. "We've never spoken to each other."

"He's not someone you want to cross paths with anyhow."

"Yeah, after seeing the way he left Bryson. I would have to agree. I've seen him around Dusty's once or twice. He's never in there for too long."

Alex set his empty plate on the coffee table. The weight of his mother's gaze pressed on him and he knew he should go looking for the phone. He covered his mouth with a loose fist and yawned hoping Tamblin would take that as cue that Alex was ready to go.

"I'm sure you have. I think everyone in town goes to Dusty's. If it's not to shop, it's usually to chat with him," Tamblin started for his mug and stopped himself. "Hey, does Dusty sell bait and tackle too?"

"Yes, Sir," Alex watched Tamblin take another slow sip of his coffee and set the mug down. "There's a small section in the store. He doesn't really advertise it because there's already a bait and tackle shop in town, but it's there in case people forget something on their way to the docks."

"I thought so."

Alex could tell he was turning something over in his mind, but he wasn't quite sure what. He shifted in his seat and looked out the window. The last bit of daylight that had remained was gone. He wouldn't be able to look for the phone now. He'd have to try again tomorrow.

"How's Dusty holding up these days? I haven't been by to see him recently."

"He shows up to work every day, but you can tell it weighs on him. You know earlier you said you wanted me to come by the precinct to ask me questions about the employees. Is Dusty one of them? Because I promise you there's no way that he could be involved with Jessica going missing."

"Dusty? Oh, god no, son. No, as much as he loves his grand-daughter, I couldn't bring myself to believe that even if it were true. No, everything with him checks out. People come and go from his store all the time. Like you said, you've even seen Timothy in there."

"Is it possible that he's involved with her or the other missing girl I've seen on the news lately?"

"I'm not convinced he is. They don't fit his demographic. The ones with poor to non-existent family life. The runaways and drug-gies. Easier for him to control someone who doesn't have anyone else to turn to. I'm willing to bet whoever took the girls saw something special about them."

"So, you think the same person took them?" Alex looked past Tamblin at his mom whose head was tilted at an angle and her blue lips were fixed into an open grin now. Buddy began to growl when her body trembled. He sat up with his ears tucked back and didn't dare take his eyes off of her.

Tamblin followed Alex's gaze behind him and whistled for Buddy to come close. "I wouldn't be surprised if it was one person. I think there are similarities, enough to even make it seem personal, but who can really say for sure until we have more to go on," he looked back at Buddy again and patted the back of the couch trying to get him away from the dining room.

"Anyhow, I'm sure you've had enough of this old man's ram-blings for one night. Why don't I go ahead and get you home?"

He walked over to Buddy and scooped the hefty boy into his arms. He was trying to wriggle his way out of Tamblin's arms stretching toward Alex's mom until he moved away from the dining table.

"Yeah, probably a good idea. I have to look for my phone in the morning before class anyway."

Alex headed for the door. Buddy had finally calmed down when his mom was no longer sitting at the table. Tamblin set him down and he waddled over to his bed and collapsed into the comfort of it.

"What does your phone look like? Maybe I can help you look for it."

Alex slipped his jacket on and zipped it up all the way, regretting he had said anything at all.

"It's a silver flip phone, but I'm not going to look too hard for it. If I don't find it, I'll get a new one."

"Tell you what, why don't you give me the phone number, and I can go out to some of the places you say you've been, and I'll call it."

Alex could feel the heat radiating off of his face.

"That's okay, really. You have other things to take care of right now that are more important than some dumb phone. Thank you though."

"You sure? I'm really good at finding things. It's sort of in my job description," Tamblin joked, but there was a hint of seriousness behind it, "Okay, suit yourself, Kiddo. Let me know if you change your mind."

There were no parking spaces open in the neighborhood so Tamblin just pulled parallel to Alex's apartment and let him hop out.

"You have yourself a good night, Alex. Come by the precinct as soon as you can, so we can clear some things up, okay?"

"Yes, Sir," Alex shut the door and started to walk away, but he turned back around. Tamblin rolled the window down when he approached the passenger door.

"What's up, Son, you forget something?"

"No. Just wanted to say thank you for inviting me into your home, Detective Tamblin. Will you please tell Ms. Lorraine thank you again for me too? I haven't had a meal like that in a long time."

Tamblin reached out to Alex and shook his hand, "You are most welcome, young man and you got it. Hey, I'll still keep a look out for your phone."

Alex started to object, but Tamblin cut him off.

"We'll talk soon."

Alex watched Tamblin drive out of the neighborhood. A chill crept into his chest and he knew his mother was back.

"If he finds the phone, he'll destroy our special place," she whispered.

"I know, Mom. I can't go back tonight."

20
Gabe

Gabe sat in the living room while Eric and Carol were busy in the kitchen. He had asked if there was anything he could do to help, but they declined, and Carol told him to make himself comfortable and get to know the girls. Peter was in a bouncy seat staring up at plastic animals dangling over his head. Every once in a while, he took a swat at one and giggled hysterically when it rattled. The girls, Elsie and Samantha sat in the couch next to his in their pajamas and stared at him in awe. This was their daddy's daddy, a man they never knew existed until their mom told them he might be coming to dinner. They watched him curiously and smiled shyly, every now and then they'd whisper to each other and laugh. Elsie was older than Samantha by two years. Elsie said she was in the third grade and Sammie was in the first.

"Do you like to draw Mr. Gabe?" Elsie asked.

"I never was very good at it," Gabe replied. "Wish I was though."

Samantha whispered in Elsie's ear and this was followed by Elsie pushing her away with a smirk on her face.

"No, Sammie, you ask him!" Samantha's face turned red.

Carol called from the kitchen. "You girls behaving yourselves?"

"Yes ma'am," they called back.

Elsie's attention turned back to Gabriel and she fidgeted with her pajama shirt riddled patterned with pink and purple ponies.

"Umm, Sammie wants to know if umm, we can call you Grandpa."

Gabe was tickled.

"I'd be okay with that."

They girls cheered.

"If you want, we can show you how to draw. That's our easel."

Easel sounded like *eeesole* when Samantha said it. She pointed in the corner of the living room where there was a plastic easel with construction paper already clipped to it. On the paper was a drawing of a baby that vaguely resembled their baby brother. Next to it was a play kitchen with plastic pots and pans piled on its stove, and next to that was a toy chest overflowing with all sorts of toys.

"Sure," said Gabe.

Their eyes lit up delighted that there was a grown-up they could teach. They took him by the hand and pulled him toward their art corner. He struggled to kneel down, and the girls rushed to his side to help him sit down. He thanked them graciously looking like a sleepy giant next to the girls and the kitchen playset. Elsie took the drawing from the easel and replaced it with a fresh sheet of construction paper. Sammie took a box of crayons from the carpet and with her tiny fingers she fished out a few and handed them to Gabe.

"Here, Grandpa," she said. "Draw a tree and I'll draw the sun."

He thanked the little girl with bright blue eyes and hair as fiery as her mom's.

"Okay; but remember I'm not very good at this."

He took a brown crayon and drew two curves near the center of the paper. He made tree limbs by drawing "v's" and then took a green crayon and made loops all around the limbs for the leaves.

The girls seemed amazed even though he knew they were just being nice, in reality the tree looked like the baby had gotten a hold of the crayons and scribbled colors together. Elsie drew the sky in a dark blue and Sammie helped draw the sun. When they were finished, Elsie wanted their new grandpa to play with their kitchen set. They gave him a plastic pot and a solid plastic can of green beans. Gabe put the pot on the stove and tossed the toy can of green beans in there. The girls laughed.

"Grandpa, you're not supposed to put the can in there!" Sammie giggled. We can't eat that!"

Gabe laughed at himself, "You mean to tell me you don't eat green beans like that? Here this will make it taste even better."

He threw in a sock he'd found stuffed in the oven."

"Ew! No!" they squealed in unison.

Elsie and Sammie got a kick out of him, and soon they were giving him more things to try and cook on the stove.

When they were done with their kitchen playset, the girls moved onto showing off their other toys. By that time supper was ready and waiting on the table.

"Girls wash up for dinner," Carol called from the kitchen.

"K!" said Sammie.

The girls jumped up and ran down the hall into the bathroom.

"Gabe, come on over and have a seat anywhere you like."

She pointed into the dining room on the other side of the kitchen. A minute later the girls were skipping down the hall back to Gabe, each taking one of his hands and leading him into the dining room. They both wanted to sit beside him at the table, so they made him sit at the other end and they each took a seat on the opposite side. Sammie smiled at him with beaver teeth. She was missing a tooth on one side. At the center of the table was a large roast beef cut and ready to serve, there were fried potatoes, homemade brown gravy, broccoli, corn, and dinner rolls, all on nice serving trays with silver serving spoons. The plates were already on the mats and there were glasses of ice water for each of them.

Carol put Peter in a wooden highchair next to her. She cut his roast beef into small manageable portions and decided that the potatoes might be too crispy for Peter to eat just yet and gave him a soft buttered roll instead. Peter reached for the meat even before she could set his plastic tray down. She took a seat beside Elsie, and Eric took his beside Sammie.

"Are the girls being nice to you?" asked Carol.

Gabe nodded.

"They've been great."

"Don't let them fool you. Sometimes I'm convinced they're little devil spawns."

Carol took Gabe's plate and gave him a heap of everything, and he ate every single bite. He couldn't remember the last time he'd eaten this good. The girls watched him eat and they tried to mimic him, taking in heaping forkfuls of roast beef and potatoes. Eric and Carol couldn't help but watch him too. Carol took small bites of her roll and set it off to the side before cutting away at a piece of roast beef.

"Gabriel, eat as much as you want. I always make more food than I should. If you want to you can take some of this home."

Gabriel nodded, indulging in this rare feast.

"Thank you. I haven't had a home cooked meal like this in a long time. It's wonderful. The roast beef is so tender and savory."

Carol was delighted. She looked over at Eric who seemed quieter than usual. He pushed the corn away from his fried potatoes and looked up at her briefly. With her eyes she asked him what had been the matter? Eric shook his head and shrugged her off.

While everyone finished their meals, the girls asked him question after question about random things which seemed like they were just asking to be asking. They asked what his favorite color was, where he lived, what his favorite time of day was, if he had any animals because they love animals, especially puppies. They were eager to tell their grandpa that they were taking ballet classes and they wanted him to come to their recitals. Carol talked about her day with the baby, and what it was like working as a physician's assistant, and what her plans were in the next five years.

"Travel," she said. I want to travel everywhere from Scandinavia, to South America, to Japan. I just want to see it all."

"Eric's momma always wanted to travel," He stopped himself from talking about her anymore and set his fork down onto his empty plate.

When the girls asked where she was, Eric intervened and told them to put their empty plates up and to brush their teeth to get ready for bed. This was met with resistance, a drawn out,

"Aww, but Daddy!" and when Eric shook his head they didn't argue. They took their plates and dropped them into the sink and came back into the dining room to give their grandpa a hug good night.

"It was nice meeting you girls," said Gabe.

"Nice meeting you too," Elsie replied.

"Umm I hope we see you again soon," added Samantha. She put a bounce in her step and did a ballerina twirl. Her voice was soft and raspy.

"I'd like that very much. Thank you."

Carol took Peter from his highchair and parked him on her hip.

"I'm going to help put them to bed and I'll be back down."

"Okay, Hon," Eric grazed her hand as she passed by.

Elsie and Samantha gave him extra hugs, and Carol leaned Peter close to him so he could give his Daddy a slobbery kiss on his cheek. Carol laughed and ushered the girls upstairs. Eric used a cloth napkin to wipe away the baby slobber and set it on his empty plate.

Gabe helped to clear the dishes, stacking all the empty ones onto each other.

"You never told the girls about your momma?"

"They don't need to know. Not yet anyway," he said picking up what was left of the roast.

Eric helped put the food way. He looked at his dad who was emptying glasses into the sink. "What'd they say when you took the box in?"

Gabe looked back at Eric as he scrubbed the glasses with a soapy sponge.

"This one got their attention. They're going to do some digging and see what they find." Gabe rinsed out the glasses and set them in the dishrack. "Eric, I'm not going to lie to you, but this has your brother written all over it."

Eric covered the roast beef in tin foil and shoved the pan into the refrigerator.

"I hope it's not him, but I can't disagree with you."

The true question wasn't who was doing this to Gabe, it was why he was doing it.

By the time Carol had come back downstairs all the dishes had been washed, the food put away, and the table wiped clean.

"Sorry it took me so long. The girls wanted me to read an extra chapter tonight and Peter decided it'd be funny to try and escape his crib for the last half hour."

She noticed that cleanup had been taken care of.

"Thanks for picking up down here."

"Least I could do," said Gabe.

"Let's pour ourselves a drink and have a seat in the living room," suggested Carol.

"I should probably get going."

"You are always so quick to try and leave Gabriel Meier, now you and Eric go plant yourselves in the living room. It has been a long day, and I'm going to pour us each a nice glass of whiskey."

Eric wiped down the counters and set the rag in the sink.

"No point in arguing with her."

Carol came into the living room with two short glasses of whiskey and handed Gabe and Eric each a glass. She came back a few seconds later with her own and sat next to Eric. She took a short sip from her glass and her eyebrows creased to a point.

"Ooh, that's strong!" she laughed and set the glass down on the end table. "Good but strong."

"You'll have to excuse her, Dad, she can't handle her liquor."

Carol swatted at his arm. They talked for a couple of hours about all sorts of things from careers to the funniest things their kids have done. They talked about their favorite movies and songs, and the places they've visited. When the whiskey was gone, they moved on to some beers that Eric had left in the fridge. They weren't big drinkers, but they did keep some on hand for special occasions which to Carol, having Gabriel come back into Eric's life was a very special occasion, hence the giant roast beef feast with all the fixings. One drink after another had made them a little groggier and a little bolder because the conversations they had avoided since Gabe first arrived for dinner were finally coming to surface.

"I wish Alex was here," Eric's head lolled. "I think he'd like this."

"I do too, Son."

"You know he used to think you didn't like him?"

Gabe set his bottle down on the end table and shook his head. "No, I didn't. I hate that he thought that of me."

"It was because you never talked to him. I told him that's just the way you were, and then when Mom died, well you know, things just got worse."

"I know."

"Gabriel, did Eric tell you about the phone call he got this morning?" Carol slurred her question and her eyes opened and closed so slowly. "He came running downs stairs at three o' clock in the morning and all Eric could hear was someone crying on the other end. I asked him whose heart he broke, but he didn't find that funny."

She rested her head against the back of her couch, eyes closing again.

"He mentioned it," Gabe looked at his son who was resting his head on the arm of the couch.

"There's nothing creepier than getting a phone call that early and hearing someone whimpering on the other end," Eric cut in with his eyes still closed. "Wakes you up real quick,"

Gabe found it comical seeing his oldest son snockered like he was. He'd never had the chance to have a drink with him until now. This was nice.

"We think it's my little brother," Eric added.

"You do?" Carol sat up in her seat. She attempted to hoist her legs onto the couch and cross them in front, but she only managed to get one leg up. Carol was a tall woman, but with all the Scotch and beer she'd thrown back, Gabe figured her legs must've felt like cinder blocks.

"Why?" She set her glass down on the end- table.

"Tell her about the packages," Eric's voice was trailing off now. Gabe imagined he'd be out like a light soon.

Gabe didn't really want to, not the way he was feeling right now. His stomach sat heavy, and he could barely focus on his son and his daughter-in-law as it was, and to have to explain it to her would be a challenge, but he tried anyway.

"Alex sent me fingernails," was all that managed to come out of the big man sinking deeper into their couch.

Carol looked at them both, eyelids heavy and barely open anymore.

"Fingernails," she said before belting out into laughter. "Fingernails?" Carol laughed until her stomach hurt and she clutched her stomach in a hysterical fit. "Let me get this straight," she said trying to catch her breath, "He sent you fingernail clippings in the mail? As what, as like a joke?"

This amused her until Gabe told her they had been whole finger-nails, and about the other package with Eleanor's ring on someone's finger, and it took her a minute to calm down from her giggling fit before she realized what he said.

"Oh, I see. Oh, no, that's not funny at all," Carol's smile faded, "That's actually pretty sick, Gabriel. Are you sure that it was your wife's ring? How would he even have gotten it?"

"She wasn't wearing it when we buried her. I'm not even sure if she was wearing it when she left the house the day she died. For all I know she could've tossed it before she got into the car. Maybe Alex found it. But there's no mistaking it. When we were newly married, she used to take it off if she was the one doing the dishes. She always set it on the edge of the sink. Well one day it had been just a little too close to the edge and when she turned the garbage disposal on, the ring went right down the drain. Clipped one of the prongs that held the diamond in place. We never had enough money to get it fixed but Eleanor, she didn't mind. Said it added character. It was the little things like that that made me love her. She was a good woman. I wish you could've met her."

Gabe went quiet and so did Carol. They both listened to Eric snoring softly. Gabe was sure that Eric already told her what an amazing woman his momma had been. Anyone who'd met her would've seen it. To Gabe she was a light in the dark, which made it that much more difficult to let go of the guilt he felt when he lost her. The thought sobered him, and he looked up at Carol who seemed to be sobering too.

"I loved her more than I've ever loved anyone in my life. It's my fault she's not here right now. I killed her," he said. He didn't mean to say it, but the words just left his mouth. He would never be able to forget the way Eric looked at him the day she died.

It had been quiet on the third floor of that ICU with the exception of soft rhythmic beeping coming from some of the patients' rooms. There was a moment of serenity, however brief, it was there, that sleepy calm before the morning storm, the deafening silence before the inevitable chaos that would forever change their lives. How would they ever recover from this? Gabriel wished he could pause time, that maybe somehow if he just held onto the calm, Eleanor would be okay, and he could fix the broken pieces of their marriage.

He found Eric, sitting alone in one of the chairs next to a vending machine, staring down at the tile floor. A blue neon glow reflected off of it. Gabe's heart lurched into the pit of his stomach when the speaker overhead signaled the code.

Eric looked up as nurses in green scrubs rushed past him and into his mother's room. He started to get up but stopped when he saw his father standing there. Gabe shook his head. The young boy cupped his face in his hands and collapsed in the seat, his father took a seat beside him. He wanted to hug his boy; he wanted to tell him that they would get through this, but he didn't know if they would. Instead, Gabe stared numbly at his calloused hands resting in his lap and let the boy cry.

"I couldn't even tell him that things would be okay. A decent parent says those things."

Carol looked down at Buster who was sleeping below her feet. Gabe hadn't meant for the conversation to turn. He wished he hadn't said anything. He looked down at his watch, it was eleven-thirty now. He stopped drinking nearly an hour ago but didn't feel well enough to drive. Carol caught him stealing a glance at his watch.

"I'll be right back," she said and wandered into the hallway, and Buster followed her to retire upstairs. After a moment she was back with a pillow and a blanket and handed them to Gabe. "You can sleep here. There's no sense in you driving home tonight. Plus, it'll be fun for the girls to wake up seeing you down here. It'd be like catching Santa only hungover and without the white hair and belly."

"Okay," Gabe smiled. "I appreciate everything you've done, Carol. If it weren't for you, Eric would've never talked to me."

Gabe unfolded the quilted blanket over him and stretched out on the sofa and stuffed the pillow behind his head. It was a down-feather pillow and he felt like his head was sinking into a cloud.

"I didn't just do it for you," Carol looked over her shoulder at her sleeping husband. "I think he needs you just as much as you need him." She turned to Gabe, "I know what I'm about to say won't make a difference, but regardless of what happened in the past Gabriel, you deserve a second chance." She touched his shoulder, a little heavier than she probably anticipated, the effects of the drink still evident. "What happened to Eleanor is not your fault no matter how hard it is to see otherwise. You argued. People argue and sometimes they storm out. Sure, you could run through all the things you would've done different, but that won't change anything now. You can't keep carrying that weight around forever." She poked at Eric and he sprung off the sofa. "Let's go to bed, Lightweight," she teased.

Eric wandered aimlessly down the hall and called back, "Night, Dad."

Carol followed Eric, but not before looking back at Gabe.

"Night, Dad," she repeated, and she cut out the light to the living room before they went upstairs.

"Good night," he said to himself and before long he was asleep.

The shrill sound of the phone catapulted Gabe from his sleep. The world spun, and his head throbbed a little. It was too dark to see anything, and it took him a minute to remember he wasn't in his own bed when he rolled onto the thick carpet. Gabe rubbed the sleep from his eyes, and he felt his way back to the couch to pull himself up. The stove light was on and he caught glimpse of a shadow moving in the dark. The phone continued to ring, and it seemed to echo in his head. He pressed the button on the side of his watch and a green light appeared. **3:00a.m.** Gabriel rounded the counter into the kitchen toward the stove light when the phone stopped ringing. He saw Eric in his white t-shirt and plaid pajama pants, his back was turned to him and the phone was against his ear.

"Son," Gabe whispered.

Eric brought his free hand up and motioned for him to come to the phone. Gabriel stood beside him and Eric lifted the phone off his ear so they could both listen. There was static and clicking on the other end, and Gabe could faintly hear a man whimpering.

"Alex," Eric said. His voice sounded concerned but gruff. "Alex, buddy, if you don't talk to me, I can't help you," Eric sounded very much like a dad in this moment, as though he'd always been Alex's dad.

There was shuffling on the other end and more fuzz. Gabe thought he heard the man say something, but it didn't come through clear enough. The man sniffled.

"I'm sorry, Eric," he whimpered, "I can't stop. She won't let me now."

Gabe and Eric were awake now. They looked at each other somewhat relieved to know Alex was alive, but this feeling was quickly followed by the realization that Alex was definitely in some sort of trouble.

"Can't stop what, Alex? Who won't? What's going on? Where are you?" Eric tried to coax more out of Alex, but after a few clicks the call went back to the dial tone.

PART III: Torn Apart, Stitched Together

1

Detective Tamblin

It usually takes about five to ten days for forensics to analyze a DNA sample, longer if it has to be sent out from a small town like Bridgford County. By that time, it might be weeks to get results. It's much faster if you have something to compare it to, and even faster when you call in a favor to some of the people you knew back in the Richmond Forensics Department. Tamblin had taken that hair sample from Alex's home but didn't have anything to compare it to, at least not at first. He had to go to Brenda's and Jessica's homes and looked for brushes or combs, swept through pillows and their laundry, even looked around their showers. He just needed one strand of hair; he needed to know if they matched the sample from Alex's bathtub. The samples weren't hard to get. On a vanity in Brenda's bedroom was a large flat brush with her hair still in it. He found a strand of Jessica's hair woven into the bottom bristles of her vacuum cleaner.

This would be the third time he tried to call to speak with his old buddy, Nolan. Third time's the charm, he thought to himself as he waited for the call to patch through.

"Nolan, what's going on, man? Tell me you got some good news. That right? Well, damn I almost put money on that one. Listen, thank you for your help, Nolan. It is much appreciated. Send Ms. Annie my love. Okay, bye now."

Tamblin put the phone down on the receiver. He still wasn't convinced. When things don't sit right it burns in your gut. That's what was happening to Tamblin. That slow burn in the pit of his stomach was likely to set him on fire if he didn't get to the bottom of it soon. He went back through his notes. How did Alex fit into all of this?

A few minutes later, one of his senior officers, Erica Hutton stopped in his doorway.

"Detective."

She looked like she had run across the courtyard to get to him.

"Hey, Hutton, what can I do for you?" Tamblin was jotting down the things he needed to do today.

"We found Timothy Beaumont."

Tamblin looked up from his notepad with his pen still on the pad. "Where?"

"Highway Patrol found him heading southbound on I-95 toward Florida. You'd think he would've swapped cars somewhere along the way, but he didn't. He was still in that POS Buick."

Tamblin followed her out of the office and across the courtyards to the other end of the station where the interrogation rooms and holding cells were. A few officers waved at him as he passed by.

"What about Tammy Baker? Was she with him?"

Hutton sniffled against the cold, "In a manner of speaking," she peered up at him from beneath her cap. "She was in the trunk, drugged out of her mind. Running a traffic ring?"

Tamblin shook his head, "I think he's too stupid to run anything, but I'm sure he knows people. I wouldn't put it past him to try and make easy money by selling her like she was cattle."

They walked into the north end of the police station. Officer Cadence was on the phone at the front desk. She pointed down the hall behind her and held up three fingers. Tamblin nodded as they walked past, their shoes clacked along the glossy tile. Hutton opened the door to the small room on the other side of the one- way mirror for interrogation room three. Timothy Beaumont was sitting quietly with his hands cuffed to the table and he was hunched over with his head hanging low. He kept his arms tucked close to his body and there were dark circles beneath his eyes which were partly closed. Tamblin looked at his thin face. The man was in his mid-forties, but he looked to be in his late fifties. He was wearing a faded yellow polo and khaki shorts like he was prepping himself to blend in with retirees down in Florida, but you couldn't disguise a man like Timothy Beaumont. While his clothes said retired golfer, his face was of the greasy salesman variety with a paper- thin smile and arched brows.

"Do you want me to go in first?" Office Hutton had one hand on the door. She was ready to get this over and done with. "You know his history with women. He's likely to show us his ugly side. His real side."

"That could work, but I get the feeling he'd be less likely to co-operate. He'll likely try to keep all of the attention off of himself by wasting his time thinking he can manipulate you."

"Good point."

Hutton opened the door for Tamblin.

"The quicker we can get this done, the quicker we can get him back to holding. I'll be watching from in here. Give me the sign and I'll come get him."

"Will do," He took a pen and notepad, and two manilla folders from the metal desk. "Let's see how much I'll be able to get out of him."

Tamblin stood in front of the interrogation room. There was a small square placard with a number 3 etched in white paint on the door. Timothy Beaumont didn't bother looking up when the detective walked in.

"I sure have been waiting a long time." Timothy's voice was slow and nasal, and he kept his eyes down at his hands as he spoke.

"Did you have somewhere else to be?"

Tamblin took a seat in front of him and dropped his things onto the table. Timothy kept quiet, the chain from his handcuffs quivered, one of his feet shook beneath the table. "You think your connections are going to be upset when you don't show up in Florida with Tammy Baker?"

"Don't have a clue what you're talking about."

"Sure, you don't. She must've tied herself up and then hopped into the trunk of your car.

Oh, by the way, I'm sure you'll be happy to know that Tammy's son is alive. We honestly didn't think he was going to make it, but he's tougher than we gave him credit for. What kind of sick bastard do you have to be to hurt a child the way you did, Timmy?"

Timothy finally looked up at the Detective. "He needed to be taught."

"Is that right? A grown ass man needed to teach a seven-year-old boy what exactly? Not to protect his sister from sick fucks like yourself?"

Timothy Beaumont finally looked up at him. A thin smile spread across his lips. "The little shit wouldn't mind his business, and his bitch mother wouldn't stop screaming about needing to leave."

"So, you couldn't get Anna Lynn and you tried to sell Tammy instead,"

Timothy raised his shoulders and let them fall again.

You smug piece of shit.

"Is that what you did to Jessica Delaney? You sell her?"

Timothy shook his head. He clicked his tongue. "Don't know a Jessica Delaney."

His answer was curt. His gaze shifted to the table and he fell silent once again. Timothy was stupid, but he likely knew how interrogations worked. He might have guessed that every once in a while, detectives found their leads by stringing different cases together.

"That's not what her mom told me. She and Jessica had a run-in with you at the Quick Save several months back. Said you called her some pretty nasty names because she wouldn't let you near her daughter."

Tamblin took a picture of Jessica Delaney from one of his manila folders and met Timothy on his side of the table. He dropped the photo in front of Timothy and leaned against the edge of the table with his fingers folded together in front of him. He looked down at Timothy Beaumont whose eyes barely skimmed the picture.

"She went missing back in September, and you're the only one that she and her mother have ever had a real problem with."

Timothy leaned back in his seat. His eyebrows were turned down into a scowl and shrugged. "Even if I did know who she was, I was still locked up back then. Check your records."

"Already have, you were just released a few weeks ago in November, but you have friends. Did you ask one of them to take her while you were gone?" Tamblin dropped the other file with Brenda Coswell's photo in front of him too. It was worth a shot. "How about Brenda, you ever seen her before?"

Timothy rolled his eyes. He leaned over Brenda's picture, pursed his lips, and let a dangle of saliva hang over her smile but sucked it back in before it even touched the picture. Tamblin had the feeling he wouldn't talk about Jessica or Brenda even if he did know them, at least not in any way that would connect him to them. Timothy changed the subject. "Who found the kid?" He was going to lead the conversation the way he wanted. "Figured he would've been dead weeks before anyone even noticed. Everyone in that neighborhood's either on drugs or hiding something. You know that don't you?

Especially the quiet ones. Didn't think anyone'd want to risk calling in the pigs. Less it was that weird pretty boy looking fucker that lives on the second floor in the next building over. Bet my left nut it was him. I should've robbed him when I had the chance," Just then his eyes skimmed briefly over Brenda's picture and then at the one-way mirror directly in front of him. Timothy stopped talking as though he'd said too much or as if he'd just remembered something.

Had to be Alex, Tamblin thought. That kid didn't look like he belonged on Timothy Beaumont's side of the tracks. He looked more like he had taken two wrong turns and gotten himself lost.

"You've gone quiet, Timmy. What's up?"

"I'm done talking," said Timothy. "Take me back to my cell now."

"You sure? Seemed like you were getting ready to tell me more about the pretty boy from the apartment next door."

The man was a cold fish now, he wasn't going to give the detective anything else. Tamblin looked back at the one-way mirror and gave a nod. "You know, I have no doubt that you'll go back to prison for what you did to Bryson Baker. Probably not for as long as you deserve, but you'll do your time, and it won't be long before you go back to your same old ways, then one day it's all going to catch up with you, and if I find out you know more about Jessica Delaney or Brenda Coswell than you're letting on, you're going find to yourself in a whole new heap of trouble."

Timothy didn't seem affected by what Tamblin had to say and before long, officer Hutton was in the room to escort him back to his cell.

2
Detective Tamblin

Detective Tamblin stopped by Brenda Coswell's home, a brick duplex style townhouse with a single driveway. It was an older neighborhood occupied mainly by senior citizens. Her sister said she'd gotten a steal on the place, and even though the neighborhood was falling apart, she said Brenda loved it because it was hers. Brenda lived one street over from the main road and it was tucked away in a quiet cul-de-sac. Her neighbor occupying the townhouse beside hers said that she and her husband always go to bed pretty early and didn't notice anything out of the ordinary, but they were deep sleepers and regrettably, hard of hearing. A horrible combination for an investigation. Another neighbor, Teresa Clark, a short woman with busy hair and thick Coke-bottle glasses, who owned the house near the mouth of the cul-de-sac said that she'd seen a black SUV in her driveway, but it wasn't unusual for Brenda to have visitors. What that meant and how she meant it, Tamblin wasn't sure, and the woman refused to elaborate.

"All I'm saying is that I heard she used to go to AA meetings. She had trouble with the sauce, and possibly other recreational activities too. Maybe cocaine. I couldn't tell you for sure," said Mrs. Clark.

Officers never did find any evidence of cocaine or other drugs, and her cabinets were clean, and while it was true, she'd been to AA, she hadn't been there in several years.

But an older gentleman had called the crime line saying he was coming back from taking his wife to the urgent care late on the night she'd gone missing. He crossed paths with a truck on the street and when his lights hit its interior, he could swear he saw a woman that fit Brenda's description. He thought it strange because her head was lolled back between the chair and the passenger side door with her mouth open. She looked like she was on something. He didn't catch a good look at the driver because he was so focused on the uncomfortable way the woman was sleeping. He thought maybe she had thrown back one too many and didn't think much of it until he saw her picture on the news.

Tamblin walked up to the brown front door with police tape stretched across it. He looked all around the door and the porch light which was missing a light bulb. There was never any forced entry, but her door was hanging wide open when he'd arrived on scene. Nothing in the house indicated any signs of a struggle. Her bed was untouched and pristine, and on the dresser, they had found a small backpack with bug spray, a fishing cap, and a change of clothes. Next to it was her tackle box with assorted lures and weights. In the back-yard there were places where the grass had been depressed as though someone had gone to the backyard and turned around. There were no signs of forced entry from the backdoor or windows either. Tamblin suspected that something must've spooked her, and she was out of there in a hurry. Her keys were gone, but the car was still in the driveway. Someone had been waiting for her. Tamblin made his way to the backyard. Tall weeds brushed against his pant legs as he did. Couldn't keep those things from growing even in the winter. Leaves crunched beneath his feet. There was a small kitchen sink window that came out further than the house. It made Tamblin think of a miniature greenhouse, and through the short sheer curtain he could see a shelf of dried flowers in porcelain vases of different colors.

Detective Tamblin noticed something peculiar in the backyard. The police tape which used to be attached to the door was now caught between the HVAC unit and the hose attached to it. The door which he knew had been locked and unvisited for at least a few weeks, was open ever so slightly. He made a call back to his department and after a few rings he was speaking to Officer Cadence.

"Hey, has anyone been at the Coswell residence since Forensics was last here?"

"Not that I'm aware of," she told him.

"Can you send a couple of them over with the van just in case and maybe another officer? The tape is down, and the backdoor is open."

"Sure thing, Detective. Just wait for them to get there before going inside."

"Okay, Cadence. I appreciate you. Tell them I'm in the backyard. They're going to want pictures. Maybe we'll get prints this time. And I know the procedure, I'm old, Cadence, not senile, I'll wait for them to get here before I go inside," Tamblin ended the call.

It wasn't long before a white van labeled Bridgford Police Department Forensics Unit on the back had arrived. They rounded the corner, ready with their kits, and were already taking pictures. There was a glass half full of water in the kitchen that hadn't been there before, and they took pictures and bagged it for evidence. Once the first floor was cleared, they searched the upstairs. Tamblin walked behind them but squeezed to the front of the line when one of the officers called him.

"Detective," Samuels, one of the younger officers called from Brenda's bedroom.

Tamblin peered in through Brenda's doorway at her perfectly preserved room. "What in the hell?" A pair of pink pajama pants and matching shirt had been laid out neatly in the middle of Brenda Coswell's bed. From where he was standing, he couldn't tell if there was anything else out of place.

"We're going to need to sweep the room again before you go in, Detective," said one of the officers.

"You go ahead and do your thing. I'm going to check and see if there's anything new where Jessica Delaney was last seen. I'll let you know if I find anything."

Detective Tamblin headed for the Quick Save. Whoever had stalked the girls was getting bold and hopefully sloppy. He parked near the back and looked under a Jeep that was already in the spot Jessica's car had been. There wasn't anything new as far as he could tell. He struggled to pick himself off the ground, asphalt pressed against his palms and his knees before he stood back up. There was a small ache in those knees and a crick in his back. Not as young as you used to be, Old Timer. Tamblin looked around, watching people driving in and out of the parking lot. Some people stared at him curiously and he pulled back his lapel to show his badge, so they'd move along. Tamblin started for the woods. The trees were nearly bare now and the ground was soft from all the raining it had been doing in Bridgford. It was cold today, but slightly warmer than it had been the past couple of weeks, his shoes sloshed over mud and wet leaves and he looked for anything that stood out to him. The smell of decaying leaves which covered most of the ground lingered in the air, and he began to doubt whether or not he'd be able to find anything of significance in here. The unpredictable weather meant that things in the woods were always changing making the small details easier to miss.

Tamblin walked around for another mile before he could no longer see the Quick Save parking lot or hear the main roads. Birds called to each other from way up in the trees. On separate occasions he saw cardinals swooping from one tree to the next, but there were mainly crows here and they cawed from various parts of the woods watching Tamblin as he passed. Up ahead he noticed that there was a dirt trail that started from the east and curved its way further north into the woods and he followed it to see how far it would lead. The path looked like it could've been a hiking trail. Tamblin didn't recall if they had searched this part of the woods in the Delaney report, but it didn't look like the trail had been used in a long time. Tamblin looked up at the expanse of blue skies between towering oak trees and then to the path beyond. He did his best to avoid stepping on the acorns and rocks. His shoes were good but certainly not meant for hiking.

He stopped when he reached the fork in the woods. One path continued straight and the other curved off to the right which seemed strange to Tamblin. It wasn't really a fork, and it didn't follow the natural order of the woods. This path had been created, possibly even used.

There were thick broken branches; and there were shrubs that were pressed down as though someone had walked through recently. Tamblin followed it. The trees crowded this side of the fork, and there were broken branches, leaves, and plants matted down into the wet earth. Whether or not these were done by a human or an animal, he would leave for forensics to decide. After a while the woods opened up again giving way to a clearing and another trail. He walked along it when he noticed deep tire marks in the ground. Tamblin had to step over a tree trunk to get to it, and as his foot came down, he heard a faint high-pitched beeping coming from somewhere nearby. He reached into his pocket to see if it was his phone, but it was only halfway through its battery life and no one had called him recently.

He waited for it to beep again, each time it did he moved in its direction. *Red light, Greenlight,* he thought. Then Tamblin's foot hit something hidden between tall blades of wet grass and mud. He looked down, half-buried in the soft ground was something silver and small. He crouched down and weeded through the grass. It was an LG flip phone. The square screen read, 27 Missed Calls. The battery icon blinked slow and steady like a weak pulse until the screen went black.

Tamblin had to go back to the parking lot to make the call to his Forensics team. He didn't get any reception in the woods and barely had reception in the Quick Save parking lot so he left his suit coat close to it so that he would know where to go.

"You'll see my car," he told them, "Take the narrow path into the woods closest to the parking lot exit and take it all the way down. I'll be standing next to the phone. I don't have reception in there, but you'll see me. I left the phone exactly where I found it."

He told Forensics to get a team to those woods as soon as possible and that he would wait until they got there. They would bag the phone for evidence and recharge the phone to see what was on it, and they would be sure to comb the woods. Tamblin hoped finding the phone would be the key to unlocking this case, and if it was, he hoped more than anything they still had a chance at finding the girls.

Tamblin walked back into the woods listening to birds calling from the trees, and the wind rustling through the branches in soft waves. It could almost be peaceful here. He took the exact same path until he reached his coat and the phone. Further ahead he caught a shimmer of water. Maybe where the rain had pooled in certain areas of the woods, but just beyond it was a small clearing. Tamblin started toward it but whipped around when twigs snapped. The crack of it echoed somewhere between the trees followed by the frantic shuffle through the leaves. He ran back toward his coat and the phone was gone.

"Oh what in the hell?" Tamblin chased after the sound. He released his gun from its holster, aiming in the direction of it. He ran against the cold with a fire in his lungs with every breath he drew in. When he saw a figure sprinting through the trees he called out: "This is Detective Tamblin with the Bridgford County Police Department! I am ordering you to stay where you are!"

But the person was not stopping. Whoever it was ducked beneath branches and zipped between the trees. Tamblin repeated himself with a warning: "If you do not stop, I will shoot!" Tamblin ran hard and fast and when he felt like he was losing him he fired a warning that zipped across the trees into some dirt. Tamblin took one dizzying turn after another, but the person was so far ahead that he lost him. Once he reached where the bullet had connected in the dirt he stopped and tried to listen for anything out of the ordinary. There was nothing. Tamblin kicked at the dirt and his foot brushed against something. It was the cell phone.

"Detective?" a voice echoed.

"I'm here. Bring a bag with you," Every muscle in his body screamed. He couldn't remember the last time he had to run that hard.

"You okay, sir?" It was one of the newer guys, Officer Marcus James. "You look like you've been dragged through hell."

Tamblin shook his head. "Damn near. Someone was in the woods. They tried to take the phone. Gonna need some guys to get out there and comb the woods. Can you do that for me?"

Officer James gave a thumbs up and was on his radio to send out for more men. Tamblin patted his shoulder and walked ahead to join the others. "I need a couple of you to come with me. There's something over there I need to check out."

He pointed toward the clearing a short distance away.

When he and two of the other officers approached the body of water, they realized it was a small pond, and beside it were two mounds of mud with tiny divots from where the rain had come down on it. Against one of the trees was a shovel. Tamblin's heartbeat drummed in his ears as they rounded the pond. "Are those what I think they are?"

One of his guys stood beside him, "Sure looks like it."

The perimeters were set, and everything was taped off. They stood under tents with lights beaming onto the mounds, and they started the excavation. Tamblin stood close as a small team began to dig. Part of him hoped it wouldn't be what they all knew it was. Because for it to be the shallow graves of the missing girls would mean their hopes of finding them alive was over. Officer James stopped digging when he reached the top of something black. Something rotten hung in the cool air. He turned his head momentarily before he dropped to his knees and dusted the mud away. Then he and another officer hoisted a black duffel bag out of the ground. Officer James unzipped the bag and spread it open. Everyone had to look away. There were multiple things wrapped tight in plastic bags, and the smell that had been unleashed was damn near unbearable. Tamblin brought a hand up to cover his nose. The odor was so foul it was almost painful to breathe.

Officer James cupped one of the bags in his hands. "Detective."

Tamblin looked at the bag the officer was holding. Tufts of light brown hair were sticking out of it. They weren't surprised to find what they did in the second mound. Body parts were wrapped in plastic this time and stuffed in a black gym bag.

The bag looked familiar to Tamblin. He'd seen it before but couldn't place it. It was, however, a relatively generic gym bag which meant he could've seen it anywhere. Still, he worked it over in his mind like a word on the tip of his tongue. He could've seen the bag in passing, but he didn't think so.

3
Gabe

Gabe stood in the second- floor hallway staring up at the attic door. There was a small cord that hung down from the handle. All of Eleanor's things had been up there since she died, and for over a decade he hadn't been able to look through them. Not that he didn't want to, but there were boxes of her old things – clothes, journals, and letters, and probably pictures from when she was still in high school, all personal things, and for the longest he felt like he had no business going through them. But Gabe missed her, and despite their failed marriage he had loved her so much it hurt, and he hated himself for never having the guts to make things right. Gabe tugged at the cord and caught the ladder that slowly emerged from above the door. He guided it with a hand until it extended down to the worn carpet.

The attic was dark and smelled of old books and linen. He pulled on an old chain above his head and the light clinked and flickered before it turned on. There wasn't much up here. Holiday decorations were stacked in plastic bins on one side and all of Eleanor's things sat in a pile in the other. He drew in a breath and exhaled slowly as if he were getting ready to see her for the first time; he took a seat next to her things and rested his hand over one of the boxes labeled **Eleanor's Books** and folded back the top flaps. He took out a book called *Revolutionary Road* by Richard Yates. The pages were worn and yellow and he could tell where some of them had been dog eared. Gabe set it aside along with other books that were much in the same shape. Others were some textbooks from when she was going to Alderson for her gen ed – *American History* and *The Principles of Anatomy and Physiology*. He dug deeper into the box and found photo albums of her when she was still a small girl. Some of them were of her and her parents in different places. There was one of her at the zoo with a parrot on her arm. In every picture she was a happy smiling, Eleanor. It made him smile too. Some of the other albums were of her and the kids. Then there was one at the very bottom of the box. It was a thin brown album. He slid it past the others and rested it on top of the pile. It had all of the pictures of her and Gabe. Most of them were on their wedding day. In one picture she was standing beside him with her hands folded in his. Another was a picture of Gabe sleeping on the sofa. When he turned another page, an unopened letter with his name on it slid between the boxes, only he didn't notice it. Instead he moved onto the next box. It held her old black jewelry box lined on the inside with blue velvet. She never did wear much jewelry, so there wasn't much in there except for a pair of pearl earrings, a gold bracelet, and an amethyst necklace.

Beneath the jewelry box was a leather journal with gilded edges and embellished with a gold cursive *E*. He opened it to the first page. She always did have the nicest penmanship, every letter was perfectly uniform, and placed on the page with care and attention. That was the type of person she was. The first page read, Eleanor Jean Meier, dated 1987 in dark blue ink. He turned another page, there was only one sentence: *I don't know what I'm doing anymore.*

On the next page there was an entire paragraph. Gabe took a seat beside the boxes. The journal was filled with entries, many of them about their sons, most of them about her unhappiness. He knew she had been unhappy for a long time. It hurt to know he was the cause of it. Gabe drew in a deep breath before reading some of the passages. These were her deeply personal thoughts; he was catching a small but significant glimpse into.

He started with a passage about dreams. She had had a dream about the farm she used to live on, running through fields of tall grass into the woods. The woods had disappeared and turned to blue sky. She had transformed into an eagle and soared as high as her wings would let her.

I was free, she wrote. *Completely, free, but when I woke up, I was lying in my bed. Gabe was sleeping right there beside me, and I cried. I couldn't help but think, what happened to us? When did I stop loving my husband?*

Gabe closed his eyes tight enough to blink away the few tears that had managed to escape before turning the page. *Gabe's never cheated on me, at least I don't think he has. I would never do that to him either. He doesn't deserve that. I guess no one does for that matter. You marry someone, you're supposed to be with them loyally and faithfully, but I have thought about it sometimes, with no one in particular, but I think about having an affair or him having an affair just to break up this dull monotonous life. What a stupid thought to have. Today when Gabe came home, we didn't even speak to each other. At least not like we used to. He can tell something's wrong and doesn't know what. He doesn't ask, but I wouldn't know what to tell him if he did. Lately, I'm not entirely sure myself. At first, I thought it was because things have been shit lately, but it feels like there's something much more than that.*

The passage ended there. Gabe thought about the last line. Many of their arguments had revolved around college, bills, and money, and for the longest he thought that was what had caused the rift. There was something more but what? Gabe thumbed through more of the pages hoping for some sort of answer. What began to unravel were endless passages of her suffering. Then he came across a passage about Alex.

Alex drew something that scared me today. It was a picture of a woman scrawled in black crayon, there was a heavy divot in her smile, where Alex had run the crayon over and over again, and he had taken a red crayon to draw lines spilling out from her body, and what scared me most was that I think the picture was of me. She was wearing the same uniform I wear at Marty's.

He turned to the last entry she ever wrote, reluctant to read it, afraid of what he might find. The page was dated, October 30th, 1988. That was one week before she died.

I can't bring myself to tell Gabe that I'm tired. I'm tired of fighting about dreams I will never achieve or the money we never seem to have, and when we're not fighting, we don't have anything to say to each other. I'm just so exhausted. Sometimes I can't get out of bed, but I have to, for the sake of our kids. I have to force myself to get up. My beautiful babies. They are my greatest gifts. If Gabe only knew, he broke my heart by not saying a word. How do you reach out to someone like that? I loved him once. I know I did, but I'm dying inside -

He couldn't read the rest; he didn't have to in order to know that Eleanor really did stop loving him. Part of him always knew, but to read it in her journal was hard to take in, and what made it worse? The situation was familiar, and it made Gabe question whether or not all marriages ended the same way. He let the journal fall to the floor and buried his face in his hands.

It wasn't until he heard Eric's voice from downstairs that Gabe realized he had fallen asleep in the attic. He looked down at his watch, he had been up there for an hour. He pulled on the chain attached to the light and climbed down the ladder.

"Dad?" Eric called from the foyer on the first floor.

"I'm coming, son."

He had that foggy-headed static feeling he sometimes got when shaken from sleep, like his head was stuck in a glass bowl. He shuffled downstairs holding onto the banister to steady himself.

"Everything okay?"

"I hope so. I tried calling a couple of times, but you didn't answer. Did you know your door was hanging wide open?"

"I must not have closed it all the way. Wind probably blew it open. Sorry I didn't hear your call. I was trying to clean out the attic."

Emphasis was on trying. He couldn't bring himself to take any of Eleanor's things out of there, but Gabe didn't think that Eric was completely listening. He was looking down at his worn Reeboks with his arms crossed tight against his chest.

"What's goin' on, son?"

Eric took a rolled-up Sunday paper from his back pocket. "I want you to look at this and tell me the honest to God truth, okay?"

Gabe wasn't sure what he meant but nodded anyway. Eric opened the paper to the front page. There were photos side by side of two young women, beautiful, brunette, with big eyes and a perfect smile, and they both had honey brown hair. **Missing** was the title in the headline.

"Who do they look like to you?"

Their names were Jessica Delaney and Brenda Coswell. Gabe only had to look at their faces to know what Eric was saying. It was the way they smiled and the way their hair fell gracefully over their shoulders, and the way their bright blue eyes stared back at him. Eleanor. They looked like Eleanor.

Gabe stared at the photographs of the women in the paper. Their likeness to Eleanor was eerie. They had the same high cheek bones and arched brows. If you could put one smile over the other, they would align perfectly. The only difference was the girl on the right was a little older and her hair was just a smidge darker, but what troubled Gabe was their uncanny resemblance to Eleanor.

"You don't think..." Eric started.

"That Alex had something to do with this?" Gabe finished. "No."

But truthfully, he wasn't sure, and the more he thought about it, the more he doubted his answer.

"Dad. He's been gone a long time. What if..." he couldn't finish his sentence.

Gabe took the paper from Eric and read through it for more information. The girls were from Bridgford County, Virginia and they had gone missing within two months of each other. There was another snippet urging anyone with information to call Bridgford County Police Department, and below that was also a number for an anonymous tip hotline.

"The number Alex called from was a Virginia area code. You think it's possible he's calling from Bridgford?"

Deep down Gabe knew it was possible. They both knew that Alex was a little off- kilter, but to the extent of possibly harming young women who looked like his deceased mother? He couldn't believe it.

"What are we supposed to do son? Call Bridgford County PD and tell them it might be your brother?"

"I don't know, Dad."

Eric looked past him to the living room. There was a picture of Eleanor on the mahogany end table in the corner of the room. Same smile, eyes same width apart.

"We might start by telling them about the packages you've gotten recently and showing them that picture."

4
Alex

As Alex was walking into his Sociology class, Catherine reached for his arm and gently pulled him back out of the room and around the corner. He turned to see her bright eyes staring up at him with genuine concern. Her lips were pursed together, and her eyebrows raised to a point in a, *What's going on with you?* sort of way.

Before he could say anything, she pulled him in close and hugged him. He nestled his face gently against the nape of her neck. She smelled so good he hoped she wouldn't let go.

"Is everything okay? I've been worried about you. Went by your house the other day, and I met some detective. Is there something I should know?"

He closed his eyes just for a minute, holding onto her embrace and feeling the slow ache as she pulled away from him. *Momma used to hug me this way.*

"I'm okay. I've been a little under the weather, and I still haven't found my phone." He feigned ignorance when she asked about the detective. "He might have been coming by to ask questions about my old neighbors. It's a really long story."

That was enough of an explanation for now, and thankfully she didn't ask any more about it.

"Since you don't have your phone. I'm making definite plans for us tonight. I'm going to pick you up and we're going out to dinner. A nice dinner, and then we're going to go back to your house to watch movies."

"I have to work tonight until eight, we're so short-staffed so I can't get out of it," Alex protested, but she would hear none of it.

Catherine shook her head.

"Picking you up at 9 pm sharp."

He saw there was no turning her down. With a quick nod she smiled at him and they walked back to class, but not before she turned around with those gorgeous bright eyes and stealing the sweetest kiss that caught him by surprise.

"In case you had doubts about whether tonight was a date or not. I took the guesswork out of it for you."

5
Alex

Alex swept the back room of Dusty's. He realized he had been doing it longer than he should have been because he found himself sweeping over the same crack in the cement floor multiple times. He had tried to go back for the phone today. He watched Tamblin in the woods, and the second the detective turned his back, he went for it. He was so close to getting it back. It was in his hands, but the detective was chasing him, and when he shot at him the phone slipped from his fingers. There was no way he could go back there now.

He didn't want to avoid Catherine, but what he told her about feeling under the weather wasn't completely false. Lately, he was feeling distant from his own mind, sort of the way he did as a child, and they were happening more frequently now. He felt as though he was on the outside looking in. The urges he felt were growing stronger, but something new was happening too. Nothing felt real anymore, and the more he tried to grasp it, the less he felt.

Dusty stopped in the plumbing aisle of the hardware store when he saw Alex staring absently at the ground.

"Are you all right, Son?" Dusty called. Behind him the sky was just beginning to turn violet.

Alex blinked a few times and began sweeping the pile of dirt into the dustpan. "Yes, Sir."

"I ask 'cause yeh been awfully distant today. I mean more than usual. Don't think I heard yeh speak more than two words."

Dusty walked to the front of the store and ran his hand along the wall behind a shelf of faucet handles and hit the switch. The neon blue electric open sign buzzed and clicked before it cut off. Dusty's store was small, it had a few aisles of hardware supplies and since the town was miles from a Home Depot or a Lowes, Dusty kept himself in pretty good business. He shuffled back in Alex's direction.

Alex scooped the last bit of dust and dirt into a Rubbermaid trashcan lined with clear plastic and set the shop broom and dustpan back in their respective hooks on the wall. In a locker beside it, he took his jacket and slid into it.

"I'm sorry, Mr. Delaney. I've been a bit distracted today, that's all."

He met Dusty in the aisle.

"I could tell somethin' was wrong. Anythin' I can do to help, Son? You needin' someone to talk to?"

Alex shook his head.

"No, but thank you. It's just that I've been missing my momma lately. I was wondering, would you mind if I took the rest of the week off so I could go visit her? It's been too long, and I think it's time we reconnect."

He watched as Dusty Delaney straightened the rack of toilet paper holders, probably running the list of employees through his head and thinking about who would fill in for Alex while he would be out. Alex was his most reliable employee, and it would leave him with Mark, the womanizer, or Arnie the one who was always on the phone. Alex figured he would go with Arnie; Mark would be the type of kid who would leave the store unattended to go skirt chasing any woman who happened to walk by Dusty's store.

"I think that's real good of yeh, Son. I know yeh haven't seen her since you ran away from home, what fifteen years now? You take as much time 's yeh need. I'll have Arnie fill in."

Dusty didn't know that his mom died in an accident when he was ten. He didn't know that when he said he wanted to visit his mom, he was going to visit the woman he had seen from the bar a few nights before --- the woman with bright eyes and honey colored hair, the woman who wore his mother's smile, and lived on 891 Camila Street. The lines between his mother and the woman were starting to blur together.

"Thank you so much, Dusty."

The old man nodded. He seemed like he had something on his mind too, more than anything relating to work. Alex didn't like prying into people's private affairs, but this was Dusty, the man who had given him a job when he moved into town and even encouraged him to go to school.

"Are *you* all right?"

Dusty looked up as though Alex shook him from a dream.

"Me? I'm as good as I can be on account of everythin' that's been goin' on with my eldest son. Yeh know his daughter, my granddaughter, Jessica, she been missin' nearly two months now."

Alex nodded absently at the old man.

"You think someone must've seen her or known somethin'. She just up n' vanished. Some people think she mighta' flown the coop," Dusty shook his head. "She a good girl. Wouldn't go anywhere without lettin' me know. If there were problems, we would've known it." Dusty looked up at Alex and gave a sad smile. "Sorry, I shouldn't dump this on yeh."

"They'll find her," Alex knew this, only it would never be the way they hoped. Dusty nodded and rubbed away the moisture from his eyes with the back of his liver spotted hand. Alex patted Dusty on the shoulder and watched as the old man started for the back room.

"Dusty?" The old man turned around. "I'm sorry."

Alex locked up behind him and made his way across the street to his truck. The deep violet skies had turned black, and the temperature had dropped another twenty degrees. It was so cold outside that the truck door was stuck so Alex had to pry it open by planting his foot against the gas tank cover and yanking on the door handle. When the door finally opened, his fingers slipped from the handle and he landed squarely on his back. Before he could pick himself up, someone was already helping him to stand. Alex looked back, for a brief moment he thought it was his mom, and his heart pounded violently in his chest. What were the chances that it would be the woman from the bar a few nights ago?

"Come on, up you go," she said helping him to his feet.

"Thanks," He brushed the dirt from the back of his jeans and shoulders. When she smiled at him, he couldn't help but smile back. "You have a beautiful smile. Reminds me of my mom's."

"What a sweet thing to say." Her smile grew wider.

The woman, or Tanya, as she had introduced herself, had accepted his offer to go back to his apartment for some coffee. With a little persuasion, he managed to convince her to drive back to his house with him instead of following him in her car on account of the roads being too icy to drive in her little car on the back roads.

"You can follow me if you want. Either way. I was just thinking it might be safer for you to ride with me."

Tanya agreed. She took out her phone and opened her text messages.

"What's your address? Just so my roommate doesn't wonder where I am,"

This was new. He wasn't expecting her to ask that, but he gave her a false one.

"Sure, it's 214 Mycroft Road."

The ride to his apartment was cozy. He kept the truck nice and warm for her as they drove down Elbow roads. She had felt comfortable enough to unbutton her black wool coat and pulled off her gloves. Her nails were painted a dark red and she sported silver rings on her thumbs and middle fingers, and she fidgeted with the fine ringlets in her hair. He tried not to take his eyes off the road too much. He didn't want her to know that he was studying her features and only seeing his mom in them. Every once in a while, he could see her looking over at him from the corner of his eye with a certain familiarity that she couldn't quite place. Yes, she had seen him before; Alex wondered if she would remember where.

The beam of his headlights caught the shine of a mist as they drove past, but he couldn't see much further than what his headlights touched. Within a short glance to his left he could only see the top of his wooden marker. The rest of it had been buried with dead wet leaves. He caught a glimpse of Mom limping on the roadside, and when he blinked, she was gone. Tanya talked about all sorts of things and Alex did quite well to seem like he was interested in what she had to say. She talked about where she grew up, her favorite places to go, what her family was like, what type of dog she had back home, and what she did for a living. She was a wedding caterer, but it had been a slow winter. No one really cared for a fall or winter wedding, at least not in Bridgford County where everything stayed dreary, cold, and damp during this time of year.

"She sure talks a lot, doesn't she?" his mom whispered, through her closed blue lips. Her breath felt like ice; her eyes were unblinking and sunken in her skull. She was sitting in the middle of the back seat looking at the woman. "Is she my new gift?"

"Yes," Alex looked over at Tanya. He wasn't sure if he said that out loud, but she didn't seem to hear him. He looked in the rearview mirror and his mother was gone.

Alex spoke little of himself but asked her questions to keep the topic off of him. When he made a left into the parking lot, he could tell that she was not expecting him to live in the shithole that he did, and she almost didn't want to get out of the car.

"I'm sorry, I should have told you. The neighborhood isn't the best, but hopefully when I graduate, I'll be able to afford something better. If you want me to take you back to your car, I completely understand."

Tanya looked at him and relaxed just a little. He wasn't forcing her to stay. There was no reason to, he knew where she lived.

"No, this is fine, really," Alex opened the truck door for her and offered a hand to help her step down from the truck. Her hands weren't as soft as Catherine's and she lacked that sun-kissed glow. She followed him upstairs into his apartment and he cut the light on for her.

"Wow, it's so chilly in here!" She hugged her jacket tight across her chest.

"Yeah, the heater is busted, but the coffee should warm us right up. Why don't you have a seat on the couch. Get comfortable," Alex headed to the kitchen.

"Actually, do you mind if I use your bathroom? I've been holding it for a while."

"Sure. Right through there," Alex pointed to the bedroom and watched her shuffle away.

He was just starting the coffee when there was a knock at the door. Alex nearly dropped the carafe. He looked at the clock on the stove. Shit. It was nine o'clock on the dot. How could he forget his plans with Catherine? He ran toward the door.

"Just a sec, Catherine!" He heard a muffled okay from the other side.

Alex sprinted toward the bedroom and shut the door behind him. Tanya wasn't expecting him to be on the other side of the bathroom door when she opened it. She almost screamed, but the carafe came crashing down too fast onto the side of her beautiful head. There was a sickening crack and blood came soaking through her hair. Surprisingly, the carafe splintered but didn't break but he had dealt enough force to render her unconscious. Alex caught her as she went down. He dragged her across the bedroom toward the recessed bookshelf. With the flat of his shoe he pushed on the bottom corner and the bookshelf popped open and tossed the carafe inside the hidden closet along with Tanya. He tugged on the string for the light. There were shears, gray packing tape, and rope in a box. He used the rope to bind Tanya's hands and legs as quickly as he could. In another corner was a black sock. He balled it up and pushed it into her mouth which wasn't hard to do because her jaw was lax, and her mouth was already partially open. He slid the sock just past her teeth and used a long strip of packing tape to hold it in place. Tanya was still breathing, barely, but she was still with him. She wouldn't be awake for another couple of hours at least. He brushed the hair away from her eyes and kissed her forehead.

"I'll come back for you," he whispered. "Promise." Alex ran out of the closet and kicked the door shut.

He greeted Catherine at the front door. A bead of sweat formed on his brow and he used his shirt to wipe it away, and his chest heaved. She was bobbing up and down with her arms crossed against her chest.

"Catherine! I'm so sorry. I got out of work late. Haven't even had time to change. Please make yourself comfortable."

Catherine squeezed past him and blew on her hands that were bright red. She slipped her heels off her feet and curled into a ball on his sofa.

"Jesus, it's almost colder in here than it is out there!"

"Yeah, I try calling maintenance, but they keep dragging their feet. I'm sorry."

Alex couldn't stop looking at her. She was wearing a black dress and thick overcoat. She smelled as sweet as vanilla, and her makeup had only seemed to enhance the beauty that was already there. The bottom of her dress had fallen open to her silk panties, and he couldn't help but steal a glance. Alex ran into the bedroom and stripped the comforter off of his bed. He wrapped her in it and his hands brushed against her thighs as he pulled the comforter over her. They were as warm and as smooth as he imagined.

"Thank you."

Catherine brought his hand to her lips and kissed his fingertips sweetly. He leaned in and kissed her forehead.

"Let me get changed and we can get out of here."

6
Catherine

Catherine drove. They went to a restaurant next door to The
Dandy Lion Pub which was one of the only restaurants in town that
stayed open late. At ten o' clock half of the restaurant
was set aside for dancing and live music. It was a big hit among
the college kids who typically chose to go there for date nights. The
hostess led Catherine and Alex to a secluded booth in the corner of
the restaurant per Catherine's request.

"Your server will be right with you. Enjoy your dinner," the
hostess with tight curls and strings of yellow highlights smiled. She
opened their menus for them before walking away.

"This is nice right?" Catherine looked around at all of the people
standing by the bar.

Despite the noise of people talking and laughing with each other,
the restaurant was cozy. There were dim recessed lights in the ceiling,
and a fake candle in a glass jar on each of the tables which added
to the warm atmosphere. In the corner of the restaurant a man was
tuning his guitar, testing each string and turning each key until it
was exactly where he wanted to be. He played a few riffs from a song
they would be playing later. Another man struck a few of the keys
on an electric keyboard.

"It's great," Alex said as he opened his menu. He never really ate much and didn't have much of an appetite lately especially now that Tanya was still in his house, and his cell phone was with the *others*. He flipped between the pages of the menu, unable to read the words on the pages. His hair fell over his eyes and he swiped it away. He stopped when he noticed Catherine watching him. To avoid any questions, he ordered a steak sandwich, fries and a coke, when the server came to the table.

"I'll have the chicken cobb salad with ranch on the side, and a sweet tea please." Catherine handed the menus back to the server and smiled at Alex. She slid in next to him and pulled her phone from her coat pocket. "Come here," she said sweetly. She put an arm around him, and he leaned in close. Catherine held the phone in front of them and snapped the picture. "This is a really good picture of us, huh?"

Alex nodded that it was as he looked at the image of himself next to a woman, he never in his life imagined would want him the way she did. He studied his own features. He had his mother's eyes, and her smile. Alex was an attractive young man, though he often thought otherwise; he thought he looked unusually pale and timid next to Catherine's outward glow.

Catherine leaned in and planted a kiss on his cheek.

"I'm a lucky girl to be out with the cutest guy on campus. Like I'm in high school all over again."

She returned to her seat across from him when the food came.

They talked about different things, mainly about school and what her plans after would be. She wanted to move to California or Arizona, some place warm and sunny. Those places fit Catherine's personality. She also told him she wanted to pursue a career in forensic psychology partly because she had seen Silence of the Lambs as a little girl, but mainly because she wanted to figure out the psyche of sociopaths. She asked Alex a lot of personal questions, and it made him uneasy, especially when she asked about his mother.

"She's a wonderful woman. We used to go this place called Peter Piper's arcade when I was little. Sometimes she would take me to the movies. We stopped going to those places when I got a little older. She just changed, and I didn't understand why, but she stopped spending time with me. So, my brother pretty much took care of me. I miss her. I've been wanting to visit her more and more lately."

He took his wallet from his back pocket and slid out his mother's picture of when she was still in her twenties. She was wearing a green dress with a square neckline, and her hair came down in soft fine waves around her face, and a smile that could light up the entire world. He handed her the picture and she looked it over and looked back up at him.

"She's so beautiful. I'd love to meet her."

Catherine handed the picture back to him and he tucked it carefully behind the clear plastic slot that ID cards usually went. So, she started distancing herself from you and your brother. Where was your dad?"

"My dad? He wasn't around much. Worked all the time, especially after Momma died."

"Died? I'm so sorry, Alex. The way you talk about her, I just assumed she was still alive."

The hazy feeling in his head was coming back along with the muffled throbbing in his ears that seemed to black out everything else. His face warmed, and his shirt was suddenly too small; it felt as though he were drowning. Alex could barely hear her calling his name, and he squeezed his eyes shut until the sound finally died.

"Alex?" Catherine reached out for his hand and gave it a gentle shake until he opened his eyes again. "Are you okay?"

"Mom," Alex shook the groggy feeling from his head, "Catherine. I'm fine. My head just started hurting for a minute. I think I'm good now."

Catherine raised an eyebrow, and she frowned at him. Alex reached out for her hand and she gave it a gentle squeeze. He didn't want her to dwell on it, he didn't want her to see him the way the others saw him. He looked over at the cover band singing to a slower piano version of an Imagine Dragons song, 'Demons'.

"Come with me," he said.

There was only one other couple on the dance floor, an older couple in their late forties. The woman's head was slumped against the man's chest and they weaved back and forth clumsily. The old man did his best to hold her up, but he too was inebriated, and eventually they wandered their way back to their table leaving Alex and Catherine alone. Alex led her to the center of the floor and placed her arms around his neck and he held her close. Catherine stole his gaze and when they danced, the rest of the world disappeared.

Back in Alex's apartment, Catherine took him by the hand and led him into bedroom. He seemed a little nervous to her, almost like he didn't want to go in there, but he didn't make any objections. There was a strange smell in the house, but she brushed it off thinking that it was because of how old the complex was and so focused on Alex. She liked his quiet charm, and it didn't hurt that he was so good-looking. Catherine shut the door. Alex was looking around the room, picking his dirty clothes off the floor; he threw them in the corner of the room and headed over to the nightstand and lit a red candle that smelled like apples. Catherine cut out the light and gently pushed him onto the bed. There was enough light from the candle to see his kind face watching her, wanting her the way she wanted him. She straddled him and pressed her lips against his. He was a tender kisser. Catherine leaned back and took his hands into hers. She delicately placed them over her breasts. Catherine moaned and she rocked back and forth over the growing bulge in his pants. He sat up and pulled her in, sliding his tongue over hers and pulling the top of her dress and black bra down to playfully bite and kiss her nipples. She cried out in sheer pleasure and undid the button on his jeans, pulling them down far enough for him to slip inside of her. She cried out again, arching her back in pleasure as he rocked her back and forth, softly at times, then rough at others until they both came. It was like nothing Catherine had ever experienced in her life; he gave himself over to her completely, eager to please her the way she needed it the most. When they had exhausted every ounce of energy they had left, Alex took Catherine into his arms and they laid together, listening to each other's slow rhythmic breathing, and before Catherine knew it, she was asleep.

It was still dark when she woke up to a draft in the bed. Catherine was still a little foggy from sleep, she looked over and noticed that Alex was no longer next to her. She didn't know that he was standing in the corner of the room and had been watching her numbly while she had slept. The candle had reduced to nothing more than a small pin of flame until it fizzled out. Catherine sat up and looked around the room when she noticed a light from behind the recessed bookshelf. She fumbled in the dark for her dress and slipped it on before making her way to it. It was partially open and behind it she heard the faintest whimper. Catherine felt along the edge of the bookshelf and managed to pull it back about an inch when it closed again. Alex had his arm up against it. She turned around and he was only inches away from her face. Before she could say anything, he kissed her deep enough to make her knees weak. He tossed her onto the bed, and they made love for the second time.

7
Detective Tamblin

Lorraine watched her sleeping husband from the bedroom doorway. He was snoring so loudly that she swore if there was a glass of water in her hand, it would've trembled. She approached him slowly and stood over her sleeping bear of a husband; the comforter was covering all but the top of his head and she pulled it down below his chin. His mouth was hanging wide open and his eyes moved back and forth rapidly beneath his eyelids. Lorraine thought about drawing the blinds to let a bit of morning light come through, but she thought it best to wait until he was awake. She was sure that the smell of coffee would've woke him up first thing, it usually did, but he had been too tired. Lorraine put a hand on his shoulder and nudged him gently. He gave one good snort before his eyes blinked open like a newborn. He smiled when he saw her face.

Howard Tamblin wiped the drool from the corner of his mouth. "What a beautiful sight first thing in the morning."

"Good morning, Baby," Lorraine kissed him on his cheek. "There's a call for you on your cell phone. I hate to wake you up so early especially on your day off, but it sounds important."

"Is it Nolan?" Tamblin propped himself up against the headboard. "What time is it?"

"No, it's Officer Hutton, and it's almost six. I could tell her you'll call back."

"I'll take the call, Dear Heart, thank you."

Lorraine handed him the phone, and pinched his cheek.

Tamblin watched her walk out and shut the door behind her before he answered the call.

"Hutton. Good Morning."

"Detective, I'm going to patch a call through to you. There's a man who says he really needs to speak to someone regarding the Delaney/Coswell cases."

"Okay. Oh, Hutton has Nolan called back yet? Do we have confirmation that the bodies belonged to Jessica and Brenda? I don't want to reach out to their families until we have confirmation."

"Not yet, Detective, but I think we all know."

"I know," Tamblin eased himself out of the comfort of his bed and down the hall into his office. The heater was on, but he felt the chill on his feet as he padded across the wood floor. Tamblin pinned the cell phone between his cheek and shoulder and slid out a pen and notepad from his desk drawer. Hutton patched the call through.

"Detective Tamblin?" The voice was older but familiar.

"Yes, speaking."

"Detective Tamblin, my name is Eric Meier. I believe I may have some information for you regarding the missing girls," Tamblin was all ears now. "Meier? Any relation to Alex Meier?"

There was a short pause on the other end.

"He's my brother. That's why I'm calling."

Tamblin pulled a steno notepad over to him and opened it up past the scribblings of false leads, grocery lists, and notepad doodles to a fresh page. He wrote down - **Mother. Phone call.** Next to the word phone call, he put a number sign and question mark and drew a circle around both. Eric was fortunate enough to still have the number on his caller ID; he had mentioned he didn't get very many calls to begin with. Tamblin could hear the clicks until Eric found the number he was looking for.

"703-555-9807. I know it was my brother. He sounded like he was in some sort of trouble."

Eric told the detective about the packages his dad had received in the mail.

Tamblin took the number down and ripped the page from the notepad, folded it neatly into a small rectangle and stuffed it in his shirt pocket.

"Eric is there any way you can get me a photograph of your mother? Are you far from Bridgford County?"

"Just about an hour west, sir. My dad and I can leave right now."

"Very good, Eric, I appreciate you. You have them call me when you get here. I'll be out for a bit, but when you call, I'll come right on back."

Tamblin ended the call and sprang to his feet.

He met Lorraine downstairs fully dressed in his slacks and a suit jacket over his button-up shirt. She turned around and handed him a plate but took it back when she saw him.

"Going into work?"

Tamblin swooped in and stole a kiss from his wife while making a failed attempt to snag the plate from her. She pushed him away and set it down on the kitchen table. He snatched a sausage link from the plate and wiped the grease on a napkin.

"I wish I could stay, Honey. You know I do. I think we're getting close to cracking this thing."

"Okay, when this is all over, I'm expecting a nice vacation somewhere warm."

"Well, that's all right," Tamblin kissed his wife's sweet lips and stole one more sausage for the road.

Tamblin met Hutton at her desk. She was reading through the morning briefings before their meeting.

"Do you ever take a break old man?" Hutton folded her arms in front of her.

"What fun would that be? Hey, Hutton do this old man a favor and see if you can tell me who this number belongs to."

He slid the yellow piece of paper from his pocket with his thumb and dropped it on her desk. Hutton, the raven-haired beauty and serious as a heart attack, wasted no time. She looked down at the number, made a call to Bell East, the local phone company and within minutes, she was writing something down on the same piece of paper. Hutton handed it back to him.

"Doesn't belong to anyone, Detective. That's a payphone. I've written down the address of where you'll find it. Hope it helps."

"It just might." He started to walk away but turned right back around. "Oh, that gentleman I was speaking to, his name is Eric Meier. He's coming up here to see me. Call me when he does?"

"Of course."

There is a small convenience store in town called the *Triple E* that Bridgford natives call, Tripoli, partly because the original owners were of Greek heritage from Tripoli, but mostly because it was faster to say. The E's were the initials of their children - Elka, the current owner, her sister Estelle, and her brother, Eduard. On the outside of the small convenience store is one payphone bolted to the wall, and beneath it was a phone book worn to shit, Tamblin wouldn't be surprised if it was the same phone book used in the eighties. There was a short sidewalk that led to the phone from the parking lot which was nothing more than square dirt patch, with trees beyond it. On the corner where cars could turn into it was a concrete lamp post that beams as bright as a lighthouse when it got dark. There were minimal patrons that came to this store because it was tucked away from everything, and it made Tamblin wonder how it had still been able to stay in business. He supposed it had its charm though, nestled smack in the middle of Elbow roads. It was a homely little store that smelled of cinnamon and pine trees. It had all the feel of a country home that you would hardly believe it was a convenience store. What it did lack however, were surveillance cameras. Tamblin wondered if they would change their minds about putting one up knowing that a potential serial killer might be lurking nearby. Triple E, like many locally owned stores closes at 5p.m. every day except for Sundays when they're closed all day. Eric Meier said the anonymous phone call came in on a Sunday, which just happened to be twenty-four hours before Brenda Coswell was reported missing, and the other call just this past Sunday at about three in the morning. Tamblin walked into the store and was greeted by that nostalgic smell of fall holidays. An older woman with silver hair was standing behind the counter thumbing through a cooking magazine.

"Welcome!" She said peering over the rim of her silver rimmed glasses. She set the magazine next to the register as Tamblin approached.

"Good morning, ma'am. I'm hoping you'll be able to help me."

He presented her with his ID badge, and she looked it over briefly before handing it back to him.

"I hope so too."

"Wondering if you've seen a man driving a black Ford come through here. Younger gentleman probably in his mid-twenties. Sharp blue eyes and dark hair. Maybe about two weeks ago?"

"If it's two weeks ago, I wouldn't have seen him. I'm running the store for my sister, Elka while she's on vacation. Sorry."

He thanked her for her time and started to walk out but she called after him. "I'm sure Elka wouldn't mind if you searched through the surveillance videos though."

"Didn't think you had surveillance cameras out there."

"Elka had one installed in one of the trees facing the parking lot because she wanted to catch whoever it was leaving empty beer bottles and cigarettes in the parking lot. Thought it might be some punk under-aged kids hanging around her store because it's so secluded. She swore she was going to find out who they were and tell their parents what horrible people they were for raising such awful children." The woman laughed. "Bit dramatic don't you think? Anyway she was right as per usual, two teenage boys – siblings, and she sure did give their parents a piece of her mind the next time she saw them in her store. After that she decided to keep it up there just in case they tried to vandalize her place or something crazy, she would have proof." She removed herself from behind the counter, scooting off the tall bar stool. She leaned her palm against the edge of the counter and hobbled toward the backroom. "Back this way."

Tamblin followed her down a narrow hall where partially open boxes filled with magazines and home goods were stacked against the wall. It felt damp back here, even the brown carpet they walked across felt like there was moisture in it, and there was the faint smell of mildew. Inside the room was a small TV monitor and a VCR sitting on a folding table. On the wall was a poster of a cat hanging onto a tree limb for dear life, and a dog staring up at it, with a terrible meme that read, *Bad day? Could always be worse.* There was also a small table lined with a checkered vinyl tablecloth. On it was a Mr. Coffee Maker with packets of sugar and creamer in a glass canister. There were granules of sugar spilled onto the table and a sticky coffee ring where a mug had been.

"You may be able to find what you're looking for in here."

She reached her hand down into a box of tapes next to the table with the TV and absently fiddled through them before making her way to the door.

"Good luck. Help yourself to some coffee if you like." She shut the door behind her leaving Tamblin alone to his own devices. Coffee sounded good, but whatever was left in the carafe had a toasty burnt smell and he decided against it. He lifted the box of videos onto the table and began searching through the tapes which were all organized by weeks.

"Elka, you made my job a lot easier," he said to himself.

He looked for the video labeled with the date Eric Meier had first received a phone call and felt like he had found buried treasure when he found what he was looking for. A piece of the label on the tape had peeled upward where it had lost its stickiness. He popped the VHS into the VCR. A grainy black and white image appeared on the monitor, there were some tracking errors on the outer edge of the video, but he could still see well enough. A week's worth of footage would take several hours to search through, and if he found what he was looking for, the tapes would be examined more carefully, but for now he just needed to see if Alex was in it. Lucky for Tamblin, the tapes started on Sunday and went on through Saturday. He didn't waste any time looking through it. The first twenty-four hours of footage was what he needed to focus on right now. He forwarded through much of it, stopping briefly if anyone resembling Alex's build or vehicle happened to drive by, but there wouldn't be any customers on a Sunday, so he pressed *FF* on the VCR to move on to about quarter to ten at night when Eric said he received the call. When Tamblin caught headlights bouncing off of the convenience store he rewound it back a few seconds to avoid missing anything. Tamblin watched as the lights turned into the lot. The vehicle parked just shy of the camera range, but he could still see part of the taillight still on. There was a shift in the truck followed by a quick jerk that could've been a vehicle door shutting, then nothing for nearly thirty minutes. Later Tamblin could see a man staggering across the dirt lot to the pay phone. Through the grainy footage he could see that the man had dark hair, of solid medium build. He was wearing a work jacket and a pair of heavy boots that looked to be soiled with mud. If that wasn't Alex, then he swore he'd hang up his detective hat a year early and make a living off selling printed t-shirts and mugs at the souvenir shop of Bush Gardens. He watched the man make a call and a minute later he dropped the phone and walked back to his vehicle. This time when the truck pulled out of the parking lot, Tamblin could see that it was Alex's black truck and it headed south the way he had come from. Tamblin ejected the tape and threw it into the box. He carried them out with him. The woman was behind the counter again and she looked up at him and then at the box of tapes.

"I've got to take these back with me to the station. If Elka has an issue with it, you tell her come find me."

Elka's sister didn't protest. She signed the forms that he needed in order to take the tapes and went back to reading her magazine.

Tamblin put a call to Hutton.

"Hey Hutton, can you send an officer to Alex Meier's apartment? It's time to bring him in for questioning."

"Detective. We're already on our way there."

8
Catherine

While Tamblin was at the Triple E only miles away from Alex's home, Catherine was just starting to wake up. She looked over at the clock ticking on the nightstand. It was eight o'clock in the morning. Alex was gone again. She wondered if he had slept at all because after they had made love for the second time, she waited for him to fall asleep so she could find out what he had behind the bookshelf, but he kept her waiting until she couldn't keep her eyes open anymore.

Catherine got up, stretched her legs, and fixed her dress. She reached for her panties that had been wedged between the nightstand and the bed and slid them on while she made her way to the window. It was a heavily overcast morning. Catherine looked down; Alex's truck was still in the same spot it had been last night. She turned to the recessed bookshelf. It was closed now, but she had to know what was behind it. Catherine felt along the edges of it, she found herself glancing toward the bedroom and bathroom doors more than she wanted. She had never seen a bookshelf with a hidden room before and didn't know how one would even open. She looked down along the edges. There was a black scuff on the bottom corner. It was a shoe imprint. She pushed against it, and the door popped open. It was a small closet, but the light was off now, and inside she saw something move. In the dimness, she caught glimpse of the string for the light and tugged on it. Catherine fell back when she saw a woman lying on the plastic lined floor. There was a large bloody gash on the side of her head. "Oh, god," she started to reach for her, but the bedroom door flew open. Catherine stumbled backward and yelped when she saw Alex in bedroom doorway.

"Morning, Catherine."

He noticed the bookshelf door hanging wide open.

"Would you mind waiting for me in the living room?"

"Okay, sure Alex," she slid past him, but not before he stole a kiss from her, not the sweet and tender kiss from last night – forced and uninvited. She broke away from his embrace and wandered into the living room. Alex shut the door, and she heard the locks turn. Catherine didn't hesitate, she went straight for the front door, unlatched the deadbolts, and turned the handle; it wouldn't open. She looked all around it, trying to see what locks she might've missed and found it at the very bottom of the door, but it needed a key. She tried for the window and pulled back on the blinds, but every corner of it had been nailed shut. A deep panic began to set in her chest. She could barely make sense of it. The man she went to bed with was not the same man she was seeing now. Catherine ran to the couch where her coat had been resting on and she struggled to get into its pockets while keeping an eye on the bedroom door and watching for the handle to turn. She drew in a deep breath, finding her phone was still in there. Her fingers shook so much that she missed the nine and instead mashed the pound sign. *Delete. Come on stupid girl, just three goddamn numbers. Nine – One - One.*

Every little sound brought her eyes to the bedroom door. Her heart pounded so hard she could hear it throbbing in her ears. It rang once, but that was too long. The operator asked what her emergency was. She didn't have time to explain. "214 Azalea Cove. Catherine Miller. There is another woman here. Please..."

She ended the call and slid the phone between the couch cushions when the bedroom door swung open. Alex stepped out, he was breathing heavy and grinning madly.

"I'm sorry I took so long, but there's someone I'm really excited for you to meet." He held out his hand to her. Catherine inched her way to him reluctant to take it; he gripped onto her fingers so tight it made her gasp. Alex led her into the bathroom, shutting the door behind them, and she saw the woman lying in the bathtub bound and gagged. Alex had met her as Tanya, but he was introducing her as his Momma. She glared up at them wildly. Her thin curls were matted down by blood and tears. Catherine could see an ugly gash on the side of her head. Pulpy clotted bits were tangled in her hair. She was wearing a green dress and there were dark stains along the square collar. It was very old and too small for her. Catherine had seen that dress before; it was the one Alex's mother wore in the picture he showed her.

"Catherine," Alex sounded delighted. He took her by the crook of the arm and pushed her forward, causing her to trip over soiled towels sprawled all over the floor. Alex hugged her from behind, as they stood over the porcelain tub.

"I'd like you to meet my mother."

He pressed his lips against her cheek.

Tears collected in Catherine's eyes, but she did her best to blink them away. Alex's gaze teetered between her and the woman in the tub, eager to get Catherine's approval. She could feel his grip around her getting tighter, and his nails were sinking further into her arm.

"A-Alex," she stuttered. "That's not your mom."

His smile fell. There was a hurt in his eyes that reminded her of the way a young boy would look if he had just been reprimanded. He let go of Catherine's arm and clenched his fists to his sides. Catherine looked down at the woman who was now shaking, she tried to adjust her uncomfortable placement inside the bathtub. Alex whimpered, and he clenched his jaws so tight she could hear his teeth grinding together, and he slammed his fists against the side of his head then against the mirror until it shattered. He beat against the walls, throwing a mad rage in the small bathroom. The woman began screaming from behind her duct taped mouth. Catherine backed herself against the wall trying to avoid his fists from making contact with her.

"Oh!" Catherine screamed. "Mrs. Meier! It's so nice to meet you!"

Alex stopped slamming his fists into the wall, he had exhausted every ounce of energy and was so out of breath that it took him a minute to calm down again. He smiled at her through clenched teeth and she forced a smile in return. To avoid having to come in contact with him she knelt beside the tub and placed a hand on the woman's cold arm, seeming to force the woman along with it with just a look. The woman squeezed her eyes shut and nodded. Catherine stood beside Alex again. He was breathing heavy, but he was much calmer now, and he looked down at the woman.

"Isn't she beautiful, Momma? Just like I told you."

She forced a nod.

"Catherine can come with me to take you to your special place."

Alex knelt beside the tub and reached for something from behind the toilet. Catherine stood over his shoulder but couldn't see what it was.

She didn't need to, the woman tensing away from Alex had let her know that it wasn't good. It wasn't until he stood up that she saw that it was a small hacksaw with blood caked between some of the teeth.

"Would you like to help me? I know Momma would be so happy if you did, right?"

The woman let out a short muffled sob, but she stuffed it back and nodded at Alex.

Catherine was focused only on staying alive. She thought she could try to fight him, but what would happen if she failed. The only good thing in this very bad situation was he hadn't bound her, yet. If she tried to fight him, then she and the woman in the bathtub might be as good as dead. Alex was an average sized man but all muscle, and she didn't want to upset him again or he really might hurt them both. No, the best idea would be to reason with him, the best way anyone could reason with a psychopath.

"Hey, Alex?"

Alex leaned in next to her, so close she could feel his warm breath against her cheek. He pressed her against the towel rack and Catherine squeezed her eyes tight as the metal rack dug into her spine.

"Can you show me where the special place is before we take her there? I'd really like to see it. Maybe I could spruce it up a little, you know? She might really like that."

"Would you?"

He looked down at Tanya who nodded vigorously and took the hacksaw from the toilet. "We should get her ready first."

He grabbed a fistful of her hair and pulled her head back. He ripped through layers of her skin. Dark blood spilled from the new tear in her neck. She shrieked so violently that it made Catherine want to jump out of her skin.

"ALEX! STOP!" Catherine was crying now. "Take me to the special place first, okay?" she sobbed. "Then we can get her ready. She'll be here. I know she will."

He stopped and dropped the saw on the ground.

"Will that make you happy?"

"So happy, Alex. Will you take me there? Please?"

Alex gripped Catherine's shoulders and pulled her in for a kiss so hard it hurt. It tasted bitter and every time she tried to pull away, he pressed harder.

When he finally let her go, he bent over the tub and kissed the top of Tanya's head. Blood was gushing from her neck in slow heavy pulses. She was looking paler by the second.

"Okay. We'll be back Momma," and for a moment Catherine was alone with Tanya.

Catherine quickly picked a towel off the floor and pressed it against the woman's neck. She lifted the woman's hands to it and spoke softly.

"I called the police. You have to try to keep pressure on your neck okay? Press as hard as you can."

Tanya nodded faintly. Catherine rushed out of the bathroom and shut the door behind her.

Alex took a set of keys that were clipped to his belt loop. He fingered through each one until he came across a black key and pushed it into the slot at the bottom of the front door and turned it. He led Catherine through it and locked the door behind him. Catherine listened for sirens, she thought they should've been here by now. He walked beside her down the stairs. It was too quiet outside. *Where were they?* He took her to his truck and went around to the passenger side to let her in. That's when the rain started. Alex's soft hair was matted down, and his shirt had soaked through. Catherine's black dress clung to her body, and strands of her hair stuck to her cheeks. Her body shook more from fear than the cold. Alex gently swiped her hair away from her face and tucked it behind her ear before helping her into the truck. She fixed her dress and he helped her with her seatbelt. Alex stared at her with those tired blue eyes; was she acting suspicious to him? She forced a smile, hoping she would hear the sirens. As he made his way to the other side, Catherine searched frantically for any sign of police cars. There were none. She jumped when the driver's side door slammed shut. Alex turned the ignition and shifted the gear in reverse but kept his foot on the break. At first Catherine wondered why he was stalling, then she heard the sirens.

9
Alex

Alex's eyes were fixed on a gentle mist collecting on his windshield. He smiled, but his eyebrows were creased with sadness.

"You called them?" His voice was soft, matching the sound of rain.

Catherine leaned against the passenger side door watching him from the corner of her eye.

"I had to. You're very sick, Alex. You need help."

Her eyes glistened, and her lips quivered as she spoke.

Alex nodded. He looked in his rearview mirror, red and blue lights flooded the neighborhood. He drew in a breath and removed himself from the truck and returned to Catherine's side. She inched herself away from the door unable to meet his eyes. Her knees shook beneath her dress as Alex reached across her lap to unclip her seatbelt. He didn't move right away. Instead, he opened the glovebox and pulled out the revolver Frank had sold to him.

"I need you to get out now, please."

Catherine hesitated. Now police cars were surrounding his truck.

"Catherine."

She nodded and squeezed past him, but as she did Alex pulled her to him and pressed the gun to her head.

"Alex."

Catherine's body was tense against his. She blinked tears and rain away from her eyes and looked to the cluster of officers with their guns pointed in her direction.

"There's a woman upstairs who needs help right now," she cried against the rain that was coming down heavy now.

***

Two officers ran upstairs to his apartment and were able to kick down the door with some effort. There were four officers positioned behind their car doors screaming for him to put the gun down but stopped when Detective Tamblin moved between them. He held his hands out in front of him. He watched Alex whisper something into Catherine's ear.

"Woah, Alex come on now. Let's keep it cool, okay? We can do this without anyone else getting hurt. This will go however you want it to go, so let's make this easy for everyone."

He glanced toward Alex's gun. Easy never seemed to be the road most criminals took when it came to surrendering. They figured it was best to go down fighting in a hail of bullets than to be brought into custody, but Alex wasn't a hardened criminal, as disturbed as he might be on the inside, he looked more like a lost little boy standing in the rain. *We might just get out of there without any incidents.*

Through the downpour, Tamblin could see Alex's eyes turning red. He was shaking, pressing the barrel of the gun harder against Catherine's temple. She winced, keeping her grip firm on Alex's forearm to keep herself from choking as he squeezed tight against her throat.

"I can't stop, Detective," Alex said finally.

"I can help you, Alex," Tamblin lowered his hands just a little."

"No. I have to do this for her, or she'll leave me again."

Alex pointed his gun toward some trees in the distance then back to Catherine. Tamblin looked but he couldn't see anyone.

"There's no one there, Alex."

Alex squinted against the rain and searched for her.

"She was right there! Momma? Where did she go?!" He was frantic now and Catherine was struggling to breathe.

"Alex, she's not there" Tamblin couldn't help but feel as though he were talking to a child and so he changed his tone drastically. "I want to help you, and you know who else does? Your daddy and your brother."

Alex briefly released the gun from Catherine's head and swiped away tears and rain with the back of his hand before returning it to her temple where a deep red impression had now resided.

"They don't even know where I am."

"Hand to God, Son. Talked to your brother earlier this morning. Name's Eric, ain't that right? He's here with me now. Your daddy too. They're waiting in the car."

Alex let go of Catherine and she fell to the ground gasping for breath. She crawled her way across the pavement toward Detective Tamblin, and officers pulled her past the barricade of car doors. He stumbled back a few steps.

"Eric's going to be real mad at me."

"He's your family, Alex. He'll want to see you no matter what. You were close right? He said you were his best friend growing up."

Tamblin waved behind him and called out, keeping his eyes steady on Alex, "Eric why don't you come on over here, Son."

***

Alex shrank when he saw his brother stepping past the police officers. Their dad stood with the crowd; his hands were cupped over his mouth. For a moment the rain seemed to fall in slow motion.

Eric stood next to Tamblin. His arms were folded against him and his shoulders in a shrug. His body shook, but he was trying to hide it. "Hey, Buddy."

"Eric," Alex swiped at his face with a free hand. "I don't know what I'm doing anymore," he whimpered. "And I can't stop, or she says she'll leave."

Eric's sniffled.

"It's not her, Alex. You know that don't you? Whatever you're seeing, it's not her. Momma," he stopped himself and drew in a breath, forcing it out slow and steady, "she wouldn't ask you to do the things you've done."

"Alex, why don't you put the gun down, Son, and come with us. Let us help you,"

Alex looked past them to a small stretch of trees in his neighborhood, searching for his mom. She wasn't there. By now people were standing in front of their houses. All eyes were on him. He shook his head.

"No, Detective. No one can help me."

He lifted the gun to the side of his head with a trembling hand. The sound of thunder clapped across the sky sending birds flying from the sanctuary of their trees and rooftops. Alex looked down. The gun slipped from his fingers and clacked to the ground. He watched the water dripping from his fingertips turn red and begin to pool at his feet.

10
Detective Tamblin

It wasn't hard for the jury to find Alexander Meier guilty; his attorney had requested that the jury find him not guilty by reason of insanity, but Alex had been fully aware of the things he had done and had used particular methods of concealing the bodies. All of the proof was there, all of it – the burial site which had only been a short distance from where Jessica's cell phone was found, the hidden closet behind the recessed bookshelf, the saw and trash bags beneath the bathroom sink, and the surveillance videos all pointed to Alex. The packages Gabe received were also taken into evidence. The fingernails had belonged to Jessica, and the finger was Brenda's. The last number that Jessica Delaney called from her phone was to a pizza place in California. Forensics couldn't figure out why she would've called that number the day she went missing, but after further investigation, they realized the corresponding letters spelled out *Name is Alex* and that was the final piece that tied him to her disappearance. Mrs. Delaney had been right: her daughter was a smart girl. She knew if she wasn't going to make it out alive, she could at least leave a clue, something that her abductor might not catch. Timothy Beaumont, after much resistance, finally admitted to seeing Alex carrying an incapacitated Brenda Coswell up to his apartment. He hadn't planned on saying anything at all because he didn't care, but he made a plea deal for his own case. This made Tamblin sick, but he stood by what he'd told him back at the precinct, Timothy Beaumont would get out of prison one day, and he would get what was coming to him.

At some point during the trial the prosecutors placed enlarged photos of Jessica Delaney and Brenda Coswell next to a picture of Alex's mother, their resemblances to Eleanor Meier were unmistakable. Tanya recovered after one intensive surgery and two blood transfusions later, and she recounted the events that took place. Catherine, as hard as it was to face him in court, had also testified. Tamblin recalled Alex's inability to take his eyes off of her, and every once in a while, her eyes would flicker in his direction.

Gabe, Eric, and Howard Tamblin were there to see the whole trial through. It was hard for Eric to hear the evidence stacked against his brother and even harder to hear, Alex's confession. He didn't know how bad things with Alex had become. Detective Tamblin felt sorry for the kid as strange as it might sound. He managed to shoot him in the arm before Alex could kill himself. Tamblin went with Alex in the ambulance. His good arm was cuffed to the stretcher while medics addressed the injury to his other arm. He would never forget what the kid said to him on the way to the precinct. *She saw me, but she wouldn't stay.*

Later, Tamblin learned that Alex was talking about the day his mother died. There had been an argument between his mother and father; Alex heard everything. She saw him on the staircase, knew he had been listening to them fighting but still left him. Nothing was ever the same for the young man after that day.

Judge Samuels deemed him "guilty but mentally ill" and sentenced him to life in the Virginia Psychiatric Hospital for the Criminally Insane, instead of the River North Correctional Center. The families of the victims were there, they listened, they cried, they were angry, and rightfully so, and they had been given the opportunity to confront Alex before he would be taken away.

Brenda Coswell's father approached the podium first with his fist clenched and heavy bags under his glistening eyes. He was trying to get words past the lump in his throat, but it was useless, and he broke down in anger against his wife's shoulder. They sobbed together. The entire courtroom sat in silence watching them grieve for their daughter. Dusty and his son and daughter-in-law shook their heads and wept too. Mrs. Coswell urged her husband to sit down and she took his place at the podium. She looked up at Alex, her nose wet and her cheeks flush with so much hate for what Alex had done. Alex sat quietly, looking to Tamblin like a frightened child, just as he had seen him at the apartment complex.

"You deserve a harsher punishment than life in a psychiatric hospital!" Mrs. Coswell cried. "You took our baby from us. What right did you have to do that? I will never again see her smile or hear her voice. I can't call her on the phone just to tell her good night and that I love her. You took that away from me. Did that make you happy? You may not fully understand the weight of what you have done to our family, and your sentence may not be as severe as the damage you have done, but I will pray every day that you get what you truly deserve!" She slammed her fist against the podium. "You hear me, you sick fuck?!" she cried. "Do you hear me?!" Her husband tried to lead her back to her seat. Mrs. Coswell screamed and lunged for Alex as they passed him. She fought so hard to reach him that Mr. Coswell had to drag her out of the room.

Jessica Delaney's sister was the next to confront Alex. She was much older than Jessica, maybe in her late thirties and looked nothing like her. The young man looked back at Dusty who was wiping his eyes with a white handkerchief. He refused to look at Alex. How could he? Especially knowing that his granddaughter's murderer was right under his nose the whole time. It took a minute for Alex to realize she had started talking, and it wasn't until she screamed his name that he turned his attention from Dusty back to her.

"Don't you dare look at my grandpa! You look at me. I hope my sister haunts you in your dreams for the rest of your miserable life. You are a murderer, you're a goddamn murderer you bastard! You took everything from us!" she staggered from the podium back to her mom, dad, and Dusty.

11
Alex

Alex put his hands in his lap. He could feel everyone's eyes burning into the back of his neck, and he was reluctant to stand when the judge asked if there was anything he wanted to say. Tamblin watched the young man avoiding eye contact with everyone in the room, but he shook his head yes, and one of the officers helped him to his feet. They walked him to the podium, and Alex steadied himself against it. He looked up at his brother, whose eyes were glistening and red. He saw disappointment in them, he must be wondering how someone could've fallen so far. His dad's legs were shaking, there were defined wrinkles in his face and hands, and there were slivers of gray mixed in his dark brown hair now. Alex looked around the courtroom, hoping to see Catherine. She wasn't here.

"Mr. Meier, please address the room. If this is too difficult, you can take your seat and you will be escorted shortly after my closing statement."

Alex shook his head.

"No, your honor. I'd like to say something, please."

Judge Samuels gave a nod, urging him to proceed. Alex looked at Dusty, whose face was buried in his handkerchief and then to Eric and Gabe.

"You couldn't have known what I really am. No one could have. Dad. Eric. Please don't blame yourselves for what I've become." He looked to the room. "I saw my mom in your daughters' faces. I tried to preserve her, but what I did was unforgivable. I took them from you. I'm sorry for it. I wish I could take it all back. I can't. I hope you find some comfort knowing I can't do that to anyone else anymore." He stepped away from the podium and the two officers at his side escorted him back to his seat.

Judge Samuels, a silver-haired, short but eagle-eyed old man cleared his throat. He had a soft, somewhat shaky voice, but it carried throughout the room with authority.

"First, my heart truly goes out to the families affected here. In all my life, I have not personally come across a case like this before today, and that is with nearly thirty-two years serving in the judicial system. The sentence has been given, but there is nothing to celebrate. In the end, Alexander Robert Meier, you robbed these girls of their lives, you took them away from their homes and their families. That is precious time you have stolen from them, and what truly saddens me is I don't think you will ever understand the full weight of what you have done. This is my reason for sentencing you to life in the Virginia State Hospital for the Criminally Insane, without the possibility of parole. You are in need of serious help, Mr. Meier. There is no punishment that would do Brenda Coswell and Jessica Delaney justice because in the end, nothing will ever bring them back. What we can do now is hope you get the help that you seem to have needed for a very long time, and I sincerely hope you get it. Court is adjourned."

Judge Samuels removed himself from the courtroom through a backdoor, and Alex was escorted out from the opposite side. He looked back at his dad and brother one last time before disappearing behind the heavy door.

12
Detective Tamblin

Detective Tamblin had received a call a few days after Alex's conviction about Bryson, the little boy Alex had saved. The kid was conscious and finally out of the ICU. A nurse he had spoken with said he was doing quite well despite two full arm casts and a neck brace. Tamblin had taken the day off to drive to go see him.

Tamblin waited at a stoplight and thought about Alex – a scared child, one who would never fully understand the severity of what he'd done. Alex didn't talk much, but what little he did say was about his mom. *She saw me, but she wouldn't stay. She promised she'd never leave me.*

At the hospital Anna Lynn was sitting on the hospital bed with her brother. She had been drawing on construction paper with colored crayons. She stopped coloring briefly and looked up when Tamblin walked in. Their social worker, Allison Parker, a beautiful woman in her mid-forties, wearing a gray dress suit, was in a seat next to them jotting notes in her planner. She smiled briefly at him and went back to her notes. Bryson couldn't turn his head, so he strained his big brown eyes to meet his. He had never seen the detective before and hadn't quite decided what to make of him.

"Hi," Anna Lynn squeaked. "My bruder woked up."

"I see that. I know you're mighty happy about that. We all are,"
Tamblin walked over to the bedside. "Hello, Bryson, my name is
Howard Tamblin. It's nice to finally meet you."

"Nice to meet you, Mr. Tamblin."

Bryson's little voice was raspy. Tamblin could tell that the kid
had his reservations about him. For a seven-year-old he had put on
a grown- up face, something only kids who had gone through more
than they should ever have to go through put up. Tamblin couldn't
say he'd blame him. His little sister sat up from her masterpiece and
looked over his shoulder.

"Wares that guy?" Anna Lynn asked.

"What guy is that, Anna Lynn?" Tamblin looked down at her
drawing. She had folded it in half like a card.

"That guy."

Anna Lynn pointed to the TV hanging on the far wall. There
was a brief nighttime news preview about Alex. It was a shot of him
being escorted into the courtroom. So many reporters were crowd-
ing around him as he was being led into the stone building. Bulbs
flashed and microphones waved in his direction.

"She's making him a card for saving my life," Bryson said in that
raspy little voice.

"Ware's he?" Anna Lynn demanded.

Tamblin looked back at the TV. Her Saturday morning cartoon
had returned, a cat mom was reigning holy hell on her two sons, a
cat and a goldfish.

"Alex. He had to go away for a while, Kiddo."

"I like him," Anna Lynn resumed scribbling on the construction
paper.

"That stinks. I wanted to meet him," said Bryson. His eyes had
drifted to the T.V. and smiled a little when Rabbit Dad caught wind
of Cat Mom's fury.

"I tell you what, you finish making that card and I'll make sure he gets it. How's that?"

Anna Lynn's head bobbed up and down and she giggled her excitement before taking her crayons to the green paper once more.

Allison set her planner on the floor next to her briefcase. She gave Tamblin a sideways glance. He gave it right back to her. If she was wondering whether or not he would actually give Alex the card, the answer was, yes. He had every intention to do so. Allison looked over Anna Lynn's shoulder to see the progress she had made. The little girl had drawn what looked like three donuts, all with arms and legs standing over thick patches of green. Above them was a rainbow and a smiley face sun in the corner.

"Looks good Anna Lynn," Allison said. She smiled at Bryson who seemed satisfied with his little sister's drawing.

"It's perfect," Bryson confirmed. Anna Lynn held it up to Tamblin. He gave a whistle of approval.

"Mighty fine, Dear Heart. I think Alex is going to love it."

Anna Lynn handed the card to him and sat next to her brother to watch cartoons. "I'll go ahead and get going. I'll come back and visit real soon. You tell me if you need anything. Miss Allison has my number."

Before he delivered the card to Alex Meier, he had one more stop to make. He drove three miles up the road past Triple E's and turned onto Alex's old campus. There weren't many people outside, but Alex told him the class and room number, and what day of the week she would be there. He hoped that he would catch her before she even made it into the building, but Tamblin had stayed with Bryson and Anna Lynn longer than he had anticipated, and he suspected that Catherine would already be in class. He rounded the large fountain sitting in front of the main building and started for the double doors when he heard a soft voice call from behind.

"Detective Tamblin?"

He turned to see Catherine standing near the fountain with her books folded in her arms. Her face was bare, not even a hint of gloss on her lips, and her eyes seemed somewhat puffy, as though she had either been crying or not sleeping. Tamblin figured it was a combination of the two.

"Ms. Miller, I was hoping I'd catch you before you went to class. How are you holding up?"

Catherine looked down at the laces of her white tennis shoes and shook her head, "Not so good. I haven't been sleeping so well these days."

He could tell. She was usually so well put together, but her long waves of hair were in tangles; her pink blouse and her jeans were deep with wrinkles, as though they had been sitting in a laundry basket for a while. Seeing her this way made him want to turn around and forget about the promise he made to Alex, and his mind had cleared just enough to question why he was doing it in the first place.

"I don't want to hold you up, Ms. Miller, I was driving by and thought I'd stop by to check on you is all. You let me know if there's anything I can do for you. I can't say I know what you're going through, but I know it can't be easy," Tamblin slid his hand into his coat pocket and grazed the edge of a folded letter he promised Alex he would deliver. Catherine Miller had been through enough. He didn't need to add to it. "I'll be seeing you." He waved and started for his car.

"Have you gone to see him?" Catherine called from behind.

Tamblin turned to face her, with much hesitation, "I have."

Catherine leaned against the fountain and set her books next to her. "I have dreams about him sometimes."

She dipped her fingertips in the cool ripples of water and shook them off before putting her hands into her pockets.

She told Tamblin that she had seen the news and they showed the woods that Alex said was the special place, and in one dream she was having a picnic with Alex near the pond in the woods where Jessica and Brenda's bodies had been found. It was as though everything was right with the world. She said Brenda and Jessica were there holding hands in white dresses singing and laughing, taking a stroll between the trees, with a swirl of gray skies above them. Alex told Catherine he loved her and promised everything was going to be okay. She wanted more than anything for that to be true. Then she would wake up hating the small part of her that still missed him.

"They're not really nightmares, but they scare me. Does that make sense?"

Tamblin understood. She worried that missing him meant that there was something wrong with her, that she might be just as sick as Alex, and the thought terrified her. She told Tamblin that she contemplated leaving town so she could be as far away from him as possible. At least if she did that much she could move on from Alex, and it'd be a hell of a lot harder to give into that part of her that wanted to see him again.

"You know, I think a change of scenery might do you some good. Some place that stays warm year round? That'd be mighty fine. Besides, I don't recommend the young ones staying here for too long. This place has a tendency to swallow people whole."

Tamblin hadn't realized it at first, but he had crumpled the letter in his coat pocket. The letter that confessed how much Alex missed Catherine, how much he hoped that she could forgive him and want to visit him someday. There were other ramblings about life in the institution, and how she was always on his mind. He even hoped that he would somehow be cured of the urges but knew realistically that he would never change. Tamblin did wonder if the letter was meant to make Catherine feel sorry for him. Was he trying to manipulate her? The detective had heard it several times, serial killers never feel true emotions, but he wondered if that was true for all of them. Maybe there was a part of Alex trying to be a normal human being, maybe there was a semblance of truth in the things he said. Tamblin hoped so, but he had never heard of a recovering serial killer. He knew eventually their demons always came back to whisper in their ears.

Catherine took her books into her arms and gave Tamblin a big hug. She thanked him for saving her life and hoped they could keep in touch. It was Tamblin's last chance to give her the letter if he so chose to do it, but he let that moment pass, and before he knew it, she was waving goodbye as she disappeared through the double doors. Tamblin shook his head. Maybe even he hadn't been in his right frame of mind. He crumpled the letter before tossing it into a tilted receptacle chained to a tree. *I'm sorry Alex, I just can't do that to her.*

Tamblin drove away from her school in his blue Monte Carlo; he knew he had made the right decision and hoped Catherine would get the fresh start she deserved. There was no reason for her to keep hanging onto Alex anymore; she needed to get her life back. Tamblin would tell Alex that he couldn't give the letter to her because she needed to move on now, and Alex would have to understand. He pulled onto the main road; there were no more stops to make today. Tamblin was finally going home.

13
Gabe

"You want me to start taking these boxes down, Dad?"

Gabriel Meier looked down at all of Eleanor's things in the attic. He figured it was really time to let her go and Eric had come over to help him do it.

"Yeah, go ahead, Son. I'll be right behind you. Eric heaved one of the larger boxes into his arms sending dust to kick up at his feet. He had to leave the box at the edge of the attic door and lower himself onto the ladder before taking the box against his chest.

"Careful."

"Yeah, I got it," and after a few minutes he was on the second floor. "Be right back. Gonna carry it out to my truck."

Gabe walked over to the rest of the boxes and beside it was the letter Eleanor had been keeping in her journal. His name was scrawled on the once white envelope, now yellow with age; he crouched down and took it up into his big hands. It was Eleanor's handwriting. Gabe could feel his heart racing in his chest. He carefully peeled the envelope back. Inside was a folded stationary, it was thick and graced with the illustration of blue flowers in each corner – the same ones hanging in her front porch the night she kissed him for the first time.

Gabe,

I know by now you must think I hate you. We haven't talked to each other in a long time. I think somewhere along the way we forgot how. We both know you've never been an easy man to talk to so I figured the best way to do it would be to write you this letter. Please just know I never blamed you for what happened to us. We fell apart a long time ago, and I have come to terms with it. I still love you Gabe but I'm so damn lonely. I feel like I'm trapped inside my own head. I feel like I'm drowning. Do you have any idea what it's like to want to reach out to someone, but you just can't? He knew that feeling better than anyone else. *It's new to me, I used to wear my heart on my sleeve. I used to love our life, but everything is different now. Is this really the end of us?*

Eleanor

Gabe folded the letter as neatly as he found it and held it close to his chest. All these years, he had it all wrong. She was crying out for help and he missed all the signs. She needed him and he wasn't there for her. He had snuffed out the bright light in his life and didn't even try to rekindle it. Gabe buried his face in his hands. "I'm sorry, Eleanor. I'm so sorry." He felt a hand on his shoulder and looked up. Eric was standing next to him. Gabe hadn't even heard him come back.

"Dad."

"I didn't save her, Eric. She needed me and I wasn't there for her," Gabe handed his son the letter. Eric sat down beside him and read it. When he was done, he let go of a deep sigh and gave the letter back to him.

"It was really hard for Alex and me to see what you and Mom were going through. I still remember a time when you two were actually happy. Then shit went sour, and I hated you every

day after she died. It took me a long time to realize what happened to her wasn't your fault. You couldn't save her, but you can't change that no matter how bad you try. So, I think it's time you let those old wounds heal."

Gabe wiped at his eyes with the back of his hand, Eric offered a hand to help him up. "Yeah. You're right, son."

He gave his son's shoulder a soft pat and they carried the rest of the boxes to the back of Eric's truck. It was a bright crisp morning. The air felt clean and smelled of chimney smoke coming from a few houses away; it was Gabe's favorite things about the winter because it reminded him of the happier times with Eleanor. They slid the rest of the boxes into the bed of Eric's blue Chevy which Eric had left running so the cab would stay warm. Gabe folded his arms against his chest. It didn't take long for that biting cold to cause his hands to ache.

"All right, I'm gonna hit the road before this snow starts. You let me know if you need help with anything else."

Eric hopped into the driver's seat and cranked the heat up as high as it would go.

Gabe nodded.

"Eric?"

"Yeah, Dad."

"About what you said earlier, thank you. If I have to spend the rest of my life making things right with you and Alex, that's what I'll do."

"I know you will. I'll see you in just a few."

Eric drove away; the first few flurries were beginning to fall.

14

Gabe

At the Virginia Psychiatric Hospital, Gabe and Eric waited for Alex in the visiting room. The procedure to get into the room was simple but still intimidating to Gabe. He had to sign in at the front desk and leave his coat, wallet, and keys in a wall locker next to the room. The receptionist behind the desk, wearing a knitted pink sweater, with sleek blond hair, gave them a rectangle paper name tag and pointed to Gabe's chest.

"Put this on the right side of your shirt.' She pointed to Eric. "Same goes for you. They need to be visible at all times. There is a twenty -minute visitation time limit."

Eric raised his eyes at her after peeling the paper from the name tag.

"Twenty minutes? That's all the time we get with him?"

The young receptionist didn't even bat an eye; she was used to hearing these questions.

"It's standard protocol to ensure all visitors have had a chance to visit with their family members. Once everyone has had a chance to see their loved ones, an additional twenty minutes will be allotted to you."

Gabe sighed. He never imagined he'd be reuniting with his son this way. He never imagined that Alex could ever be capable of doing the horrible things he'd done to those girls. He didn't realize just how broken he was.

The security guard led them through the metal detector and directed him into the visitation room. They sat at a round plastic table and matching plastic chairs. Two of the walls that separated a hallway and the nurses' station from the room were instilled with large plexiglass windows. There were small security camera domes in each corner of the room. A soft melody played from a speaker box built into the wall on the far end. It had the sterile feel of a well-lit hospital room but all the looks of a nursing home under tight surveillance. There were two other patients talking quietly with their family members. The patients, one man likely to be in his mid-forties, and a young woman, that Gabe guessed was barely more than twenty, wore orange jumpsuits. The man was clean shaven, with dark bags under his eyes. His hair was being tousled to the side by a much older woman, Gabe suspected was his mother. His eyes were wide, and he sat calmly while the woman and an older man with white Santa Claus hair talked to him softly. The young woman sitting at the other table was fidgeting with the sleeve of her jump-suit. She was talking about random things that didn't seem to make any sense. Gabe could hear her saying things about a cat that lived in her mattress, and the story would then switch to her accusing a young woman sitting across from her about stealing bracelets.

"Dana, you put them in your purse, I saw you! Where's your fucking purse?!"

Dana spoke to her in a soft voice, but Gabe could see her face flushing. It wasn't long before an orderly came in to assist her. He put a hand on the patient's shoulder.

"Okay, okay. I'll be good. I promise. Christ, you don't have to be a dick about it, Steve!"

The orderly removed his hand from her shoulder and stood by her until he was sure she wouldn't be any more trouble. Dana apologized for her sister's behavior, and when the woman had settled down, Steve went back to the nurses' station through a secured door that required a keycard to get through. Not long after, Alex was being escorted down the hall by an orderly in a full white uniform. Gabe watched them pass the plexiglass window. Alex stared straight ahead with his shoulders slumped. The young man kept a loose grip on Alex's arm. He gently led him to Gabe. Alex kept his eyes low to the ground. By the looks of it, he had lost a bit of weight, his orange jumpsuit seemed one size too big. He was much paler than he usually was.

There was a short electric buzz at the door followed by a heavy pop and the orderly pushed the door open. He directed Alex to Gabe's table. It had been too long since he had seen him. To the world he was a sick man who had done horrific things to innocent women. To the world he was a monster and labeled a serial killer, and while it was all true, Gabe hoped somewhere hiding beneath the monster, was still the little boy he remembered.

Eric rounded the table to greet him. Though they were older, they looked exactly the same. Eric stood a little taller than Alex, and he looked down at him like a parent whose child had strayed too far from home. Alex looked up to him with his shoulders close to his body. His tired eyes could barely meet his brother's gaze. Their bond was still there. Gabe could see it. Eric's jaws tensed, and Gabe could see the outline of those muscles working themselves into a fight against the tears that he was surely holding back. Eric reached for Alex and drew him in, and his baby brother buried his face against his chest with his eyes squeezed shut. Eric whispered something to him that Gabe couldn't make out, and Alex nodded still with his eyes closed, now with moisture collecting in the corners. Eric kissed the top of his head before letting him go and sat next to his dad. He swiped at his eyes with the back of his fingers and turned his head away to clear his throat. Gabe and Eric watched Alex take the plastic seat across from them. This was a young man who didn't look like he could hurt anyone, and yet he had. It was difficult for Gabe to grasp. Alex's lips pressed into a faint smile, and his eyes only briefly met Gabe's.

"Hi Dad," Alex said in a soft voice, just as timid as he had always been.

"Hi Son. It's been a long time."

Epilogue
Alex

At night when Alex would lie awake in his cell, he would look at a wallet-sized picture of his mother showing the way she truly was, the way he remembered her. He would kiss her photo and clutch it close to his chest. Sometimes she would visit him in his dreams, and in those moments, he was a child again. They would be together on a summer day laughing and playing at the beach with sand in their wet hair and a breeze against their salty cheeks. Then she would hug him the way he remembered -- gentle, motherly, warm. It lasted only for a short time, and in those moments, he wished he could hold onto her forever, but inevitably she would disappear, and Alex would wake up reaching out for her, only to find the mother who was not Momma sitting at the edge of his bed. It would be too dark to see her face, but he would know that she was there -- the weight of her eyes on him, the festering stink of decay that filled the empty spaces in the room and clung to his mattress, and that awful grin. His psychiatrist had said that the mother he was seeing was a manifestation of his trauma and guilt, but to Alex she was very real, and she let him know it every time her hand gripped his shoulder, and each time she waited in the shadows with outstretched arms beckoning him to give into his urges. And just like her, his compulsions were always there. Hiding. Waiting. Slowly chipping away at his sanity piece by piece.

ACKNOWLEDGEMENTS

First and foremost, I'd like to thank my wonderful husband, Matt, and my children, Marcus and James, who believed in me even when I didn't believe in myself. It took a long time for me to get here, but you encouraged me to keep going. I love you so guys so much. Thank you to my editor, Laura Ellen Joyce, who saw the potential in my novel and went through it with a fine-toothed comb. I was so nervous about the editing/revision process, but you helped make the process less intimidating. Camile, thank you so much for answering my questions about the police procedure for collecting evidence. I'm so grateful to have met you, and I can't wait to see your screenplays on the big screen one day. Dr. Sadr, you are probably the first person to ever read any of my novels, and I'm so grateful for the encouragement you had given me. Thank you to my TPW Angels and all of my other amazing group of friends, you know who you are. Thank you for believing in me. Thank you to Kaitlin, Victoria, and Natalie for reading my novel and giving me incredible feedback. Lastly, thank you to my parents for fostering my imagination and allowing me to dream big. I love you.

CPSIA information can be obtained
at www.ICGtesting.com
Printed in the USA
LVHW100306110522
718489LV00005B/71